TOP DOWN TO CALIFORNIA

JENNIFER SKULLY

Redwood
Valley
Publishing

GET A FREE STORY!

Join our newsletter and receive **Somebody's Lover** for free! You'll also receive for free both Jasmine's **Beauty or the Bitch** and Jennifer's **Twisted by Love**!
Plus you'll get the scoop about new releases and sales, as well as subscriber-only contests. Sign up at **http://bit.ly/ SkullyNews**

TOP DOWN TO CALIFORNIA
A ONCE AGAIN NOVEL

Book 8

The ride of her life with a super sexy co-driver...

It's been forty years since Noreen Kincaid spent that carefree summer in the Florida Keys, but she's never forgotten one steamy second.

After too many bad relationships, she's sworn off men, but when she inherits her uncle's classic red Corvette, memories of sultry nights driving with the top down beside the town's sexiest bad boy, Cutter Sorenson, return unbidden. On a whim, she decides to drive the vintage convertible from Florida to her home in San Francisco.

Cutter Sorenson never forgot Noreen Kincaid or that summer they shared riding in her uncle's smokin' hot convertible. Does she think she's going to drive off with the Corvette he's put his blood, sweat, and tears into maintaining for the last forty years? The car he thought would be his when his good friend Mortimer passed on? Not if he can help it. There's only one thing to do—drive to California as her mechanic, and try like hell to convince her to sell him the car.

But when old passions spark and their nights grow steamier than anything they shared during that Corvette summer, Cutter has to admit she's the girl he never got over. It's not just the car he wants, but the woman she's become. But how can he convince a woman who's been burned too many times that he's the man she's been waiting for?

Snap on your seatbelt and take off for the drive of a lifetime in this second chance holiday romance.

ACKNOWLEDGMENTS

A special thanks to Bella Andre for this fabulous idea and to both Bella and Nancy Warren for all the brainstorming on our 10-mile walks. Thank you also to my special network of friends who support and encourage me: Laurel Jacobson, Kathy Coatney, Shelley Adina, Jenny Andersen, Jackie Yau, and Linda McGinnis. As always, a huge hug of appreciation for my husband who helps my writing career flourish. And to fabulous Wriggles who is crying for her dinner. And it's only 1:30 in the afternoon! She starts earlier every day!

"The old man had five hundred thousand dollars?" Valerie's voice rang with incredulity, a hint of scorn thrown in. She'd never had much use for Uncle Mortimer.

The morning sun streamed through the bay window of Noreen Kincaid's kitchen. Late March could still be chilly in the San Francisco Bay Area, but the sun warmed her enough to push up the sleeves of her sweater.

Laying the estate lawyer's letter on the table, she smoothed the creases beneath her palms. They all looked at her expectantly, her daughters, Grace and April, her sister, Valerie, and her best friend, Tammy Barlow.

Noreen had been flabbergasted when she received the letter from Uncle Mortimer's attorney. Five hundred thousand dollars? And he'd left it all to her? How did her uncle even have that much money?

Uncle Mortimer had been what their mother called the black sheep of the family. Though he'd gone to university like all the Kincaids, he hadn't done much with his life, at least according to their mother's standards, squandering his education by moving to Key West and chartering fishing boats. He was like Humphrey Bogart in *The African Queen*, taking tourists out on the water and living in a shack on the shore. And, his family thought, barely able to support himself.

Noreen had never seen him that way. She'd liked him. He was carefree, doing what he wanted with his life, and he never seemed to need much. Not like their mother, with the big house, the jewels, the fancy cars. In her teens, Noreen had gone out to Key West four summers in a row. She'd gotten to know her uncle, learned to accept him and love him just the way he was.

"His lawyer writes that Uncle Mortimer owned several fishing boats," Noreen synopsized the letter. "He never used all the money he earned." That sounded like Uncle Mortimer, just living his life, frugally and simply. "It says here that the trustee's instructions were to liquidate everything, giving all his captains the right of first refusal to buy the boats." She pulled the letter close. Even at fifty-seven, she didn't need reading glasses yet, and she could see the fine print easily. "Since we're his only living relatives, we get the money."

Valerie snorted. "You mean *you* get the money. Mom's going to be so pissed."

Noreen searched for disgust and anger in her sister's voice, but she didn't hear it. Valerie was divorced with two sons, both of whom still lived in the Bay Area. Working as a customer service manager for a manufacturing company, she wasn't struggling, but she could use the money far more than Noreen. Yet nothing in Valerie's voice begrudged Noreen the windfall.

Their mother, however, could be a different story.

Valerie, sixty now and three years older than Noreen, had chosen not to visit their uncle on Key West when they were teenagers. Leaving her boyfriend, whom she'd dated all during high school, was out of the question, and then university became her priority. Flying out to Key West to stay with an uncle she barely knew never interested her.

Yet Noreen had still made her decision. "I look at it as family money, not just mine. We're splitting it." She looked at her beautiful daughters. "And you too. You can do whatever you want with the money. Even buy a house."

"But Mom." Grace didn't add anything to that, the shock clear on her pretty face. With long blond hair she usually wore up in a bun, she took after Noreen far more than April, her younger daughter, did.

At thirty-four, Grace was a purchasing specialist for a leading department store chain with a major online presence. She loved her job, was well-adjusted, and one quarter of the money could be a down payment on an attractive condominium somewhere in the San Francisco Bay Area. And April, twenty-six, with dark, curly hair like her father, was fresh out of veterinary school and doing an internship. The money would go a long way for them both.

The only one she'd left out was her best friend, Tammy. Despite being the mother of three, Tammy had few wrinkles and almost no gray in her brunette hair. Maybe that came from being happily married. A successful marketing executive, she didn't need the money the way Valerie and the girls did, especially after the inheritance she'd received from her mother.

When Noreen looked at her, Tammy smiled, understanding the way best friends did without having to say a word.

"That's generous of you," Valerie said, her voice warm, as if she meant it. They could have been twins with their blond hair and their mother's face. They both dyed away the gray, but Noreen had cut hers to just above her shoulders, revealing some of the curl, while Valerie still wore hers straight to the middle of her back.

"But that money was for you, Mom," April said.

Grace echoed her. "We didn't even know Uncle Mortimer."

"That was my fault. I should have sent you out there to spend time with him. And even gone with you. We all could've gotten to know him better." She shrugged, the tug of guilt around her heart. "I guess life just gets in the way."

It was more accurate to say her mistakes had gotten in the way. Noreen wasn't proud to admit she'd been married four times. And each time she picked the wrong man. After the first divorce, she'd reverted to her maiden name, and she'd always kept it after that. Maybe that should have been a sign to her. But her first marriage produced Grace, and her second gave her April. And while the marriages had been mistakes, her sweet daughters made the turmoil worth it. But then there'd been marriages three and four.

She'd flown out to visit Uncle Mortimer only once after she'd graduated from university, and that was years ago. Obviously he hadn't held that against her. She'd phoned him though, and later they kept up with each other through video chats. But how long had it been since she'd talked to him? At least three or four months. He was eighty-eight, for God's sake. She should have checked on him far more often.

Guilt wormed its way through her stomach. She hadn't even known he'd died until the letter arrived, calling the lawyer immediately to learn that Mortimer had a heart attack two months ago, dying almost instantly. He'd wanted no fanfare, and his ashes were scattered at sea per his request. She hadn't even been there for a final goodbye.

Maybe Uncle Mortimer wanted it that way.

Valerie looked at her. "You really, *really* don't need to do this. I mean, you're the one that spent time with him and called him. You knew him a lot better than I did."

Noreen touched her hand. "I want to do this."

She didn't say that her sister needed it more than she did, which made it sound as if Valerie had made mistakes with her life. But she'd divorced only once. And part of the reason Noreen had more money was the divorce settlements she'd received, some of which she'd put in trusts for the girls' educations. She'd done well on her own too. As a freelance editor, instead of taking a flat fee from clients who could ill afford to pay her at the time, she'd received payment as a percentage of future royalties. And she'd made the right choice because several of those authors had gone on to become bestsellers.

Her choice in men, though, had never been her strong suit. One would have thought she'd learned her lesson after two divorces, but no, her choices had sucked every time. And now she'd sworn off men. Well, actually, she'd sworn off relationships and marriage, but she still planned on enjoying a casual liaison every once in a while. When she found the right partner.

But Valerie had made good choices. Her marriage simply hadn't worked out. Maybe it was just luck that Noreen got where she was. And now she could afford to share her windfall with her sister, and of course, her daughters.

She held up her hands, warding off their protests. "I won't hear any more about it. I'll contact the lawyer and make the arrangements. Uncle Mortimer had four beneficiaries, not just one."

Then, picking up the letter, she held it to her chest. And her smile felt as if it stretched across her face. "The only thing I'm not splitting is his 1959 Corvette."

Tammy gasped, throwing her arms wide. "He left you the car?" She was the only one at the table who knew just what that car meant.

Noreen nodded, making herself dizzy with excitement.

"He left the car to me, specifically. He said I'd always loved that Corvette and he wanted me to have it."

"Oh yeah." Tammy winked at her. "I know you love that Corvette."

Noreen wouldn't say it out loud, not with her daughters right here, even if they were adults, but she'd lost her virginity in the Corvette. And she wanted that car. She wanted the memories that came with it. She called it her Corvette summer, the summer she'd turned seventeen, the last summer she spent on Key West with Uncle Mortimer. There'd been a very special boy, and the things he taught her in her uncle's Corvette had been the best of her life. Although that could be nostalgia. After all, she was fifty-seven, menopausal, and fast approaching Medicare and old age.

"I thought Uncle Mortimer was a beach bum," April said.

"We all thought he was," Valerie was quick to answer. "Your grandmother always said he'd never make anything of his life. And we believed her." She tapped the letter Noreen was still holding. "Until now." She rolled her eyes as if she were April's age. "But you know your grandmother."

Their father had died twenty years ago, and their mother remarried a few years later, moving to France with her new husband. Living in an extravagant flat in Paris, they attended the opera, the symphony, special exhibitions at the Louvre, and took elaborate vacations across the continent. Her expectations had always been high.

"Mom is going to be pea green with envy when she hears how much money Uncle Mortimer actually had." Valerie's eyes twinkled. She'd love getting one up on their mom.

Noreen smiled, raising a brow. "And the Corvette." Not that Mom would consider anything other than a Bentley. "Anyway, Uncle Mortimer's will stipulates that I have to physically go out to Florida to claim the car."

"You mean you have to drive it back here?" April was aghast.

She gave a one-shouldered shrug. "I can ship it if I want. I just need to go out there first."

"How much will it cost to ship the Corvette?" Grace was always the practical one.

Noreen had received the letter a week ago and told no one, not wanting to be bombarded by everyone's opinions. Now she'd made up her mind, and that was that.

"I'm not going to ship it," she said to collective gasps filling her sunny kitchen. Grace and April spoke almost in unison. "You've gotta be kidding me," from Grace and, "What would Everett say about that?" from April, who punctuated with a smirk.

Everett was Noreen's fourth husband. Up to that point, her taste in men had been awful. Until Everett. He'd seemed like the perfect man, handsome, funny, smart, a brilliant lawyer, highly successful, ten years older than her, polished and charming. Too bad she hadn't discovered how controlling he was until *after* she'd married him. Over time, he'd tried to cut her off from her friends, even from her family. He told her what to wear and who to see, always chastising her for staying out too late or drinking too much or going on spa weekends with her sister or Tammy or the girls. He even refused to let her fly alone to see her mother in Paris, insisting he needed to go with her to "protect" her. Not allowing her to see her mother unless he came along was the last straw.

"Everett would never let you drive cross-country all alone," Grace agreed.

Noreen divorced him a year ago, and she was only now getting herself back. Maybe Everett and his controlling ways had fueled her decision to drive the car across the country. Everett would never have allowed it. And there was that word. No one *allowed* her to do what she wanted. She just did it. This cross-country trek from Key West to San Francisco, top down all the way, might very well be her way of thumbing her nose at Everett.

Or maybe she just wanted to relive the memories of her Corvette summer as she sky-rocketed across the country in a gorgeous classic car.

"Why on earth would you want that old rust bucket anyway?" Valerie asked. But Valerie didn't know everything about Noreen's summers on Key West.

Tammy smiled knowingly. "It's not an old rust bucket. It's a red and white 1959 Corvette. And it's probably worth beaucoup bucks too."

Valerie snorted. "Knowing Uncle Mortimer, it's sitting in some old shed covered with seagull crap."

Grace pointed a finger at her. "But you didn't think he had five hundred thousand dollars either. Maybe we're all in for a big surprise."

Finally, Noreen had her say. "Uncle Mortimer loved that car. It was already over twenty years old when I was out there. And it was pristine."

"But that was forty years ago, Mom," April said. "And he was like, what? Eighty-eight years old when he died?"

"Yes," Noreen admitted. Another pang of guilt soft-shoed through her belly, and she wished she'd reached out to her uncle more often.

"Didn't he have a mechanic?" Tammy asked, that knowing glint still in her eye.

"He's long gone by now." She sent Tammy a glare but couldn't help the flutter around her heart. "But I'm sure Uncle Mortimer would've had somebody looking after the car. And," she tapped the letter. "His lawyer would've told me if the car was a rusted hulk."

April expelled a breath. "I'm worried about you being out on the road all by yourself."

"Maybe it would be better to sell the car," Grace said, her gaze thoughtful. "Those old cars are massively expensive to maintain and insure. And they're gas guzzlers. With the price of gas right now, it's going to cost a fortune to drive it across the country."

Grace was the focused one, looking at all the angles, doing the research, pushing for the better deal. That's why she was the top buyer at her company, snagging better prices than anyone else. Noreen loved both her daughters with all her heart, but she recognized the differences between them. April was the gentler one. She'd worked hard to be a vet, but she had a soft core. Even as a child, she'd fostered injured animals. Noreen remembered a time April had rescued a bird attacked by its own bird family, and she'd cried for days when she couldn't save it.

But Noreen wouldn't let their fears get in her way, and she tapped the letter again. "I have an inheritance here which will pay for the gas and nice lodgings along the way. So I'll be safe."

"But shouldn't you save that money for a rainy day?" Grace sounded like the mother in this relationship.

Noreen didn't discuss her finances with her girls. She lived in a three-bedroom home in the Belmont hills, on the peninsula just south of San Francisco, one she'd bought after the divorce. It wasn't extravagant, though she'd remodeled and put in a hot tub. She liked her luxuries. But she knew Grace's thoughts. Mom wasn't getting any younger. She was fifty-seven, with old age creeping up fast.

But Noreen didn't feel old. She was in the prime of her life. And she had to make up for the five years she'd wasted being controlled by Everett. "I have enough money for a rainy day, sweetheart. And I want this car. I'm driving across the country, and I don't care how much the gas will cost."

Tammy punched the air. "You go, girl."

April joined in Tammy's enthusiasm. "We support you, Mom. One hundred percent."

Then she nudged Grace, who added, "Just keep in touch, call us every day, and let us know how you're getting along."

"When are you leaving?" Valerie wanted to know. "I could come along, if you like."

Noreen's heart raced. "Are you kidding? I mean, it's going to take me two weeks." She could do it in a week if she drove five hundred miles a day, but she wanted a leisurely trip. She'd never driven across the country, and enjoying the sights was just as important as the drive itself. "It would be great if you could."

She hadn't relished making the trip alone. There was just something about appreciating tourist sites and eating good food with someone else, sharing the journey and that sense of awe when you looked at a monument and felt the rarefied air around you.

Valerie closed her eyes for a moment, then looked again at Noreen. "I'll see what I can do. And if I can't make it the whole time, maybe I can fly out and meet you part way."

She obviously regretted the spontaneous offer and was struggling for a way to get out of it. Valerie didn't work from home the way Noreen did, and with a demanding boss, she couldn't take off without several weeks' notice. Besides, her sons had a lot more issues than Grace and April. Valerie often lent them money, though *lend* wasn't the word because they never paid it back. And both boys, when they lost a job or ran out of money, came home to live in their old rooms until they got on their feet again. With Valerie paying for everything, even their food and phones.

So her sister couldn't afford the time off, or the airfare

either. And if Noreen offered to pay, she'd risk offending Valerie. It was better to keep the inheritance from Uncle Mortimer for a rainy day. And Valerie had a lot of rainy days.

Noreen would make this trip on her own. And it would be top down all the way!

2

I t took over a month to make all the arrangements with her uncle's lawyer, and it was mid-May before all the documents were completed and ready for Noreen's signature. The money would be disbursed in another week, but she could take possession of the Corvette whenever she was ready. As long as she came to Florida to get it.

Tammy drove her to the airport. Grace had a business trip to Dallas, the company headquarters, and the veterinary hospital April worked for was over in Santa Cruz. Valerie had finally decided she couldn't take time off work since one of her sons was moving back in.

"I told you she wouldn't make it," Tammy said.

"I know." Noreen didn't even heave a sigh.

Instead of dropping her off, Tammy had parked the car and come inside for a leisurely breakfast in an airport restaurant. Noreen had already checked in her bags, leaving plenty of time before the security check. Since most people rushed to get through the long line, the restaurant was relatively empty, and they'd found a quiet corner table.

Tammy stabbed a few lettuce leaves. "It doesn't mean she doesn't love you."

"It just means her responsibilities are greater right now."

Noreen could edit anywhere, but since she'd had a month to plan, she'd rescheduled her clients, finishing up two jobs ahead of time and pushing out a third with the excuse that the author was notoriously late finishing his manuscript and would appreciate the extra time. She was free. And she'd have a fabulous trip. Even if she was on her own.

"I wish I could come with you." Tammy sighed wistfully.

Noreen snorted a laugh. "Like when could you ever take off a full two weeks?"

Reaching across the table, Tammy patted Noreen's hand. "I'll be there with you in spirit." Then she finished her forkful of salad before adding the kicker. "So tell me why you really wanted to drive this car all the way across the country instead of just having it shipped."

Noreen smiled, letting her thoughts drift inward. "You know exactly why."

"Because that car is a symbol of the best times of your life?"

Tammy knew the whole story. That's what you did the first year at university with a brand new roommate who just seemed to get you. You spilled all your secrets, all the highs and lows. And that summer on Key West had been Noreen's biggest high.

"You're not expecting that he'll still be your uncle's mechanic, are you?"

Noreen almost choked on her sip of coffee. "You've got to be joking. If he was still my uncle's mechanic after forty years, then he would be the biggest loser in the history of losers. No, I'm sure he's moved up and out."

"Oh my God," Tammy gasped. "You're such a classist. What's wrong with being a mechanic?"

"There's nothing wrong with being a mechanic," Noreen backpedaled. "I just meant that you have to move on from who you were when you were eighteen. That was just a high school job for him." Except that she'd never felt he was particularly ambitious.

"I forget. What's his name?"

It rolled smoothly off her tongue. "Cutter Sorenson." Just saying it made her stomach flutter.

Tammy dropped her voice. "But don't you want to see him again?"

Noreen shook her head. "Are you kidding? He's probably bald."

"Bald can be sexy." Tammy winked.

"With a massive beer gut and a plumber's crack," Noreen finished, and they laughed together.

She hadn't been in love with Cutter Sorensen. It was pure lust, which made it even better. And she wanted to preserve every sexy moment she'd spent with Cutter in her uncle's 1959 Corvette.

Without today's reality ruining yesterday's memories.

"Don't tell me you're not dying to see your first love again." Tammy gave her an eloquent smirk.

She and Tammy had been assigned to the same dorm room at university, which was only a year after her last summer on Key West. The memories had still been so vivid back then, unchanged by time and marriage and babies and bad decisions. She'd shared the story with Tammy just as Tammy had shared her secrets, the good, the bad, and the ugly.

Noreen made a face. "You know very well Cutter wasn't my first love. He wasn't a love at all. He was just a boy I saw during the summers."

"Right," Tammy scoffed. "That's why he was the best sex you ever had. Because he didn't mean anything to you." There was truth to that, but Tammy's tone was mocking, as if she'd always believed there was more to the story. "And he was so much better than any of your husbands."

Noreen winced inwardly. That wasn't something she liked to dwell on. Her four failures shamed her, even if she knew the blame wasn't all hers. She told herself she was a poor judge of character, as if that absolved her. But in the end, it didn't work. If you keep repeating your mistakes, you have to ask yourself what you're doing wrong.

She tried to explain about Cutter yet again. "What we did was only so good because there wasn't all that emotion attached. We were best buddies, and experimenting with each other just seemed like a good idea. No broken hearts left behind, and the memories aren't polluted by agony." She grimaced, and her salad suddenly seemed unappetizing. "Not like marriages gone bad when all you remember is the anger and the fighting and the bad times. The misery paints all your memories so you can't even remember the good times anymore." She shrugged her shoulders and picked up her coffee cup to sip the strong brew. "I don't think I truly remember what sex was like with any of them because I only remember the bad times."

Tammy's face softened. "Are you sure there's not one single good memory?"

Noreen smiled fondly. "The girls." Then she shrugged, a frown turning her lips down. "But it's different for you. You've been married for thirty-five years to a good man who doesn't hit you, cheat on you, lie to you, or try to control you."

Tammy scoffed from deep in her throat. "Like that means I haven't had bad times? Or bad memories? Like that six months when Frank and I barely spoke to each other because..." She spread her hands on the table. "I don't even remember why we stopped talking. I just remember how angry I was all the time."

"Because he sold your Starbucks stock just before the first stock split and bought a motorcycle." Noreen remembered.

Tammy gritted her teeth and puffed a big huff into the air. "I knew we should have hung onto that stock. One share is now equal to sixty-four shares."

Noreen laughed. "See, you're still following the stock price." She raised a brow, lifted a corner of her mouth in a light smirk. "But then Frank bought you a helmet so you could ride with him, and you insisted on getting your motorcycle license so you could ride by yourself."

With all the noise in the airport hallways, Tammy's out-loud laugh went unnoticed. "Just like on *The Simpsons* when Homer bought Marge a bowling ball for her birthday. And she insisted on taking lessons with a sexy French bowling instructor." She waggled her eyebrows lasciviously.

Noreen grinned. "Admit it. You loved riding that motorcycle with Frank. You never even went out by yourself."

Tammy's eyes lit up as she lowered her voice. "That thing was so sexy. Sometimes we got back from a ride and headed right into the bedroom to tear each other's clothes off."

"As I recall—" Noreen winked. "—you didn't always wait until you got home."

Tammy shivered. "Those were the days." With a smile and a devilish glint in her eyes, she said, "After you leave, I might have to rush right over to his office and lock the door while I have my wicked way with him."

Noreen wasn't envious of how good Tammy's marriage was or that her love life had only gotten better after menopause and the kids had moved out. She was simply saddened by her own monumental failures and dismayed that her best memories were forty years ago with a handsome eighteen-year-old boy.

It was even more depressing that her uncle's Corvette meant so much because she wanted to recapture the essence of those memories. The laughter seemed to die inside her, and Noreen sobered up, glancing at her watch. "I should get in the security line now."

But Tammy didn't let her go. "Honestly, I understand what you're saying about the memories. But I also hate to hear you say that your whole life has been a waste."

Noreen took a mental step back, straightening, "It's not a waste. I've got the girls. They're the most important thing. And I love my work. I'm actually happy."

"I know, I know." Tammy waved Noreen's words away with a flutter of her fingers. "I just meant that it would be nice if you had a good relationship. At least once."

At least once. Tammy had summed up Noreen's life in those three words. She'd never had a good relationship, and that was just freaking sad. And preventable if she'd been a better judge of character.

"It would've been nice," she said, trying to sound casual, and probably failing. "But I made my own choices, and I chose badly. I don't have it in me to do it all over again." She leaned in, held Tammy's gaze. "I swore off men after Everett. I'm sure I'll enjoy a fling now and then," she added when Tammy scowled. "But I'm never falling in love again. And it's actually great that I couldn't find anyone to go on this trip because I want to be the kind of woman who can enjoy life on her own." She felt stronger saying it. "I'm happy just the way I am."

"I agree," Tammy said. "You're happy. You're in control. But—" Noreen thought she'd make a fairytale wish about some silver fox Prince Charming finding her along the road, but Tammy only added, "I still want you to call me every day so I know you're okay."

"You sound just like the girls." They both laughed. "I promise I'll call, Mom."

After hugging goodbye at the security gate, Noreen waved one last time before Tammy disappeared. Goosebumps suddenly raised her skin.

And she was filled with the sense that this trip would be a momentous turn in her life.

STEPPING OUT OF THE AIRPORT DOORS IN THE EARLY evening, the muggy Miami air hit Noreen like a wet rag. The temperature might not have been that much higher than what she'd left behind in the Bay Area, but even in mid-May, the humidity made her clothes heavy on her. Funny that she didn't remember the humidity being so bothersome when she was a teenager. But then she'd been like a local, used to the weather, and usually wearing a bathing suit and cutoff shorts, ready to jump in the water at a moment's notice.

Of course, menopause might have changed everything.

She shrugged out of the white sweater she'd worn on the plane, glad to find her Uber sitting at the curb. The air conditioning blasted her as she climbed in, and she sighed out her relief.

She'd chosen a downtown business hotel close to the address of Uncle Mortimer's lawyer. From the freeway, Miami was like any other city, a lot more palm trees, but other than that, it was buildings and industrial parks, hotels and, of course, gridlocked cars.

They finally exited onto a boulevard lined with palms and packed with tourists wearing shorts and brightly colored shirts. The Uber driver dropped her with her suitcase and computer bag. In the time it took to walk from the car to the hotel doors, her blouse stuck to her back. Then, thankfully, she was in the air-conditioned lobby.

Finally in her room, she thought about changing and going out for dinner. On the west coast, it was only four o'clock. But she couldn't face the humidity again. Floridians would probably laugh at her, saying she had no idea what real humidity was like since it was only May. Thank God it wasn't July or August. But she ordered room service anyway. In hindsight, it would have made more sense to take a very early flight to arrive in Miami by the afternoon, making it possible to meet with the lawyer on the same day. But Noreen had long ago decided against oh-dark-thirty flights in order to gain a few more hours of daylight on the other end.

Around nine and not at all tired, she stepped into her bathing suit and meandered down to the hot tub. In her flip-flops and a towel wrapped around her, she ordered a champagne cocktail. What was a soak in the tub without a champagne cocktail?

The tub and pool deck were empty, and the water was glorious, easing all the aches and pains of travel. She'd taken a nonstop to Miami, but regardless, it had been five hours in a seat and almost painful to stand up. Putting in her ear buds, she listened to an audiobook, sipping her champagne until she felt like a boiled lobster.

Of course, she woke the next morning at five o'clock while it was still dark outside. The minute the sun rose above the horizon, she headed out. It was neither hot nor humid, and she walked the Miami streets all the way to the beach, taking off her shoes to stroll the packed sand, runners and speed-walkers passing her. A gorgeous sunrise silhouetted pelicans skimming across the water's surface and sandpipers foraging at the surf's edge.

After showering off the salt and sweat, she decided informal dress was good enough for the lawyer's office. After all, this was Miami, and she was the client. Wearing capri pants and a bright blue sleeveless top, she headed out of the hotel. The walk wasn't far, and she soon stepped into the high-rise's massive lobby, pushing the elevator button for the twentieth floor and Mr. Theodore Howard's law suite.

After being escorted into his office, she was surprised to find him dressed in a tropical shirt and linen pants.

Theodore Howard was a short, trim man in his sixties, and shaking her hand, he asked. "Coffee or tea? Or would you like lemonade?" He rubbed his bald head, waiting for her answer and glancing at his secretary, who hadn't left the office.

"A cup of decaf coffee with cream would be fabulous," she told him. When his secretary returned momentarily, Noreen wet her lips with the delicious brew. Theodore Howard obviously ground first class beans.

After the pleasantries, he got underway. "I apologize for the need to fly all the way out here to take possession of the car. I tried to talk Mortimer out of that stipulation, but he couldn't be swayed."

"Uncle Mortimer definitely liked to do things his way, Mr. Howard." She unzipped her computer bag and pulled out a folder.

"Please, call me Teddy." He suddenly reminded her of Telly Savalas, the actor who'd turned bald into sexy. Although he'd been far beefier than Teddy.

"Thank you, Teddy." She laid a paper on his desk, with all the account information he would need. "Here are our Social Security numbers, bank account numbers, and routing numbers for the transfers."

He slid the sheet over with one finger, picked it up, looked for a long moment, as if he was reading carefully. "Are you sure you want to make this split?" He speared her with a look. "There's no obligation for you to do so."

"I'm absolutely sure. If you transfer the money from the estate, then there's no gift tax. I read the trust, and it says the money comes to me or any of my designated beneficiaries. So I designate my daughters and my sister."

"There's no problem. It's just such a large amount, I wanted to make sure."

"I'm sure."

She signed all the documents, two of which had to be notarized, and conveniently, Teddy's paralegal was a notary.

When everything was completed, she asked, "Is there anything else I need to provide before I take possession of the Corvette?"

"Nothing. As I said, being Mr. Kincaid's trustee, I've liquidated all his assets, including his house, such as it was, and all the boats. Now all you have to do is pick up the car." He opened his desk drawer and removed a keyring, sliding it across the table.

She asked, wincing even as she did. "And it's really road-worthy for a cross-country trip?"

Teddy laughed, his eyes twinkling. "As I assured you over the phone, your uncle kept his boats and his car in flawless condition."

She'd checked, of course, but she wouldn't feel totally secure until she saw the car for herself. "May I have the address of the garage where you're storing it? I can have an Uber take me there right away."

He tipped his head questioningly. "But it's down in Key West."

She felt her skin blanch. She'd assumed the Corvette was in Miami because that's where the lawyer was located.

"Here's the garage in Key West." He handed her a business card. "Budget Auto Repair were Mr. Kincaid's mechanics."

She read the address. "I'll have to rent a car. I didn't

realize I'd need to get all the way down to Key West." The drive could take three or more hours, especially if she hit heavy traffic.

"I'm sorry I wasn't clear."

She smiled. "I should have asked." Palming the key, she stood.

It was all good. She hadn't expected every detail to go just the way she planned. She could handle any deviation.

And screw Everett for thinking she couldn't do anything on her own.

3

With the added fees for dropping off a rental car in Key West, it turned out to be cheaper to take a puddle jumper to the island, and she arrived midafternoon.

The plane's route followed the Overseas Highway connecting the Florida Keys with the mainland, a two-lane slice of road and bridges that went all the way to Key West at the tip. Handling both domestic and international flights, the small airport was bustling. Key West was a year-round tourist destination, especially with snowbirds coming from the north to enjoy Florida weather in the wintertime.

Noreen didn't know how she'd feel coming back after all this time, but there was a little kick around her heart, just like she'd felt when Teddy Howard handed her the key to the Corvette that morning.

She grabbed a taxi and gave the driver the address, and they headed out. The shops and restaurants were still colorful and cutesy, although the names had changed. Segway tour groups dotted the roadways, while teenagers wearing skimpy bikinis and cut-off shorts hung out by ice cream parlors and shops featuring key lime pie on a stick. Fish restaurants abounded and the briny scent of the sea air filled her nose. Boats bobbed in the harbor, and tourists gathered round small kiosks advertising a day of snorkeling or fishing or para-sailing. Just as they had all those years ago, flocks of chickens clucked, pecked the ground for seeds, and wandered wherever they wanted, sometimes stopping cars to cross the road.

So little had truly changed. It didn't seem so long ago that she'd been one of those teenagers savoring key lime pie on a stick.

The taxi driver wended through a couple of back streets and pulled up in front of her destination, Budget Auto Repair. She stepped out to the sound of electric tools and a radio blasting *Margaritaville*. What could be more appropriate on Key West?

The driver left her standing at the edge of the road, her rolling suitcase beside her, her laptop bag over her shoulder. Before her loomed four open bay doors, the interiors filled with cars of varying makes and vintages, two of them on lifts high in the air. More cars packed the parking lot.

But she didn't see her uncle's Corvette, *her* Corvette, among the Jaguars, BMWs, and Mercedes.

Rolling her bag through a door beside the bays, she found the office surprisingly neat. The four vinyl chairs in the waiting room lacked the telltale grease stains she would have expected. The floor was clean of dirty footprints, and the glass countertop sparkled, not a single smudged fingerprint on its surface. The computer and printer appeared new, maybe even state-of-the-art.

She turned just as a short man entered from the garage, a fringe of hair in disarray around his bare pate. Wiping his fingers on a rag, he asked, "Can I help you, ma'am?"

The use of *ma'am* had never offended her, finding it a term of respect and politeness, not just a remark on the gray in a woman's hair. Besides, this guy, with the heavy lines on his face, was probably older than she was.

"I'm Noreen Kincaid. Theodore Howard from Miami gave me this address, saying my Uncle Mortimer's Corvette is being stored here."

"Mortimer." He grinned and bobbed his head in acknowledgment. "Real sorry for your loss, ma'am. Mortimer was a great old guy. He was on the water right until the end, and he sure had a good, long life."

"Yes, he did."

"We're sure going to miss him around here."

"I'll miss him too." The twinge of guilt curdled her stomach again. She couldn't remember the last time she'd video chatted with Uncle Mortimer. Christmas? Yes, it was the holiday. She felt this man's eyes on her as if he was silently asking why she'd never been out to visit her uncle in his old age? Why she'd come *after* he was gone and only to claim his car? It didn't seem good enough to say she'd been busy getting married four times and raising two daughters.

"Car's out back." He jerked a thumb over his shoulder. "She's all locked up safe and sound. Let me get her mechanic. He's got the key."

He skittered back through the doorway into the garage, and she watched as he spoke to a man bent beneath the hood of a vintage car she couldn't identify.

It was a good sign her uncle still had a mechanic for the Corvette. She hoped it meant that Teddy Howard was right about the car's pristine condition. Opening her purse, she found the keyring she'd stowed in the zippered pocket so she wouldn't misplace it, and wrapped her fingers around the key as if it were a talisman.

But looking up again, she lost all sense of comfort, all sense of her surroundings, all sense of time and place.

The man's head almost skimmed the doorway as he

stepped through. Her skin prickled as he wiped his hands on a rag, his stained overalls baggy on his lean form, the rolled sleeves revealing the corded muscles of his arms. But it was his hands she remembered. He'd always had strong hands. And yet they could be so tender. He was older, but so was she. His hair, once dark and curly, was now mostly silver. And there were lines at his eyes that hadn't been there at eighteen, grooves beside his mouth.

She'd thought he was a man back then, but looking at him now, she realized he'd been just a boy, and she'd been just a girl. But he was all man now. Prime beefcake. He'd turned into Jeff Chandler, her favorite silver-haired movie hero from years ago, when she was a kid sitting in front of the TV watching black-and-white classics, especially *Return to Peyton Place*, about the young ingenue writer and the big city editor. It was probably when she'd decided she wanted to be an editor.

Cutter Sorenson, even in his stained overalls and grease beneath his nails, was the spitting image of her long-ago movie idol. And he gave her heart palpitations the way he always had.

Or maybe that was just a hot flash.

"Well, well, well," he drawled. "Noreen Kincaid. A blast from the past." He stuffed the dirty rag in a pocket and folded his arms over his impressive chest, his first name stitched on the pocket.

She wondered if he thought she'd weathered the years as well as he had. His gaze raked her from her short, bobbed hair, freshly washed and blow-dried this morning, to her mini-malist makeup with all the right touches, to the silky sleeveless blouse and fashionable white capri pants, to the sparkly blue polish on her toes.

The humidity, however, had turned everything limp, from her hair to her makeup to the blouse sticking to her body.

His gaze finally returned to her face. "Love the toes," he drawled. "Wearing that color for anyone in particular?"

The words would have stolen her breath if she had any left.

She'd always worn sparkly offbeat colors, even back in high school, greens, blues, neon orange, never pastels. Cutter had loved the colors. Everett had made her put the funky polishes away, saying they were slutty. They'd only been married three months, and she'd worn those colors the entire time they'd dated. She should have known there was a problem right then and gotten out. But she'd already made three mistakes, and she'd wanted to make it work this time. So she'd thrown the bright bottles away and brought out the pastels.

And bought a sparkly blue polish, as well as mint green, the day she filed for divorce.

Cutter Sorenson scratched that same sore spot.

"I'm ready to see my car now," she told him, sounding imperious and demanding. It wasn't how she'd intended to come across, but he was baiting her.

"*Mortimer's* car is out back." He stressed her uncle's name, and then, as if dismissing her, he marched through the door, back out to the garage bays.

She had no choice but to follow. Not intending to get off on the wrong foot, she'd done it anyway when he made her think of Everett. She'd just never expected Cutter.

Good Lord, he was still working as a mechanic in a little shop on Key West. He hadn't changed in forty years.

Except to grow excessively attractive.

He moved fast, and she left her suitcase and computer bag in the office to rush after him. By the time she made it to the second bay, he was already outside and turning the corner. She found him at a set of four garages behind the station and already fitting a key in a padlock. When she reached him, he was rolling up the door.

She lost her breath for the second time in just a matter of minutes.

There it was, still magnificent with its shiny red paint and contrasting white side cove on the door, its windshield clean of even a speck of dust or dirt, and not a single bug on its headlights. Except for a personalized license plate that read *XB-70*, the car hadn't changed in forty years.

And it brought back all those memories.

She could almost feel the wind through her hair as Cutter raced along the Overseas Highway. Even more, she could feel his lips on hers, his hands on her body.

Which was exactly what she didn't want to feel right now.

Suddenly a bundle of nerves, she stared at the gorgeous car. She knew how to drive a stick, but the Corvette was old, the clutch hard to push in. And she expected to drive it all the way across the country?

Maybe her daughters were right, she was crazy.

But Cutter was talking, his eyes on her, still that deep chocolate brown that had always made her shiver when he looked at her. "She's in good shape. I'd like to make an offer."

An offer? Did he want to drive her cross-country? God, could she handle that? Then again, it would be nice to have a mechanic along. But what if he wanted more? What if *she* wanted more?

"I can give you a fair price for her. I won't cheat you. We'll look at prices on the internet so you know it's a fair deal."

And suddenly she understood his offer. It wasn't about her at all. He wanted to buy the Corvette.

"It's not for sale." The words snapped out of her harsher than she'd intended.

She loved the car. She'd loved it since that first summer on Key West when she was fourteen years old. And she'd loved it when she was seventeen, the last year she'd visited. That summer with Cutter. It was a part of her youth. It was a part of *her*. With so many memories attached to it, she couldn't let it go.

But she couldn't explain any of that to this man. A man she didn't even know anymore.

His lips thinned as he looked at her. "Mortimer would have wanted her to go to someone who knows how to take care of her."

"But he left it to *me*." She tapped her chest. "I might not be able to work on the car myself, but I can find a good mechanic."

He eyed her for a long moment, then tried another tack. "It's going to cost you a fortune to ship it across the states."

She lifted her chin. How the conversation had turned adversarial, she didn't know, but she felt the tension rising off him, felt it vibrating inside her. "I'm not shipping it. I'll drive it back to California."

His eyes widened with shock. Then he laughed, a short bark of sound that grated along her nerves. "You've gotta be joking."

She narrowed her eyes, pursed her lips. "I'm not joking. That's why I flew all the way out here."

"You," he pointed at her, "are going to drive this car," he stabbed a finger at the Corvette, "all the way to California?"

She glared at him as if he was saying she was incapable. "I can drive a stick. And, if you'll recall, you taught me how to drive this car."

That seemed to stop him a moment. As if he suddenly remembered all the *other* things he'd taught her. As if he remembered the tastes, the kisses, the touches. Exactly the way she did.

Then he steamrollered right over her memories. "It isn't just driving it. She's a classic beauty. But she's old and she's got her issues. She's the proverbial car that only got driven to church on Sundays."

Noreen laughed as humorlessly as he had. "Uncle Mortimer never went to church."

"You know exactly what I mean." He rubbed the hood of the car as if it were a woman. "She's delicate. She needs a gentle hand."

"If you've taken such good care of her over the years, she should be just fine crossing the country." She found herself calling the car female just like he did.

"You don't get it. Things break easily. You need to know how to handle her."

She wondered why men talked about cars and boats as if they were lovers. "Look, I've got a long drive ahead of me. I don't want to argue with you. I just want to get on the road."

He gaped at her. "You mean right now?" He made a sharp wave in the air, his tone caustic as he said, "Today?"

"Yes, today. There's plenty of time to get across the Overseas Highway and back to the mainland. Today," she stressed.

"But, but," he stammered as if she'd robbed him of words. "She's not even prepared. She needs an oil change, a lube job, new spark plugs."

She scoffed from deep in her throat. "Wasn't that already done? You knew I was coming."

"Sure, I knew you were coming. But I didn't know you were actually driving the damn thing all the way home."

So. The car was no longer a woman; now she was a damn thing. "Didn't Mr. Howard tell you that?"

"He told me you wanted the car, and that if I wanted to buy her, I'd have to talk to you. He never said anything about a cross-country drive."

Maybe Teddy had thought Cutter could change her mind. Maybe, when she finally got here, Teddy didn't believe she'd actually want to make the trek. It didn't matter. "How long will it take to do the oil change and the lube and change the spark plugs?"

"It certainly won't be done today," he snapped, then added, "Do you actually think you'll get that damn suitcase in the trunk?"

She'd forgotten about her suitcase back in the office. He'd obviously noticed. "Yes, I intend to put my suitcase in the trunk."

"Don't you remember *anything* about this car?" He stepped forward, audaciously grabbing her hand and dragging her to the back. He inserted a key—he obviously had his own that she'd insist on getting back from him—and opened the trunk lid, flourishing a hand across the space.

Okay, she hadn't remembered. She'd brought her biggest hard-sided suitcase, because, after all, she'd be on the road for at least two weeks. The Corvette's trunk was cramped, she had to admit. The problem, really, was closing the lid.

"Maybe I can fit it on the passenger seat."

He snorted loudly and raised his hands in wonder and disgust. "You are *not* putting a suitcase on the fine leather of that front seat."

"It's my car," she said, wanting to go up on her tiptoes so he couldn't tower over her. "And I can do whatever I want."

How had they become so angry with each other? It wasn't supposed to be this way. She'd expected to find a gentlemanly mechanic who would hand over an immaculate car and wave her goodbye. She hadn't expected Cutter or this hostility.

Was it because he wanted the car? If he really wanted it, why hadn't he just bought it from Uncle Mortimer years ago?

She hated starting off her trip with a bad taste in her mouth.

Even more, she wanted to keep all her good memories of Cutter, of her summers on Key West, of that last, glorious Corvette summer. Closing her eyes a long moment, she breathed deeply, then opened them again to stare at him in the gloom of the narrow garage. He was too close and instead of reeking of grease, he smelled of some sexy aftershave. Or maybe that was just *his* scent.

"We got off on the wrong foot." She kept her voice as polite as possible. "I'd really like your help getting the car ready for the drive back home. I'll pay you for time and materials, just like any other job, and I'll buy another suitcase that fits in the trunk. And I promise not to put a lot of junk on the front seat. When do you think you can have it ready?" She held up a conciliatory hand. "Please, take as long as you need."

His face shifted, or maybe it was just his eyes, the blue irises deepening even back here in the gloom. His mouth loosened from that tight-lipped lock he had on it. "Sorry. I'm just surprised. I thought we could come to an agreement about the car. After all, you haven't seen her for forty years. I thought you wouldn't be interested in keeping her."

The stab of guilt once again nicked her insides. She hadn't seen the car for forty years, or Uncle Mortimer for almost that long. A compulsion rose in her to explain how complicated life had become, how hard it had been to get away. Now, she barely found the time to get out to France to see her mother.

But those were excuses. She'd taken the girls to Disney World. She could have come down to the Keys. They would have loved it.

And yet she hadn't visited.

Cutter added, "I still think it's a bad idea to try to drive all the way. That's a lot of miles. She's not used to it." He closed the trunk lid with a snap, stroking the shiny red paint.

She decided to stroke his ego. "You've been her mechanic for the last forty years, right?" When he nodded, she went on,

"So she's in the best shape of any classic car. And I feel confident she'll make it."

She didn't know if it worked. He still eyed her with skepticism. "I can have her ready the day after tomorrow. And I've got an extra duffel at home you can pack your things in. The soft sides will help."

How was she supposed to fit everything she'd brought in a duffle? She hadn't wanted to rely on finding a laundromat. Maybe she could leave behind a few of her shoes. But she'd brought her favorites.

Really, what had she been thinking?

And yet she snapped up the offer immediately. "Deal. Thank you. I'll find a hotel for a couple of nights." She looked at the beautiful lines of his face a long moment, noticing again how well he'd weathered the years. "I really appreciate your help. It'll make the trip a lot easier on me." Then she stuck out her hand.

He shook it. She noticed the grease under his nails and in the lines of his palms. Still a mechanic after all these years.

But that meant he was the perfect man for the Corvette.

Standing in the office doorway, Cutter watched her walk away, wheeling that ridiculous suitcase she'd actually thought would fit in the Corvette. She'd even suggested putting it on the pristine red leather seat as if it was a luggage rack. The woman didn't understand the XB-70. Hell, she didn't even ask what the license plate meant. She didn't understand the car's intricacies or know how to talk the XB-70 through a rough start.

But damn, Noreen Kincaid was pretty. Even prettier than she'd been at seventeen. The sparkly blue on her toes was mind-altering, and more than just his mind too, somehow reminding him of the sounds she'd made, the way she'd tasted, the way she'd...

Don't go there. No can do. He needed to keep his head on straight. Both of them. This was about the car and nothing more.

He shuddered to think that if she encountered a problem on the road, she'd probably call some chain store grease monkey who didn't know a lug wrench from a sledgehammer. Not that he wasn't a grease monkey. Just look at his fingernails. Though he used the orange pumice scrupulously, he never got them completely clean. He'd never cared before.

Until she walked into the shop.

But what he really cared about was Mortimer's car and how she was treated. The XB-70 was more than a classic Corvette. She was the man's legacy.

Noreen Kincaid, no matter how much she'd loved the car when she was seventeen, couldn't possibly know how to treat her like the beautiful lady she was. He didn't even blame Noreen. He just wished Mortimer had sold him the car years ago.

And now, in only a matter of days, he had to figure out how to get Noreen to leave the XB-70 behind when she left for California.

❧ 4 ❦

Key West was not, by any means, a metropolitan city. It didn't have freeways or four-lane boulevards. It was quiet streets, mom-and-pop eateries, and wall-to-wall tourists. Noreen loved the vacation mood now as much as she had in her teens. But after the third hotel with no vacancy, she sat on a bench and retrieved her phone to search.

In the sunlight, it was hard to see her phone screen, but she finally found an Airbnb with available dates. It was little more than a shack, but then Uncle Mortimer's home had been a beach shack and she'd loved it. One room with a kitchenette, a tiny bathroom with a stall shower, and a front porch with a view of the ocean through the surrounding cottages and palm trees, she snapped it up before it disappeared. When the details arrived, she realized she could walk rather than call an Uber, and she started off, rolling her suitcase behind.

A gaggle of college kids in a top-down BMW slowed beside her to ask if she wanted a ride. But the moment she opened her mouth—whether to say yes or no, even she wasn't sure—the driver gunned the engine and peeled off down the road, laughter filling the air in their wake. Until a knot of traffic up ahead stopped him.

"Serves you right, creep," she muttered under her breath.

If it wasn't for the humidity, she would have been fine, but as it was, she'd turned into a wet rag. When she finally reached her shack, she needed a long cool shower.

For a single person over two nights, it was perfect, with a comfortable foam mattress on a double bed, a reading lamp between two chairs, and a coffee maker in the kitchenette. She discovered ground coffee in the freezer, and in the fridge, small creamer cups that weren't past their sell-by date. She couldn't ask for more. There was no TV, but the house guest book had the Wi-Fi password.

Comfortable on one of the cushioned chairs on the front porch, she decided the coffee was the best she'd ever had. She wasn't right on the water, but a stretch of beach was visible through the two cottages opposite. Palm trees swayed in the breeze, and the sun sparkled on lazy waves. Other people might have wanted a cool drink, but the delicious brew filled her stomach and perked her right up.

Pleasantly relaxed after the shower and her coffee cup finally empty, she headed inside to peer into her luggage. She hadn't thought about the Corvette when she packed. Her only excuse was that it had been so long. Even so, it was embarrassing.

Sorting her clothes and paraphernalia, she made three piles: must-haves, maybes, and definitely-can-do-without. But darn, now she'd have to ship the suitcase, which was probably more expensive than buying a new one back home.

Cutter had given her his number, and when she finally glanced at her watch, it was after six. He'd be done with work by now.

And she needed that duffel if she wanted to figure out exactly what she could bring.

Risking a call, she put on a cheery voice when he answered. "Hi, it's Noreen. You mentioned a duffel so I can pare down my stuff, and I wondered if I can come by to pick it up. Where do you live?"

She prayed it wasn't on the other side of the island. Or even on another key.

"Where are you staying? I'll bring it to you. As I recall, you arrived in a taxi," he drawled, sounding as if he couldn't believe her stupidity.

He hadn't been callous or sarcastic when they were kids. Cutter had always been sweet, despite his bad-boy exterior. But then maybe life hadn't been kind to him.

"That's really nice of you. I appreciate it." She gave him the address.

Arriving fifteen minutes later, his hair was damp as if he'd just stepped out of the shower. He wore a Jimmy Buffett-style print shirt and baggy cargo pants, and his fingernails were almost clean.

He pulled out the camouflage duffel he'd tucked under his arm as she stepped aside in the doorway to let him enter. His scent wafted over her, fresh soap and shampoo and that sexy aftershave that tantalized her more than it should.

He was so tall, so big, the cottage suddenly felt cramped.

All he said after eyeing her place was, "Nice and simple." Then he looked at the bed where she'd spread out her piles. A heap of sandals lay on the floor.

Following his gaze, she said primly, "A lady can't wear the same pair of sandals day after day."

He snorted. "That looks like a different pair of sandals *every* day." Then, amazingly, he smiled. "We can fit most of your things. It's the hard-shell suitcase the trunk lid won't close over." He sniffed the air. "I smell coffee."

Noreen pointed to the coffee maker. "It's fairly fresh. I only made it a little while ago."

"Thanks." Grinning, he helped himself, taking it black. He didn't look like a sugar-and-cream man. Coffee in hand and looking at the piles on the bed, he said, "I can help you pack."

"I'm quite capable of packing." She didn't exactly snap the words at him, but close.

He seemed unoffended. "I'm good at packing tight. Getting a lot into a small space."

The comment wasn't sexual, and yet she blushed anyway, turning away from him to hide the heat in her face. She'd been so comfortable with him during all those summers on Key West. Yet now he was like any other stranger.

Except for the memories.

"Come on. I don't bite, I promise."

Okay, maybe he was being sexual, but she ignored it.

She glanced at the piles laid out on the bed, then the duffel. "Thank you. I appreciate the help."

The portable air conditioner, which had been just fine before he arrived, now seemed incapable of keeping up with the heat in the room. Noreen fanned herself.

First, he pointed at her cosmetics bag. "You really need everything you've got in there?"

She put a hand on her hip and give him a mock glare. "Yes, I need every single thing."

He shrugged and tucked it into one end of the duffel. "Jesus, that's heavy."

"A woman has needs," she said between her teeth. Then regretted the words immediately.

When he stopped and looked pointedly at her, she pretended that hadn't sounded sexual.

Then he shrugged. "Which pile do you absolutely need?" he asked, recognizing that she'd already sorted.

She put a hand on the nearest stack of clothing.

"The secret is to roll." He grabbed the shell blouse on the top, rolling it neatly and expertly, then stuffing it in the bag.

Noreen watched, fascinated. He was an amazing packer. The pile of clothes dwindled and yet the duffel wasn't filling up.

He waved a hand at her lingerie pouch. "You need to leave all that in the bag?"

She snatched it up, not wanting him to paw through her panties. "It absolutely needs to stay in the bag."

Taking it from her gingerly, a smirk crossed his lips. Then he rolled the pouch and stuffed it in. In the end, they got through her entire pile of maybes as well. But the duffel was packed so tightly, she wouldn't be able to find anything.

And they hadn't tucked in any of her sandals.

"Honestly," she said, not wanting to sound whiny, "I can't wear the same sandals every day. And I need a pair of walking shoes."

"I have just the thing for that." Pulling a crumpled cloth bag from a pocket of his cargo pants, he asked, "Which ones do you want to take?"

"Those, those, and those." Two pairs of sandals and her tennis shoes, plus slip-on thongs.

He plucked them out of the pile, shoved them in the bag, tied it off, and tossed it on the bed next to the duffle. "There. That will fit in the trunk."

He stood back, hands on his hips, terribly proud of himself as he studied his handiwork. She looked from her suitcase to the duffel. Admittedly, she hadn't packed tight, but he'd done an astounding job. And she gave credit where it was due. "Thank you. That's great."

He followed her gaze to the suitcase. "You could probably ship that back home."

She eyed the bag. "I thought about that, but it's cheaper

to just buy a new one. It's not as if I spent thousands on luggage."

"We can get the other sandals and that extra pile there —" He pointed to the definitely-can-do-without pile. "—into a medium-size box, and it shouldn't be too expensive to mail."

There was nothing all that important, except the sandals. They were her favorites, all of them. "Thank you."

"We've got a ton of boxes at the shop. I'll find something for you." They were silent a moment. Then he asked, "Have you eaten dinner yet?"

She shook her head. "I concentrated on packing instead."

"I know a great fish place."

She wondered why he was being so nice to her. But she was hungry. "Fish sounds good."

She'd pictured empty soda cups and carry-out containers filling the back, but his jeep was surprisingly clean. And the wind blowing through her hair felt glorious.

Stopping at the shop, he found the perfect box, large enough to handle all her leftovers. And it wasn't even grease-stained. He'd also put her suitcase in the back of the jeep so she didn't have to worry about how to dispose of it.

The meal was divine, a flaky rockfish freshly caught from the waters that surrounded the key. He wanted to know what she did, and she told him she was a freelance editor, but telling him about the girls, she didn't mention they had different fathers.

But Cutter deflected every question she asked, and she ended up knowing only that he'd gone off island for a few years before moving back permanently. And that he'd always taken care of Uncle Mortimer's Corvette.

When she would have passed on dessert, he said, "You've gotta have the key lime pie. This place serves the best."

"We sure do," the waiter agreed with a smile.

"Only if you share with me," Noreen said, not wanting to eat the whole thing by herself.

"Deal."

The coffee was delicious, even if she'd ordered decaf, and the key lime pie was to die for. With two forkfuls left on the plate, she pushed it at him. "You have the rest. I can't take another bite." It was her waistline she worried about.

Cutter had no such qualms, finishing off the pie. "Are you really sure this car is what you want?" He leaned back, coffee mug in hand, and after the question, he raised it to his lips, looking at her over the rim.

Right. Here was the point of all his friendliness. He wanted the car.

"I'm sure I want it," she said, keeping her tone polite.

"You'll need to find a really good mechanic. You can't just take her to any schmo down at the mini-mall. Not even for an oil change. It's a specialty car."

She managed not to grit her teeth. "I'm sure I can find a good dealer who specializes in classic cars and get a great recommendation."

He snorted, but didn't belabor the point. "Do you have a place to store it? You can't leave her out on the driveway in the elements, not even with the cover on it."

"I have a two-car garage."

"Have you thought about the expense? She guzzles gas, she needs regular maintenance, and replacement parts are expensive."

"Uncle Mortimer seemed to handle it."

He put a thumb to his chest. "He had me. I got the parts wholesale and didn't charge him an arm and a leg for the labor. He paid me mostly by letting me drive the car whenever I wanted."

She got it then. Cutter loved the car like it was his own. He'd driven it whenever and wherever he wanted. He loved working on her, emphasis on *her*, and that's why he'd done everything so cheaply for her uncle. It was a labor of love.

But she still couldn't let the car go. "I'm prepared for all that. Uncle Mortimer left me a nest egg that can handle it."

His nostrils flared slightly. "I'll make an offer better than you'd get on the open market."

She didn't want to be rude. Instead, she was completely honest. "I loved that car when we were kids. I know it'll guzzle gas on the trip home, and I know it'll take a lot to keep up the maintenance. But it reminds me of all the freedom I had during the summers I was here. And since Uncle Mortimer left it to me, I think he intended for me to remember all that." She didn't say that she loved it for the memory of all the things she and Cutter had done in that car.

He opened his mouth as if he had something important to say. Maybe the reason why the Corvette meant so much to him. Instead, he said, "You never asked how Mortimer died."

"Mr. Howard—" She didn't call him Teddy. "—said he died of a heart attack."

"It was more than that." He signaled the waiter for a refill on his coffee, as if the story required a long chat over a fresh cup.

She took a refill as well and added more cream, settling in.

"It was like he was tying up loose ends," he went on as if they hadn't been interrupted. "He had me do a thorough check of the car, change all the fluids, the hoses, everything. He went up to his lawyer in Miami a couple times, and he had me help him clean a bunch of old crap out of the house. Then he took the Corvette for a long drive. He hadn't done more than tool around Key West in years."

A wave of guilt washed through her for having ignored Uncle Mortimer since Christmas. He'd died two months before Teddy's letter arrived, for God's sake, and she hadn't even known.

"And he started asking around about who wanted to buy the boats. He told me he was too tired to charter anymore. Not that he'd taken out a charter in years. But he liked to fish early in the morning on a clear day when the ocean was smooth as glass."

Cutter's sharp features softened, as if he were thinking of all the fond memories of her uncle. Mortimer had never married, he'd never had children. But he had his fair share of lady friends. And yet in the end, all he'd was his car and his boat.

She wondered if that's all Cutter had. If that was why he wanted the Corvette. Because it was all he had, even it wasn't his.

"You may remember," Cutter said, leaning forward to prop his hand on his chin. "Mortimer wasn't the neatest guy. But when he went out fishing that last morning, there wasn't a single dirty dish, not even a spoon or his coffee mug, left behind in the house. His laundry was done, his bed made up with fresh sheets. I know because I found sheets in the dryer." He breathed in deeply, holding it, then sitting back again and letting it out in a long, sad sigh. "I found his boat drifting. The rod was right beside him and a bait bucket on the other side. There were three fish in the cooler. It was obvious he'd gone just like that." He snapped his fingers. "But he knew it was coming, and he didn't want to leave a mess for anyone. Not you, not me."

"That's why he cleaned everything up before he went. Just in case," she finished for him.

He nodded his head. "I think he wanted to meet his end on his boat with a fishing rod in his hand. And that's exactly what he did." He looked at her. "He went out on his own terms, where he'd loved life best, on the water. Me." He tapped his chest. "I want to go in my car."

She was quiet a long moment. "I'm happy Uncle Mortimer went the way he wanted to. Not everybody does."

"Mortimer always said he wanted to pop off, no long, drawn-out illness. And he certainly didn't want dementia to get him." He put a finger to his temple. "The old guy might've been slowing down, but he still had it all up here."

"He went out in style, his own way, the way we all should go." Happy for her uncle, she was also sad he hadn't called her to say goodbye, that she hadn't called him just to check. She tipped her head, finally getting it. "You scattered his ashes at sea, didn't you?"

He nodded. "Yeah. Just me. He was a weird old bird, and he didn't want anyone hanging around and getting all weepy. He didn't want a funeral. But I had a big barbecue bash in his honor."

She gave Cutter a long look, his strong, handsome features, his wide shoulders, his broad chest. If he was anything like Uncle Mortimer, he had another thirty years left. But she guessed where Cutter was going with his story. "Why do I get the feeling you're telling me a sob story so I'll sell you the car?"

He chuckled, set his mug down. "Is it working?"

She shook her head. "No. In fact, it's having the opposite effect. I want to drive cross-country in Uncle Mortimer's Corvette from the Florida Keys to the Pacific Ocean, top down all the way. And when I'm home, I want to drive over Highway 17 to the Santa Cruz Beach Boardwalk. I want to tool down the coast highway from Half Moon Bay to Carmel. I want to drive over the Bixby Bridge and down to Big Sur." She leaned forward, both hands on the table. "And if I find I'm not driving the Corvette at least every other weekend, then I'll call you. But for right now, it's not for sale."

IT WASN'T EVEN DARK BY THE TIME HE DROPPED HER OFF.

But her words still rang in his ears. Santa Cruz, Half Moon Bay, Carmel, the Bixby Bridge on the way to Big Sur. He could see her flying down the highway with the top down, her sunglasses shading her eyes and a smile on her face.

He relished an image of her racing across the Bixby Bridge, the wind in her hair and a smile on her kissable lips.

She'd talked about the memories the car had from their youth. But hell, he had his own recollections of her and that car. So many seductive memories, so many hopes and dreams. But those weren't enough. What he needed to hear was about the trip she wanted to take. What he wanted to be sure of was that the XB-70 wouldn't sit on her driveway untouched, that she'd drive it, that she'd love it, that she'd keep Mortimer's spirit alive in it.

He wouldn't buy another sports car, not yet. Maybe all he had to do was wait her out.

Before she could get out of the Jeep, he said, "You haven't driven the car in forty years. She's got a stiff clutch and a tricky gas pedal."

She set her mouth in a stubborn line that he remembered so well. "I know how to handle the Corvette."

She'd always been that way. When she made up her mind, she wanted what she wanted, and she was tenacious about getting it. Even relentless. He'd admired that about her back then. And if he hadn't wanted the XB-70 so badly, he'd have admired her tenacity now.

It was sad that she'd have to change the license plate. He'd helped Mortimer pick it out. Okay. He'd been the driving force behind it. He loved cars, he loved boats, he loved aircraft, just about anything with a motor. And the XB-70 was his favorite bomber jet.

"Sure, you can handle her, but it would be a good idea to take a test drive. I can do the maintenance in the morning

45

and pick you up in the afternoon. And if there're any kinks, we can work them out."

The stubborn line of her mouth slipped away into a smile, as if she suddenly saw the brilliance of his suggestion. "You're right. Thanks for the offer."

He could have let her take the car out tomorrow on her cross-country jaunt where she could either sink or swim. And if she sank, she'd be back here lickety-split, begging him to take the XB-70 off her hands.

But in all good conscience, he couldn't do that to Noreen. He couldn't do it to Mortimer's memory. And most especially, he couldn't do that to the XB-70.

"No problem," he said. "Let's say three o'clock."

She smiled and hopped out of the Jeep.

He watched her walk up the path in her tight, white cropped pants. She still had a nice ass. You weren't supposed to look at a woman's ass these days, or even call it an *ass*, let alone comment on it. But she made a damn pretty picture. She always had. And back then, she'd liked the way he looked at her, the desire in his eyes as she sashayed for him, teased him, drove him crazy.

Of course, now he had to mind his manners.

But he wouldn't stop looking. He enjoyed looking at her way too much. Always had.

W hile Cutter worked on the Corvette the next day, Noreen wandered the town. In ways it was different, the shops changing names, facades, and paint jobs. Duval Street, the most popular tourist destination and the heart of Key West, was home to a vibrant collection of hole-in-the-wall bars, historic haunts, funky shops, galleries, and outdoor cafés. Some buildings had been torn down and rebuilt, maintaining the style but now fresh. The street layout remained the same, with cottages, homes, and shacks off the main roads.

Down at the water, she removed her shoes to feel the sand beneath her feet. For the most part, Key West lacked the wide expanse of beach tourists enjoyed in Hawaii. But the snorkeling on the coral reefs made up for it. At this particular beach, a long pier stretched out over the water, and Noreen walked along it looking for stingrays, but didn't spot any.

Heading back, she easily found the road leading down to her uncle's house. The shack had been repainted, now white with blue shutters and blue trim around the windows. It was cute and cheery, with a row of sandals on the porch, from little kid to big man, and a sand pail tipped over next to them.

Her heart lurched once again, thinking of what she'd missed. Or more aptly, what she'd neglected. Why was it that people got so busy with their lives they forgot important things, like beloved uncles? The phone calls and video chats didn't make up for it. He'd died out on the sea in a boat, alone, even if Cutter said he'd gone out exactly how he wanted to.

For lunch, she splurged on grilled spiny lobster with a navel orange butter sauce for dipping. Peak season was late summer, but she found a place that served them. Unlike Maine lobster, spinys lacked claws, and the meat was delicious. Though a favorite of hers, she hadn't tasted one since that last summer here on Key West. And instead of waxing nostalgic about the town the way she'd wanted to, she couldn't rid herself of the sadness and guilt.

With a couple of hours before she'd meet Cutter for their drive, she found an unoccupied bench on one of the public boat docks. Watching parasailers out on the water, she drank in the ocean's beauty and the sea air scent. And gave herself over to thoughts of that summer, of Uncle Mortimer, and the free rein he'd given her, like nothing she'd ever had at home.

Running around every summer with a group of island kids, including Cutter, they were gone all day. What did they call that now, free-range kids? Although she'd been in her teens. With a little money in her pocket, she could have lunch out, a soda or key lime pie or some candy. She'd loved every moment of those summers.

In the evenings, Uncle Mortimer cooked the fish he'd caught that day. She'd never had fish like that, before or since. Often a group of his friends dropped by, everyone bringing something to add to the table. It felt like a party every night.

Sometimes a lady stayed over with Uncle Mortimer for a

few days. Noreen had thought he was old back then, but he'd only been in his forties. She never questioned who his ladies were or where they came from. Her mother would have had a fit if she'd known, bad influence and all that. Sometimes Noreen heard them in his room, a sigh, a groan, but it never creeped her out.

When she arrived home at the end of that first summer, her mother had said she was as brown as a berry, and it wasn't a compliment. But she'd let Noreen go back the next summer, and the next, until that last summer before her senior year in high school. And she'd started noticing Cutter as more than just one of the gang.

It hadn't been infatuation or even love. It was just a growth stage. If it wasn't for that humiliating incident at the end of her junior year back home, her Corvette summer might never have happened.

But being with Cutter wiped out the mortifying memories. And they'd made so many sexy new ones. Memories she'd never forgotten.

Memories that seemed to come back full force whenever one of her marriages went bad.

THE ROAR OF THE APPROACHING SPORTS CAR THUNDERED IN her chest even inside the cottage.

That's what she called the rental, a cottage instead of a shack. It sounded more elegant.

Stepping onto the porch, she locked the door. And there he was, flipping a U right in front of her, gravel spraying across the road.

The car was a beauty, a shiny bright thing in the heat haze of the day. And he was the kind of driver a car like that needed. Cutter had been sexy and good-looking as a teenager, but now he was downright gorgeous. He was George Clooney and Patrick Dempsey and Brad Pitt, all rolled into one. Better yet, he was the embodiment of her favorite classic actor, Jeff Chandler, tall, ruggedly handsome, totally sexy.

Slipping his sunglasses down his nose, he looked at her over the rims. Okay, with those aviator sunglasses, maybe he was Tom Cruise in *Top Gun: Maverick*.

Then he climbed out of the car, holding the door open for her, waiting.

And her stomach sank. Now she had to drive it, with all her stops and starts. And Cutter witness to her ineptitude.

She'd been so bold last night, telling him she could handle the car. But she was actually a bit terrified. It had been so many years. She was used to driving regular cars. The Corvette was a beast. Not that she'd let Cutter know how she felt. To him, the Corvette was a lady.

Honestly, what she remembered the most about riding beside Cutter was his hands on the wheel. Uncle Mortimer had let him drive the car even when he was fifteen. She could still hear her uncle's voice. "It's just an island. Anyone can drive on an island."

And later, what she remembered was Cutter's hands on her.

She noticed his hands now as he helped her into the car. He'd always had such strong hands from all his work on cars. And God, the things those hands could do.

But she couldn't get all hot and bothered now. That was years ago. They were different people. And she'd made mistakes over men far too many times to want to repeat them.

He hunkered down beside her in the door's vee. "Remember, you have to keep it in neutral to start her."

She rolled her eyes like the girls were so fond of doing to her. "Yes, Dad, I remember," she mocked him.

"Then start her up for me." His voice was low and sexy, as if he was asking her to start *him* up.

Her body wanted to shiver, but she kept that to herself.

The car started right up, and she almost high-fived Cutter.

"Good job." He rose slowly, gracefully, giving her an up-close view of his chest, his powerful thighs, and everything in between.

She was breathless all over again.

Rounding the hood of the car, he slid into the passenger seat, turned to her, and said imperiously, "Home, James," as if he were some rich dude and she the chauffeur.

Just like she remembered, the clutch was a beast. She'd been driving an automatic for years, having gotten rid of her manual Honda before she married Rodney, husband number three. It was like riding a bicycle, wasn't it? You never truly forgot.

She pushed down the clutch and shoved the gear into place.

Of course, she let the clutch out too fast, and the car stalled before taking off. "Dammit," she said under her breath.

"She wants to pop right back out," he said. "You have to take charge, make her go slow."

Did he have to talk about the car as if she were a woman? Especially when everything he said had sexual undertones.

Had it always been that way between them?

Not at first. They'd been buddies, part of a gang, hanging out at the beach, sitting by bonfires, sneaking beers and occasionally something stronger.

Until their Corvette summer when she'd made her demands, wanting to take control of her life instead of letting other people push her around and make her feel worthless.

And she would take control of this clutch, just like she'd gotten what she wanted all those years ago.

She started again, and this time she forced the clutch to go slow. She took control. The car didn't install, and although she pulled away from the gravel shoulder with a couple of hiccups and a few jerks, they were rolling.

"You've got her now. She's putty in your hands." He crooned the words, rubbing his hand over hers on the shifter.

She got the car into second gear easily, then into the third, the engine powering down the road. Of course, the Corvette didn't want to go thirty miles an hour. She wanted to hit the highway where she could sprint, and then race.

Good Lord, she sounded like Cutter.

"Just take her around on back streets for a little while, get her used to the feel of you before we wind her up."

They tooled around the grid of back roads for twenty minutes, which forced her to shift more as they turned corners. Pushing in the clutch came easier to her, and the wind didn't blow her hair all over the place.

Until Cutter said, "Are you ready for Duval Street?" Being Key West's main drag, traffic would be at its heaviest. "Then we can head out along the Overseas Highway for a bit."

She nodded. Although the thought of the stop-and-go traffic on Duval Street made her twitchy. She was okay going from first to second and second to third, but getting under way from a full stop would be more difficult. She didn't want to stall again or take off with that herky-jerky start.

She compared it to driving on the San Francisco hills. Even when she'd mastered her stick shift, she'd sometimes stall on those hills.

But if she was going to take the Corvette across the entire country, she'd need to get used to traffic.

Duval Street was a steady flow of cars, stopping and starting, as someone backed out of a parking spot, or someone slid in, or a pedestrian jaywalked in front of her. Thankfully, she didn't stall again, didn't even stutter. She could have crowed, but Cutter would roll his eyes at her.

After fifteen minutes, he said, "You're doing great. Let's get on the Overseas Highway. You can open her up out there."

The Overseas Highway connected the Florida Keys to the mainland and was often choked with tourists. A two-lane road most of the way, through towns and across bridges, she doubted the traffic would let her truly open up the Corvette's engine. On a regular freeway, the one hundred miles would take a couple of hours, but on the Overseas Highway during the day, it often took four hours. Maybe she'd be lucky, and the traffic wouldn't be too bad.

She and Cutter had usually gone late at night when he could really wind up the car.

In the mornings, more cars were heading into the Keys, in the afternoons they were heading out. And that was true today. But once they were out of town, she picked up the speed to at least forty-five, sometimes even fifty-five.

And it felt marvelous. She didn't care what the wind did to her hair.

She wanted to be seventeen again, flying along the highway with her hands in the air. Sometimes she'd knelt on the seat. Until she heard her mother's voice in her head, yelling at her to be safe, and she'd slither back down and strap in, Cutter laughing at her all the way.

Before the Seven Mile Bridge, they hit a snarl, tourists driving slowly so the wife could take pictures, and she turned around on Cudjoe Key, half an hour from Key West.

"You want a burger?" Cutter asked, jutting his chin at a restaurant by the road.

And there it was, the Snack Shack. "Oh my God. I can't believe it's still here?"

"It's changed owners a few times. But they always kept the name. And the menu's pretty much the same too."

She breathed out in awe. "The Thousand Island Burger." The quarter pound burger was smothered with Thousand Island dressing, tomatoes, pickles, and lettuce. It was the dressing that did it. "I haven't had one in years. Do they still make them?"

She heard the excitement in her voice, as if she was seventeen again. They'd eaten here all the time, and she'd never been able to finish a whole burger. Cutter always finished it for her.

He grinned. "They've still got 'em."

"Do they still do the trays on the side of the door?"

"Yeah." He snarled like a rabid dog. "But no one's putting a tray on the side of the XB-70."

She tipped her head. "The XB-70?"

He put his hands up in the air, gave her a look, and clucked his tongue like an old lady. "Didn't you even look at the license plate?"

She shoved the gear into Park and climbed out of the car, walking around to the front. Then she came to his door when he didn't climb out. "What does it mean?"

Pulling his phone from his pocket, he swiped and tapped, then held it up to show her a photo. "It's a long-range supersonic bomber."

She snorted softly. "Uncle Mortimer got a license plate for a bomber plane?"

"He sure did." He winked at her. "When you get her California plate, you need to make it the same one. She won't feel like herself—" He patted the dashboard. "—until she has her correct name."

She folded her arms. "You chose the plate, right? Don't tell me Uncle Mortimer picked it himself."

When he grinned, she knew the truth. He'd conned Uncle Mortimer into buying that vanity plate.

She decided to tease him. "When I get to California, I was thinking of something more along the lines of *MYCORVETTE* or even *MYBABY*."

He made a disgusted sound deep in his throat, shoved the door open, forcing her to step back. "*MYCORVETTE* might be okay. But *MYBABY* will only shame her. She doesn't want anything cutesy." He stalked to the door of the Snack Shack and held it open for her.

"Then how about something like *ONEHOTLADY*?"

He let the door slap shut behind them. "She knows she's a lady. She doesn't have to advertise it."

At the counter, he ordered two Thousand Island burgers with fries.

The place looked just the same, green vinyl booths with swirling green Formica tabletops, and a green checkerboard linoleum floor. Except that it all looked new, as if the owners updated while still keeping the original feel of the restaurant.

Few people were inside, only two tables taken, everyone else staying outside for car service. It was so delightfully 1950s. Even way back when, Cutter wouldn't put the tray on the side of the car. They'd always come inside.

The burgers took seven minutes, just as they always had, and Noreen slid into a booth in the corner where she could see the Corvette.

It was amazing how many people stopped to look, exclaimed, pointed, ran their hands over the hood with reverence.

She was a showpiece.

God, she really sounded like Cutter, giving the car a gender.

But she was a beauty.

"How about *MYBEAUTY*?" she suggested when he slid the tray onto the Formica tabletop.

"How about XB-70," he said, making it an edict rather than a question.

"How about having some fun?"

Pulling his phone out once more, he tapped away. "Look." Excitement threaded through his voice. "The license number is still available in California. Except you can't use the hyphen, just a space. But that'll work."

"You're crazy." Then she tasted the burger and groaned. "Oh my God, this is even better than I remembered."

He chomped into his burger, wiping the sauce off his chin with a napkin. "I haven't had these in years. I'd forgotten how good they were."

"And so simple."

"But they make their own dressing. It's not some crap out of a bottle."

The burger, and Cutter biting into his, threw her back to that Corvette summer, driving out here for a late dinner, then flying along the Overseas Highway, pulling off onto a key, and finding a secluded spot after the sun went down.

In the Corvette, Cutter had taught her everything she wanted to know, everything she'd *begged* to know.

It was with him that she'd learned to love sex. And it had become a lifelong love. Even if nothing had ever been as good as that summer with Cutter.

Maybe that was just a trick of memory, the way everything grew in your mind over time. Something merely bad became terrible, and something good became better than anything. Or maybe it was the memory of her catastrophic failures. Failure tainted everything. And now, at the ripe old age of fifty-seven, her chances for future great sex were slim.

She couldn't help herself then. It was a compulsion to look at Cutter, to remember.

But it couldn't, absolutely wouldn't, be the same. Despite how good he looked. Despite how good time had been to him. But today's reality couldn't compete with yesterday's memories. And when it didn't measure up, everything they'd done back then would be tainted too.

No, she could not have sex with Cutter. Not even one night. Not even though she'd drive away in the morning and never see him again.

She smiled as if her thoughts hadn't turned erotic or maudlin. "I don't care if I have to use a bottled dressing, the day I get home, I'm making these burgers for my girls."

And with that, she pushed away the thought that she might miss out on the last best sex she'd ever have in her life.

6

Cutter had kept the car overnight, wanting to make a few last-minute adjustments before Noreen took possession. And the following morning, an Uber dropped her off outside the garage. After a few days in Florida, she was more acclimated to the humidity, and she could have walked, but slinging the duffel over her shoulder as well as her computer bag, plus the shoe bag, was too much to ask.

She'd called the girls last night, then Valerie, assured them all she was fine, that the car was in tiptop shape and would make it all the way to California. She didn't tell them about Cutter or that drive to Cudjoe Key and the Thousand Island burgers. She didn't even tell Tammy, not asking herself why, although she suspected it was because Tammy would have told her she was an idiot for not getting him into her bed for old time's sake. Or maybe she just wanted to hug the experience close for a little while. She could always tell Tammy later.

Cutter had parked the car in the middle of the lot.

"Oh my God," she squealed like a teenager. "You even washed the car. Thank you."

The Corvette's red paint shone like satin. Yesterday she'd been nervous about driving it, but today, she took in its full grandeur. The white cove on the door, a striking contrast to the red, was buffed to a shine, the leather seats freshly polished.

She felt a momentary pang for stealing all this beauty from Cutter. It was obvious he loved the car. And yet she couldn't let it go, not even knowing how he felt.

"No problem," Cutter said, lacking any inflection. "I changed all her fluids. Everything should be fine."

He opened the trunk and threw in the duffel and her bag of sandals. They fit with a little extra room. She'd undone Cutter's amazing pack job to retrieve her toiletries bag and fresh clothing, and things hadn't gone back quite the same. In the end, she'd put the toiletries bag in last since it was the most difficult to pull out, and decided the best thing to do was lay out whatever she wanted for the next day.

"Thank you so much. How much do I owe you?"

A frown creased his brow. "Nothing. It's my sendoff to Mortimer."

Seeming almost offended, he turned away, and she added, "I really appreciate it."

He trailed a hand along the car's body, and she thought it wasn't offense he'd felt. It was his way of saying goodbye to the car.

Feeling as if she needed to make things right with him, she said, "Thank you for taking me out yesterday to get used to driving the car. And I appreciate your help on the packing too." She waved a hand at the closed trunk. "Now I might actually have room for a couple of souvenirs along the way. I mailed my extra stuff yesterday. The box you found was perfect."

She babbled like a child telling her mom all the mundane details of her day. But really, there was nothing left to say.

She climbed behind the wheel as Cutter's three coworkers stepped out of the garage to watch. She put on her sunglasses and tied a scarf over her head to keep the hair out of her eyes.

Cutter laughed for the first time. "You look like Tippi Hedren right out of *The Birds*."

She laughed with him. "The scarf tied under the chin is so fifties and sixties. And it matches the Corvette perfectly."

With a smile, she suddenly felt free, the way she had when they were teenagers.

Making sure the car was in neutral, she started the engine, pushed in the clutch, and shifted into gear. It was time to go. Thankful Cutter had taken her out the day before, she managed to drive away without stalling.

Turning onto the road, she fluttered her fingers, and in the rearview mirror, the mechanics waved her off.

All except Cutter.

HE TOLD HIMSELF HE DIDN'T FEEL A SINGLE EMOTION AS she drove away. Except about the car. He still wanted the XB-70. But there wasn't another thing he could do to get Noreen to sell.

After she drove the Corvette yesterday, that look in her eyes doomed his desire. She was hooked. He'd seen her excitement, but even more he saw lust, not for sex but for the open road with the top down. Maybe it would be sated after driving cross-country. But then, his lust for the XB-70 had never been sated.

If truth be told, he'd never lost his lust for Noreen either.

He'd dreamed of her lithe body for years. But even more, he'd dreamed about her laugh. She'd always had a beautiful laugh. She still did. He'd never met another woman with a laugh as magical as hers.

And when she laughed yesterday, he knew he never would.

Not that he cared. He liked his life here on Key West. At fifty-eight years old, he was satisfied with his accomplishments. He no longer needed a woman with a beautiful laugh. That dream had died a very long time ago.

But he still lusted after the car.

Had any morning ever been so glorious?

With the top down and the salty sea air filling her up, the joy was up there with the first time she held each of her daughters in her arms.

This was why she'd wanted Uncle Mortimer's car. This marvelous feeling.

She was relatively early and most of the traffic on the Overseas Highway was heading in the opposite direction, toward Key West. She flew along, only slightly over the speed limit. In her gorgeous red 1959 Corvette, it wouldn't be a good idea to catch a cop's eye. And she didn't need to speed. It was enough to feel the wind blowing around her and the sun on her head.

The Overseas Highway was a hundred-mile stretch—give or take—that connected each of the Florida Keys and the mainland. In the summer, it would be clogged with tourists on vacation and teenagers out for joy rides.

But now, in the middle of May, it was almost a dream drive. She sailed over bridges and through towns on the different keys. She passed over the Seven Mile Bridge, the longest bridge on the keys. They'd used it for a scene in Arnold Schwarzenegger's movie, *True Lies*, although they hadn't blown up the real bridge. The ocean beneath was an amazing shade of blue-green. Beside her was Old Seven Mile Bridge, originally a railroad bridge, and popping out of it was

Fred the Tree, an Australian Pine that grew right out of the bridge itself.

The traffic grew heavier and slower after that, but it didn't dampen her mood for the drive, except that the car's temperature gauge was rising. Should she call Cutter? No, it was probably normal, or Cutter would have said something about watching the temperature. She couldn't remember what it had been like yesterday.

She tugged the scarf from her hair, wanting to feel the wind off the ocean.

Another hour farther on, she headed off the highway to snap a picture of Big Betsy, the giant lobster, on Plantation Key, and use the restroom. She would have bought a coffee, but the Corvette didn't have cup holders. Ten minutes later, she pulled up outside a Winn-Dixie, buying a small Styrofoam cooler to hold drinks and a sandwich. Remembering Cutter's horror when she suggested putting her suitcase on the passenger seat, she set the cooler in the footwell.

Stopping at a bird sanctuary, she ate her sandwich beneath a shady tree, watching huge pelicans diving into the water for tiny fish. She contemplated how far she wanted to go today. Miami for sure, but as far as Daytona Beach? She decided on Miami, not wanting to push the car on the first day.

Her plan was to drive up the coast, then across Interstate 10, stopping wherever she wanted. Without a schedule, she could push on through and do the trip in a week if she wanted. Or take two leisurely weeks. It was all up to her and how she felt each day.

The car had cooled while she ate, and the temperature was fine when she started out again. But by the time she'd passed through Key Largo—of Humphrey Bogart and Lauren Bacall fame—and started across the stretch of bridge and highway that led to the mainland, it began climbing once more.

She again considered calling Cutter. He would probably just laugh at her and ask if she planned on calling him every hour to make sure the car was okay. But it was worrying her.

When she reached the mainland, things became dire. Pulling off the highway, she stopped in a marina parking lot, and getting out, she stared helplessly at steam puffing from beneath the hood. She could have looked inside, but what good would that do? She wouldn't know what she was seeing anyway.

There was nothing to do but grab her cell phone and call Cutter.

He answered with, "Yo." Was that glee in his tone? But then he couldn't guess she was calling with a problem.

She could do nothing else but blurt out, "I think the car is overheating. There's steam coming out of it."

He was silent a moment, and she detected a noise like a man beating his head against the wall. Then he muttered something that sounded like, "Women." Yet it could have been anything, a groan of pleasure that she was already having trouble and would rethink selling the car.

"Where are you?" he said tersely.

"On the mainland. I'm about fifteen or twenty minutes from Florida City."

He mumbled something else she didn't understand before he asked, "Was the temperature gauge getting hot?"

"A little. But I pulled off and let it cool down just after Big Betsy the lobster."

"Jesus," he muttered. "Why didn't you call me then?"

She didn't admit she'd been afraid he'd call her an idiot. "I didn't realize it was a big problem. I don't know the car well enough."

She could hear his deep breaths, as if he was trying to calm himself. And finally he said, "All right, I'm on my way."

"You want me to just sit here until you arrive?" It could take three hours.

He sighed, heavily, full of all the exasperation a man could feel about a woman with a broken car. Especially the XB-70, a beautiful 1959 Corvette.

"I was going to say," he said in clipped words, "that you need to call a tow truck. Here's a number." He rattled it all off so fast she couldn't remember it all.

"Wait a minute, let me just put it in my notepad." She typed it into her phone when he repeated it. "The area code?" He gave her that too.

"I know them," he said. "They'll treat you right. Just tell them it's the XB-70, and you need a flatbed. Don't let them tow the Corvette, got that?"

She wasn't sure what irritated her more, his tone or those added words, *got it*, like she was stupid.

Then again, he was frustrated. She should have called him when she first noticed the temperature gauge. That had been her instinct, but she'd let pride get in her way.

She'd proven almost right away that he was a more capable owner for the Corvette.

He stopped at the house long enough to grab an overnight bag.

He wasn't happy about it. Of course he wasn't. Whatever was wrong with that car, he would fix it, and then she'd be on her merry way. It wouldn't change her mind about selling him the Corvette. So he wasn't happy. The drive was just a pain in the ass.

He wasn't happy about seeing her again either. Of course he wasn't. Depending on what was wrong with the car, they might have to wait for a part, but he certainly didn't plan on driving back tonight.

He wasn't happy that they'd probably have dinner together. Or spend time reminiscing. Or that he'd probably laugh with her. He'd have to hear her laugh again. And that would make him want things. Good, sweet, hot things. And that just wouldn't work.

So he wasn't happy at all. His heart rate didn't race at the thought of seeing her. It was just your normal, everyday rising blood pressure because of the inconvenience.

Noreen Kincaid was one hell of an inconvenience.

He called Zeke at the repair shop in Florida City. "Hey, man," Zeke said without even saying hello. "Some lady just called. I think she stole your Corvette." He followed that with a big boom of laughter that filled the Jeep through the Bluetooth.

"Then I'm glad you caught her." And Cutter added, "You're taking a flatbed, right?"

Zeke laughed again. "Oh yeah, man. She was real specific about that."

Cutter chuckled. Of course she'd been specific. He'd put the fear of God into her.

"You think you could pop the hood and look under when you bring her bring in? I'm on my way, but it'd be nice to know what I'm looking at."

"Sure thing, boss." Zeke punctuated with another laugh. "She's got a mighty pretty voice."

"I hadn't noticed. After all, she stole the XB-70."

Zeke snorted. "I told you to get the old man to sell you that car years ago."

"I tried, I tried."

But he hadn't tried hard enough. And he sure as heck didn't know why Mortimer had decided that his niece needed the Corvette more than Cutter did.

Maybe the old man really was going senile.

Zeke No-Last-Name was big, Sasquatch big, with long, beefy arms that looked as if he could bench press a cow. Or a woolly mammoth.

His rusty gray beard and mustache twitched in what might have been a smile as he lifted the Corvette's hood. Thankfully, it had stopped steaming. He tugged on this, tapped on that, wiggled a hose. Then he stood, hands on his hips, and laughed.

Noreen didn't see what was so funny.

"Well, little lady," he said in a John Wayne drawl. "Looks like you've blown your water pump."

In her mother's vernacular, she was fit to be tied. "That's not possible. Cutter went over the entire car before I left. He changed the oil, all the fluids, the spark plugs."

Zeke's beard and mustache twitched again. "Guess he didn't check the water pump." He bellowed another laugh that echoed across the marina. "Let's get this baby back to the shop, and I'll see what parts I've got on hand."

He maneuvered the car onto the flatbed in less time than it took to blow-dry her hair. And in a courtly gesture, he helped her into the cab of the tow truck.

"So you're going to fix it? Cutter's not coming?" She could only pray.

Zeke's belt of laughter in the cab was enough to split her eardrums. "You're joking, right? No one touches the XB-70 but Cutter. Though he might let me fetch and carry for him. Or make the coffee."

Darn. Cutter was on his way.

And she absolutely did not want to see the look on his face when he found out she'd blown his water pump.

7

Four hours later, Noreen, seated on a tall wooden stool, watched as Cutter and Zeke huddled beneath the Corvette's hood.

Zeke's shop was another Budget Auto Repair, obviously a chain store, which was probably how Cutter knew him. The garage was clean and bright, its walls painted white, its floors gray concrete, its bays filled with tall tool chests, air compressors, and bins of nuts and bolts. Zeke's guys had quit work on the dot of five, just after Cutter arrived, and now it was the three of them.

While they'd waited for Cutter, Zeke had given her a loaner, and she'd booked a hotel room. Even if they finished the car today, she wasn't getting on the road again tonight. She'd planned on staying in Miami anyway, only an hour away, but she figured she'd start fresh in the morning for Daytona Beach, or even St. Augustine.

Zeke said for maybe the tenth time, "You're damn lucky I had the right water pump in the stockroom." He stood, stretched his back, then sprawled once more over the car.

Cutter didn't say anything, like he hadn't the other nine times. He'd given a profuse, "Thanks, buddy, you saved my bacon. Otherwise, I'd have had to drive all the way back to Key West to get one," at the very beginning, and that was it.

It was rather nice, too, that he hadn't yelled at Noreen. He hadn't scowled. He hadn't even muttered, "Idiot woman," under his breath.

Zeke was a talker, about his wife and his three little Sasquatch boys, about the car they'd had in yesterday that was beaten to hell but which he still got running, about the race he went to last week, about the great show he'd binged, except that it might have been too bloody and violent for Noreen.

But even with all the talk, he never stopped working. Despite what he'd said about only fetching for Cutter, the two worked side by side.

And finally, Cutter stood straight, stretched, and declared, "That should do it." He pointed at Zeke. "Fire her up."

The big man overflowed the front seat. As he turned the key, the motor roared to life, and he gunned it a few times for good measure.

Noreen had never understood what that accomplished. After a few seconds of the noise, she put her hands over her ears. Then Cutter slammed the hood, circled his hand in the air, and Zeke cut the engine.

"Looks good, sounds good," Cutter said. Then he peeled off his grease-stained overalls and threw them in a big bin. "Tell Lydia thanks for loaning you out."

Zeke gave an awe-shucks shrug. "My pleasure, boss." Zeke liked nicknames. Cutter was the boss, probably because he was more than ten years older than Zeke, and she was the little lady. Maybe he just didn't remember her name.

"Thank you. How much do I owe you?" she asked. "I'm so grateful you dropped everything to take care of this." Works in progress filled the bays, and Zeke had moved out another car to accommodate the Corvette.

"No worries," he said. "He's got you covered." He jerked his head at Cutter, then glanced at the phone in his pocket. "I better get on home to the little lady." Ahh, so all women were little ladies. At least his wife wasn't his old lady.

He shucked his dirty coveralls and, like Cutter, underneath he wore cargo shorts and a button-down surf shirt. "You'll lock up?" he asked, looking at Cutter.

Cutter nodded. "Sure."

When the big man was gone, she said, "You don't have to pay Zeke for me."

At the sink, washing his hands, he said over his shoulder, "Zeke just helped because he loves the XB-70. He doesn't want payment." Drying his hands on paper towels, he turned to her. "And I screwed up," he admitted. "I should've seen the water pump had an issue and replaced it back at the shop. So it's my cost, not yours or Zeke's."

"But it's my car. I should have paid you for the work you did yesterday. Or, at the very least, paid for the parts."

Cutter shook his head, turning to toss the wad of paper towels in the trash. "I did all that for Mortimer. You don't owe me anything."

It gave her a twinge that he hadn't done it for her. She didn't know whether to fight him or thank him.

Instead, she thought about his long drive, and unless he stayed the night in Florida City, he had another long drive back, admittedly without all the traffic. "Thank you. Can I at least take you to dinner before you head back?"

She was starving. It was well after six, and she usually ate early.

He took so long to answer that she thought he'd say no. "Yeah, sure, that would be great. Cuban?"

Did he remember how she'd loved Cuban food? Almost as much as a Thousand Island burger. She nodded. "Perfect."

"I know a great place. We can walk," he added. "It's just across the street and down the block."

And boy, was he right. He ordered at the counter while she grabbed a vacant table. The food was delicious. Her *ropa vieja* over rice, tender shredded beef cooked in tomatoes with onions and green peppers, was amazing, while Cutter devoured his *pernil*, slow-roasted pork served with rice, black beans, and fried plantains. Even though the place was a hole in the wall, it was packed, with many more people ordering takeout.

"We checked all the hoses with the new pump, so you should be good to go." Cutter glanced up from his roast pork. "Unless you want me to take her off your hands."

She laughed. "Did you sabotage the water pump just so I'd sell you the car?" She spoke with a smile, taking the accusation out of her words.

"No." He grinned. "But would it have worked?"

She wagged her finger at him like a teacher who'd caught him writing curse words on the chalkboard. "It's going to take a lot more than a busted water pump."

Then he asked, "Have you got some sort of road service?"

She nodded. "Triple A."

"Good. Because she's like an elegant old house. She always needs repairs." When she opened her mouth, he cut her off. "I'm saying this seriously, not to scare you off. Just like a beautiful old home, sometimes she needs new pipes or new wiring, new this, new that."

"I understand she's a classic. But you've kept her in amazing shape. I'm not worried."

He snorted. "Yeah, but I don't want you calling me from Biloxi and begging me to come out and fix her."

Now why did that give her an idea? She didn't blurt it out right away. She mulled it over while she relished her *ropa vieja*, and sipped the tangy, sweet margarita.

Then finally, she said it, because why not. All he had to do was say no. But maybe he'd say yes. "I've got a proposition." She held up her hand before he could speak. "Don't say anything until I've finished."

He smirked. "Obviously, I'm not going to like it." Then he slugged back a long swallow of beer.

He probably wouldn't, but she made her proposal anyway. "Why don't you come along with me as my mechanic?" He snorted a laugh, and she added, "I said not to say anything until you've heard me out."

"I didn't say anything. I snorted."

"That's even worse."

He held his hands up in surrender. "All right, I won't snort or laugh or say no until you're done."

That wasn't terribly encouraging, but she went on. "I'll pay you. I don't expect you to lose a paycheck. We could be like James Dean and his mechanic. He always took his mechanic along."

Even though he'd said he wouldn't, he laughed. "Yeah, and look what happened to them. His Porsche Spyder creamed by Donald Turnupseed in a 1950 Ford. And the rest is history."

"His mechanic wasn't killed."

Cutter rolled his eyes. "The mechanic was badly injured, but yes, unlike James Dean, he survived. So did Donald Turnupseed."

She crossed her eyes at him. "All right. Let's forget about James Dean and his mechanic. I'm serious. I'd pay for your accommodations and food as well, so you won't be out of pocket."

Still, he frowned. "You don't need to freaking pay me."

"But I don't want you to lose money."

She wasn't sure, but he might be glaring at her now. "I can actually afford to take a week off."

Maybe they were arguing, but he hadn't said no, and her heart did a little jig. Until she suddenly thought there might be a woman who wouldn't want him taking off on a cross-country trek. Why had she just assumed he was single? "But maybe there's a girlfriend or someone who wouldn't appreciate you taking the time to drive with me?"

He puffed out a disgusted breath. "If there was a lady friend, she probably wouldn't have liked me having dinner with you either. So the answer is no, there's no one."

Now she let her heart do the full jig. "Okay. Good. But it might end up being two weeks. I don't want to push the XB-70 too hard every day." She hoped using the pet name would get him on her side.

Because the more she thought about it, the more she wanted it.

"Even two weeks won't stop me from paying rent," he growled.

She might be offending his masculinity. She didn't know how much mechanics made, especially not on a tiny island like Key West. "Can you spare the time? I mean, if there's not a bunch of big jobs lined up?"

"We don't get big jobs."

Her hopes rose. Then she added, "And I'll pay for your flight back home too. Maybe you even want to tour around San Francisco? Have you ever been there?" She knew nothing about him except that he'd lived a few years off island. Other than that, he was a mystery.

"I've never been to San Francisco," he said without inflection.

Under the table, she crossed her fingers. "What do you think?" Thank God she wasn't trying to hold her breath, because he took so long to answer she might have passed out.

"If I go," he said, followed by a long pause during which she could actually hear her heart beating in her ears. "I reserve the right to keep trying to talk you into selling the Corvette."

She wanted to punch the air. Until he said, "And that's a big if."

At least he hadn't given her an unequivocal no.

HE WAS NUTS FOR EVEN CONSIDERING IT. IT WAS A CRAZY idea. Of course, she thought he worked full time. He'd only been at the shop that day because he knew she was coming by to inspect the car. Not that he expected her to want to drive off with it, for Christ's sake.

He was a free man, at least in the short term. He could do it. And he'd never taken the XB-70 cross-country. He and Mortimer had driven her up to Daytona Beach to watch the Daytona 500, and a few times Mortimer had gone with him to visit some of the Budget shops around the state, but that was the extent of the XB-70's travels.

He was intrigued enough to wonder how the car would do.

But seven to fourteen days with Noreen Kincaid?

He'd lose his mind.

She'd want luxury hotels and five-star restaurants and require a lot of pampering. Not that she'd been a complainer in her teens, but that was forty years ago. Who the hell knew now? And she'd want to talk incessantly. He could handle constant chatter from Zeke because they were working on cars. He never really had to listen.

But Noreen Kincaid would want to be listened to.

On the other hand, he'd been bored lately. Not just lately, but for a while. He wasn't unhappy. He still loved working on cars, that would never end. He'd built a Cobra replica from the ground up, restored an Austin Healey and a Mercedes-Benz 190SL, and of course, he'd worked on Mortimer's XB-70. And he'd enjoyed starting up that first Budget Auto Repair twenty-five years ago, being "management," expanding over the years until there were franchises in every city across Florida. He'd morphed from mechanic to businessman, and despite hating being stuck in an office, he spent way too much time doing just that while overseeing his management team. The most fun he had these days was venturing out to visit the various franchises, Zeke's included.

And he'd been feeling the need for something new and different.

Maybe he just needed an adventure. Like two weeks driving his favorite car across the country with a beautiful woman he used to have the hots for. Big-time hots. The kind of hots you never forgot.

"On the other hand," he said, enjoying the way her eyes lit up, the changing shades of blue as he paused a little too long for her liking.

Until she had to ask, "On the other hand, what?"

Her eagerness made him smile. "On the other hand," he finally gave her. "A little adventure might be fun."

She gasped. "Oh my God, this is going to be such an adventure. I promise." And she actually believed what she said.

He watched her eyes change again. "But only *if*," he stressed the word, "I decide to go." He enjoyed the shifting emotions on her face as he drew everything out. From a smile to pursed lips to a frown between her eyes to a grin again, as if she knew what he was doing. "We need a few rules," he said.

She scowled, which on her was playful, even sexy. "What rules?"

Yeah, what rules? He made something up on the fly. "First, you don't get to do all the driving."

She pretended to consider that, crooking her mouth this way, then that, propping her chin on her hand. "I guess it would be nice to have a break so I can look at the scenery."

Damn right she'd need a break. The XB-70 was a beauty, but she was a beast. It wasn't like driving a Chevy or a Ford with all the bells and whistles.

"And I want to pick some of the stops we make."

She pretended not to like that either, narrowing her pretty blue eyes. "Like where?"

He thought for a moment. "Like Sedona. I want to see the red rocks."

Her eyes went wide, as if he'd surprised her. "Sedona is great."

"And I've never been to Vegas."

"You've never been to Vegas?" Shock dropped her mouth open a moment. Then, as if she considered fighting him on it, she took a long time getting around to saying, "I can do Vegas."

"And anywhere else along the way," he added, "I'd like a say."

She nodded solemnly, as if they were signing a contract. "I agree to that." Then she asked, eyeing him suspiciously, "What else?"

So he laid it on her. "I'm not taking your money and I pay my own way."

Her lips turned stubbornly stiff. "But—"

He held up his finger. "No buts."

She didn't use the word again, but it was still there. "I'm asking you to be my wingman and work on the car if it breaks down. That's worth something."

His mind went to a whole bunch of places he'd like to go with her. Badly. It had been forty years, and he remembered every exhilarating moment they'd spent in Mortimer's Corvette. But he sure as hell wasn't making it a price of going along. Not that she meant it that way. She was over fifty-five. Women didn't want sex after that point, right?

He looked at her stylishly cut hair, the smattering of different colors in the blond, a little red, a little brunette, a little gold, even a few strands of silver. And she'd kept in shape. Christ, yes, her curves made him drool. But still, she was his age, and women after that certain age just weren't interested anymore.

Damn, he needed to grab his steering wheel and pull it back to the straight and narrow. Getting worked up with impossible ideas was ridiculous. He'd learned that long ago when she left Key West for the last time. "I don't live paycheck to paycheck," he said. "I can pay my own way. And —" He leaned forward. "I have one more rule."

Her gaze turned shadowed and wary. As if she knew this was probably the thing she couldn't live with. "What?"

Then he laid it on her. "I reserve the right to keep on trying to talk you into selling me the XB-70."

She sat back, taking her margarita with her, sipping it. "You can keep asking as much as you like." She swirled the margarita in her glass. "And I reserve the right to say no."

He tapped the table. "Fair enough."

"Do we have a deal?" She waited. He could almost see her excitement shimmering around her.

He was sure he heard her heart beating all the way across the table, but he drew the moment out a little longer, liking the way her breasts rose and fell as she breathed. The clothing she wore appealed to him, the blousy tank top baring her shoulders, not too young for her, but not matronly either. Her plum-colored lipstick enticed him, especially now that it was almost gone, as if someone had kissed it off her. And her sparkly blue toenails damn near drove him crazy.

And he whispered, "Deal."

NOREEN WANTED TO PUNCH THE AIR. HE WAS GOING WITH her. She wouldn't have to worry every second that something would go wrong with the car, leaving her stranded. Her road service would have helped, but now she'd have a mechanic who could fix anything on the Corvette. He didn't even want payment. Although that made her feel guilty. She'd have to find ways to pay him back, maybe a few gourmet meals. And she could put all the hotel charges on her card. She could make it work.

And then she turned to practicalities. "We need to go back to Key West and get your stuff for the trip."

He shook his head as he swigged his beer, his lips pursed around the bottle. "Since I didn't know the problem when I left Key West, I brought a bag with me, enough for a couple of days. No sense going back for more. I can buy anything I need along the way."

He wasn't like her, needing his stuff. Cutter Sorenson would never over pack. "You think we can fit it in the trunk?"

"It'll squish down. The problem with your suitcase was the hard corners. The trunk lid wouldn't close over them."

She didn't want to throw any roadblocks on the trip and let it go. "I'd planned to stay a night in Miami, but since we're stuck in Florida City..." She went through her thinking of earlier in the day. "I'm considering Daytona Beach or St. Augustine, which is only another hour farther along, and they have some really cute bed-and-breakfasts there."

His answer was immediate. "Daytona."

"Oohkay." She drew out the word. "Is there something special you wanted to see?"

He scoffed deep in his throat and punctuated with an eye roll, as if she should know. "Daytona International Speedway."

"Ahhhh." She elongated the sound, stalling. "The Speedway."

"In the old days," he said, as if they weren't born during those old days. "They used to race on the sand. It's heavily packed there. Those old races were f—" He stopped himself before saying the word, but she got the idea. "They were amazing. I've watched a ton of videos."

"So you've never been to the Speedway?"

"Of course I've been to the Speedway," he said with a grimace and a note of disgust. "But only on race day. During the week, they have a tour where you walk on the track."

She raised her hands and made a *wooo* noise like the seance ladies in *The Ghost and Mr. Chicken*.

He gave her a dressing down with his eyes. "I guarantee you'll be amazed."

"I'm perfectly fine just lying on the beach while you take the tour."

He pressed his lips together before saying, "New rule."

She jumped in. "We've already signed the deal. You can't add new rules."

He ignored her. "New rule. We both have to see the sights the other one chooses."

Oh, that was dangerous. She started thinking up crazy things she could force him to see. "Deal," she snapped before he could imagine she had an ulterior motive.

Whipping her phone off the table, she tapped on the rental app she'd added to her phone just for this trip. "I'll find us a place to stay in Daytona Beach."

"There are plenty of motels along the main drag. No need to book ahead."

She looked at him over the top of her phone. "And my new rule is that we book ahead. I don't want to end up sleeping in the Corvette."

"It's impossible to sleep in the XB-70."

She smiled, like a jungle cat about to pounce. "So it's good to book ahead."

She pushed the microphone and spoke her destination and date. And up popped a gazillion rentals. She pared it down. "Oh my gosh, this place is fabulous. It has two pools and three hot tubs, a mini golf course along with ping-pong and badminton. It's a fabulous resort."

"A resort means a million little kids," he said in a growl.

She tipped her head, giving him a look. "You don't like little kids?"

"I like them in their proper place. Just not in my hot tub."

She had to agree. A hot tub was for relaxing, and little kids never relaxed. "This place has an adult-only pool, sauna, and hot tub." She turned the phone for him to see.

He frowned, hesitated, then pulled a pair of reading glasses out of his shirt pocket and propped them on his nose. She wanted to laugh, but held it off. He hadn't worn reading glasses for the menu, not tonight, and not the other night in Key West. Which meant he knew the menus. She wouldn't admit that she wore specially designed contact lenses for reading and distance.

He flipped through the photos. "It looks disgustingly expensive."

She took the phone back. "Au contraire," she said in a bad French accent. "It's excessively cheap. Probably because they have a room available only for a night, and this is last minute. Most people want to book a resort for a week or more." Then she turned the phone once more to show him the cost.

Behind his reading glasses, his eyes widened. But all he said was, "Sounds good."

She booked it before she lost the deal. "Okay, done."

"I'll give you cash," he said.

"I'm treating you to the resort." Then she added, "You paid for dinner tonight and you can buy lunch tomorrow."

When he shrugged, she decided she'd won.

❧ 8 ☙

They headed out the next morning on the four-hour drive to Daytona Beach, stopping first in Miami where Cutter looked up a secondhand store while Noreen drove. He found two pairs of cargo shorts, three shirts, and swim trunks.

And there she'd stopped the shopping spree. "You are *not* buying underwear from a secondhand store."

He didn't intend to. He actually had standards. But it was fun to let her go on thinking he would have. They dropped by a Walmart and he stocked up. "I bet a lot of places will have a washer and dryer," he said before getting excessive in his purchases.

And if there wasn't, he'd toss out the dirty stuff and buy more. Like Jack Reacher, who never carried more than a toothbrush.

They ate breakfast before leaving Miami and didn't stop for more than a bio break until they reached Daytona Beach. She'd made him slather on sunscreen for the drive as if he hadn't lived in Key West all his life.

"I want to drive with the top down, and we don't want to get sunburned," she'd said.

That made him smile. She was such a mom, especially when she wore that cute scarf over her hair, driving 1950s style.

They didn't fight over who would drive. It was good to let her get used to the XB-70's eccentricities. And he had to admit she was a good driver.

But the best thing about driving with the top down was the lack of useless chatter. The roar of the wind drowned out any words that passed between them. He was comfortable and closed his eyes, having driven this road far too many times for it to retain its novelty.

They arrived in Daytona Beach in the early afternoon. Being midweek, the schools weren't out for the day yet, but tourist traffic still clogged the main drag.

Stopped at a light, Noreen said, "It's too early to check in. What do you want to do until it's time?"

He slid his sunglasses down his nose and looked at her over the rims. "Daytona International Speedway for the tour. Remember?"

She pursed her lips as if she'd been hoping he'd forget. "I'll drop you off and take a walk on the beach. Then I'll come back for you."

He shook his head. "Absolutely not. We agreed. I pick a place to visit, you pick a place. And we both go."

"Did I actually agree to that rule? I think you said it, but I didn't actually agree to it." She pulled away from the light, punching the gas, and the car leapt forward. But he didn't miss the snarky words and tone or the tilt of amusement on her plum-colored lips.

"You're not weaseling out of this," he insisted, raising his voice to be heard. "After all, I agreed to come along with you."

She growled. "All right," her voice snippy, "how do I get there?"

He directed her, allowing himself a smile. When she chose, he was sure she'd make him pay. Jesus, what if she picked a shopping mall?

❧

OKAY, IT WOULDN'T HAVE BEEN HER CHOICE, BUT THE Speedway was actually impressive. The tour itself wasn't packed with people, just two guys from Texas and a couple from the Midwest, the husband a NASCAR fanatic who could name every driver that ever won the Daytona 500.

Despite the lack of a crowd, their guide maintained his enthusiasm, a middle-aged man—"Call me Gary"—preceded by a paunch that rivaled Santa Claus. He knew the entire history of the Speedway and the Daytona 500, and he gave it all. "The tri-oval track is two-and a-half miles long, but there's also a road course for sports cars and another for motorcycles. So you can see how versatile it is."

Enthralled, the NASCAR fan listened as if Gary was a driver, while the wife covered her yawn with her hand. But Gary wasn't deterred. He recited stats, regaled them with tales of the great crashes, got a tear in his eye recounting the names of the people who'd lost their lives.

Then they climbed on the minibus for a trip around the track. Cutter looked at her as if he knew she was bored out of her mind while he enjoyed every moment of the tedium.

She smiled at him from behind her sunglasses. "Wow, this is really cool, isn't it?"

He simply grinned.

He was a good traveling companion. She'd expected him to pick on her driving the way Everett had, to the point where she'd let him do all the driving so she didn't have to bear the criticism. But Cutter had relaxed in his seat and might even have fallen asleep.

The track was what Gary called a tri-oval, with an extra turn so there was less banking than a regular oval track. She'd never actually seen a race and always thought of a racetrack as being flat, except for the turns, but this was banked all the way round. The steep turns were almost a slingshot up, around, and out the other side.

Gary bellowed out, "Y'all want to walk on the track?"

They all punched their fists in the air to match his enthusiasm. Once outside the bus, Noreen realized just how steep the turns were.

Cutter held out his hand. "Come on, let's climb."

She took his hand and let him pull her up. "How do they even drive on this?"

He didn't explain aerodynamics, just smiled. "It's pretty amazing to walk on it. I've always wanted to do this. But—" He shrugged. "I've always been on race day and would've had to stay an extra day if I wanted the tour."

"Then I'm glad I could help fulfill a lifetime dream for you."

He barked out a laugh, and she thought he was about to make some snide remark, but then he pulled her to the top, and they turned to the amazing view of the Speedway, the spectator stands, and from up here, she could make out the road course as well, punched into the interior of the Speedway.

Holding Cutter's hand, she closed her eyes, imagined the roar of the engines, the heart-pounding action, and her blood raced like the cars.

"Maybe I'll have to see a race one day," she ventured.

He smiled. "Maybe you will."

And she thought about seeing one with him. Which was impossible, of course. They only had two weeks at most.

Finally, Gary called them all back to the bus. The NASCAR fan and the two guys from Texas had made it to the top. The wife stayed with the bus, texting on her phone.

Stepping off the bus at the end of the tour, Cutter grabbed Gary's hand, shook profusely, slapping him on the back. "That was great, man. I never knew all that stuff about the track. You're amazing. Thanks a million."

Gary beamed under his praise. And Noreen gripped the man's hand in both of hers. "That was the best, really the best,"

It took so little to make a person's day. And they left Gary with an enormous smile on his face.

As they climbed in the car, it was check-in time at the resort. "I miss my dashboard GPS," she told Cutter as she pulled her phone out of her purse to look up the route.

"You can add an aftermarket one." Then he grinned. "But maybe the best thing about the XB-70 is not knowing where you're going. And not caring about it either."

Maybe that was a metaphor for his life. He'd never known where he was going, and that's why he was still a mechanic on Key West. But it certainly didn't seem to bother him.

The resort was on the main drag, fronting the beach. After she'd checked them in, Cutter carried their belongings up to the room. His duffle much smaller than hers, they'd both fit in the Corvette's trunk along with her computer case, shoe bag, and the small cooler. So there.

"Wow," Cutter said as he dropped everything in the suite's small foyer. "Not bad digs, Kincaid, you done good."

A large bathroom accompanied the bedroom, with a second bathroom just off the hall. The well-outfitted kitchen had all the appliances, including a blender if they wanted margaritas. A living room with a sofa bed, two chairs, dining table, and a flatscreen TV looked out over the balcony to the beach and ocean beyond.

She turned to Cutter. "I'll make you a deal."

He raised a brow with a skeptical glint in his eye. "What deal?"

"I'll pay for the room if you take the sofa bed." She smiled widely. "And if you barbecue some shrimp." She jutted her chin at the gorgeous ocean view and the barbecue on one end of the balcony.

He made a face, narrowed his eyes, looked at her a long moment. "Deal." Then he held out his hand. "Let me have the keys, and I'll get the groceries."

She couldn't say why she froze for a second. After all, he'd been driving the Corvette far longer than she had. He knew every quirk. And he loved that car. He'd never hurt it. Yet in the next moment, she realized that for one second, she'd been afraid he wouldn't come back, leaving her all alone.

He raised his brows. "Never have put a scratch on her, never will," he said, as if he guessed her thoughts.

"Uncle Mortimer would turn over in his grave if either of us scratched her."

He winked. "That's why we scattered his ashes at sea."

The guilt pang hit her again. She should have helped Cutter scatter her uncle's ashes. But she hadn't even known he'd died.

She tossed him the keys and smiled away her thoughts, even if she couldn't smile away the guilt. "We're going to need margaritas too."

He gave her a little bow, flourishing his hand. "Your wish is my command."

Then she handed him one of the card keys. "I think I'll walk on the beach while you're handling all the domestic chores."

His laughter echoed all the way down the hallway.

Ten minutes later, she was on the beach, relishing the feel of sand between her toes.

Though most schools hadn't let out for summer vacation, the beach was still relatively crowded. Kids built sand castles, sunbathers drank in the last rays of the day, giggling teenagers frolicked in the sand, and the shouts of a volleyball game rang out across the beach.

Noreen figured Cutter would be gone at least forty-five minutes. Then he'd have to heat the barbecue. She had time, and she gave herself over to the sand beneath her feet, the salty scent of fresh ocean air, and the delicious warmth of the day. Out here, the humidity didn't bother her.

Smelling the barbecue even before she unlocked the door, her mouth watered. Besides taking care of the car, there were definite advantages to having Cutter around.

He'd already blended the margaritas and salted the rims.

When he saw her, he hooked a thumb over his shoulder. "I was just waiting for you to get back before I put the shrimp on the barbie," he drawled like the famous Australian and picked up the plate of seasoned, skewered shrimp.

"Oh my God, you're fast."

"I'm fast when I want to be." He winked. "But I take my time when speed isn't a need." Turning, he carried the plate like a waiter.

That absolutely had to be a sexual innuendo, but she didn't mind.

Just before he closed the balcony door, he added, "And in this case, I bought the shrimp already skewered."

His laughter floated through the closed glass door.

The guy was too funny. He just might be a good companion on this trip. Especially since the margarita tasted delicious on her tongue.

Finding a salad kit in the refrigerator, she put it together with tomatoes, cucumbers, and avocado, finishing up when he came in with the cooked shrimp.

He kissed his fingers. "Perfection. Even if I say so myself."

They ate on the balcony, and after the first scrumptious shrimp, she gave him his due. "You're right. Perfection." The evening was perfection too, the sun beginning to dip, casting shadows across the sand, the air pleasantly warm.

He held up his margarita and toasted. "To good driving days, a good start to the trip, and to the Daytona International Speedway."

She had to laugh as they tapped glasses, and she gulped the delicious margarita, giving herself a momentary brain freeze. Then they dined in comfortable silence, enjoying the food and watching people walk along the beachfront and pelicans dive-bomb into the sea.

And she wanted to know more about him. "So you've always been Mortimer's mechanic?"

He snorted a laugh. "You think I'd let some other grease monkey touch the XB-70?"

"Of course not. I should have known." But Corvette maintenance wasn't where she was heading, and he forced her to ask more. "Didn't you ever want to do anything else? Besides work on cars, I mean."

He shrugged. "A man has to live up to his skill set." He held up a hand, fisting his fingers. "I'm good at what I do. And I like what I do. I've got freedom. I could never be tied down to a nine-to-five desk job."

"But you work for an auto shop. What's it called?" She couldn't remember the name.

"Budget Auto Repair," he said with a straight face.

"That was the name of Zeke's shop too."

He nodded, finishing his last shrimp.

"So that's how you know each other, because you both work for the same chain?"

He was silent a little longer this time, finally saying, "Yeah." Which was not very enlightening.

"But you're still working on the shop's hours, so you're not really free."

Neither was she. Though she had her own business and she worked from home, she still had deadlines set by her clients. She might juggle things if someone wanted a rush job—or she wanted to take a cross-country trek—but she was ruled by what other people wanted from her. And yet, because she could take her work with her, she had the freedom to get up and go. Not that she planned to work on this trip since she'd scheduled around it.

But Cutter had to be there when his boss told him to.

"I'm good at what I do," he said, slouching back in his chair and propping his feet on the railing. "And when you're good, people let you call the shots, telling them when you want to work and what you want to work on. If I feel like taking a day off to fire up the XB-70 or take out the boat for some fishing, no one tells me I can't."

But working that way, how could he have saved up enough money to buy the Corvette? Not that his money situation was her business. Maybe he expected her to give him a cut rate. Or maybe he'd thought Mortimer would leave the car to him since he'd cared for it for so long.

Honestly, she didn't know why Uncle Mortimer hadn't done exactly that. Or why he'd put in his will that she had to come to Florida if she wanted the car.

But whatever her uncle's thoughts had been, the car was hers.

Cutter studied her. "Do you enjoy your job?"

She didn't have to think. "I love editing. I have a hand in helping perfect a masterpiece. It's like reading someone's thoughts right out of their head and giving them shape."

"You get to call your own shots too."

"But whenever someone's paying you to do something, you're not totally free."

"Don't you think Mortimer was free to do whatever he wanted? He took out a charter only if he felt like it, and if he thought a potential customer was a dickhead—" He shrugged, grinning. "He went fishing on his own and told them to pound sand."

That sounded like Uncle Mortimer. "But he had a bunch of boats and captains working for him." Not that she'd understood that when she was a teenager. She thought he'd had only his boat. It wasn't until the attorney contacted her and told her what her uncle had amassed that she realized he'd owned several boats which supported him and gave him the freedom he'd craved.

Cutter sighed, staring out at the setting sun as it cast brilliant colors across the drifting clouds and the waves. "Freedom is being able to do what you love. And when you love it, someone paying you to do it is like the icing on the cake."

A scoff rose up her throat. "I don't do it for free, not even for friends." Then she heard how ugly that sounded. And tightfisted. Especially when she knew Uncle Mortimer hadn't paid Cutter to work on his car, at least not beyond driving privileges.

She sounded like she was judging him.

Instead of jumping all over her words, he asked, "So what does a freelance editor do?"

Over dinner the other night, she hadn't explained. "I provide developmental editing, which is working through the holes in an author's plot, characterization issues, lack of motivation, and pretty much anything that doesn't make sense. I also line edit where I look for grammar, sentence structure, word usage, clarity. And I copyedit, proof."

"I remember now. You wanted to be a New York editor."

"Yeah, that's what I wanted. It just never happened." And here she was grilling him about why he hadn't done more with his life than being a mechanic, when she'd never fulfilled her dream either.

Maybe it was okay that your dream changed. She'd had kids and marriages to worry about. And Cutter just had himself. Or did he? She hadn't asked if he'd ever married or had kids, only if he had a current girlfriend. "I had the girls to take care of. Do you have any kids?"

A snort welled out of him, and he shook his head. "Never been married either. I'm not even like Mortimer, with a couple of nieces or nephews."

She remembered he was an only child, but she wouldn't pry into why he hadn't married. She'd never expected him to. He hadn't seemed the marrying type.

"I guess you like your freedom," she said.

He shrugged again. All his shrugs seemed to have different meanings, from I-really-don't-care to you've-gotta-be-kidding. But he said, "It wasn't intentional. Key West is a different kind of place, and it takes a different kind of person to live out there. There're no big shopping malls with a bunch of department stores. No Costco." He laughed, adding a little twist of his mouth. "But we've got great food."

She sighed, staring out at the ocean, the reflection of the sun dappling the waves with color. "I totally get it. I need my mall and my Costco and my Super Walmart."

He agreed with a half smile. "Most people need their Super Walmart."

It wasn't for her to fault his lifestyle choices. But she could never have lived on Key West. She could never have handled men of her uncle's or Cutter's ilk, men content to be charter captains or mechanics so they could have the freedom to do what they wanted when they wanted. But then, neither of them had families to support. And her prime motivator had always been making sure her girls had everything they needed.

She could never have married someone like Cutter, who worked only when he wanted to.

And yet, she'd been a terrible judge of character in the men she had picked.

Could a life with a man like Cutter have been any worse?

9

Cutter could have told her he'd never married because he never found the right woman. He could have told her he'd been looking for someone like her. Not her specifically, but someone *like* her, the fun-loving, try-anything girl she'd been that last summer. But not the kind of woman who'd go stark raving mad on an island a hundred miles from the mainland and all the good stores. There weren't a lot of women like that just floating around.

His attending university hadn't come up between them that summer. And until Noreen couldn't stop talking about how badly she wanted to finish high school and head off to college, it hadn't come up for him either. Maybe it was the fact that she'd assumed he wouldn't go for higher education or that perhaps she'd even thought he couldn't make it, but after she was gone, he'd worked hard and applied for scholarships. And he'd headed up to Gainesville, earning his business degree. After that, there was an office gig at a big corporation in Miami. He could have found a job in any big city, could even have gone to San Francisco and shown Noreen that he wasn't some nowhere guy who lacked ambition or aspiration.

But he'd hated the work, hated living in the city, and after sticking it out for an agonizing three years, he'd returned to Key West. Once the place was in your blood, you never got it out. He wanted the laid-back style. He didn't even mind the tourists.

But how could you explain that to a woman who needed a fancy mall, Costco, Super Walmart, and family? Not that there was anything wrong with malls or Costco or Super Walmart. Or families. Hell, he headed out once a month to stock up. He just didn't want to live in a place that was big enough for Costco or Super Walmart.

He didn't begrudge her those things, and the evening had certainly been pleasant. But to her, he was still a nowhere guy without ambition.

Maybe there was an irony in where he'd ended up. He'd left Miami and the office job he'd hated, and yet now he was back spending too much time in an office. But at least he was the one in control, and he could take off when he liked, even make a jaunt across the country. And he still had Key West.

What if he told Noreen about the franchises? But no, he was long past having to prove himself.

When they finally went to bed, the pullout sofa was comfortable to sleep on. Luxurious digs weren't his style anyway. In the morning, after they'd packed up their stuff and headed out to the car, she asked, "Do you want to drive?"

He didn't wait a single second for her to change her mind. When the XB-70 was beneath his ass and her wheel in his hands, he felt energized. Driving her was like riding a bucking bronco. She had a mind of her own, and you had to tame her.

Once they'd strapped in, Noreen asked, "Any preference on where we go?"

All he cared about right now was getting on the road. Exactly where they went didn't matter. Driving was all about the road beneath them and his hands on the steering wheel.

"You choose," he said.

"How about heading for Tallahassee today? Let's go up the coast and stop in St. Augustine for brunch."

"Sounds good to me."

The coastal byway took an extra twenty minutes versus the freeway, but the scenery was worth it. He drove the road faster than she would, but Noreen didn't seem to mind. Her sunglasses shaded her eyes, her scarf held her hair down, and her sunscreen protected her face.

She didn't chatter at him constantly, and he didn't think that was just the wind drowning her out. He actually enjoyed driving with her, and they were in St. Augustine in ninety minutes.

"Oh, look, the Castillo de San Marcos." She pointed. "Let's visit."

Had she always been so enthusiastic? He could only remember one thing she'd been enthusiastic about, sex, the kissing, the touching, the pleasure. And he'd loved it all, the silky feel of her skin, the way she...

Jesus, he definitely had to stop his mind from going there.

"Sure, sounds great." He remembered touring the old fort on a school trip when he was in elementary school. There hadn't been much money in his house, not for touring and vacations, but back then, school trips were subsidized for kids like him.

He was lucky to find a parking spot, but it meant a walk to the Castillo, and by the time they got there, the line to enter snaked almost to the sidewalk. But Noreen bounced ahead. Yes, the woman seemed to bounce, and she stopped a docent patrolling the line, talking animatedly.

Racing back to him, she said dramatically, "Oh my God, it's at least an hour, and that's if we're lucky. Can you imagine what this place is like in the summer or at Easter break?"

He glanced at his watch. "We have time."

She shook her head. "I'm starving. I want brunch. Let's skip the Castillo and eat."

He looked at the line he didn't relish standing in and nodded. "Okay, if that's what you want."

"Let's get a few pictures first. I need to send something to the girls."

"How old are they again?" Girls implied they were teenagers, but he knew they were older. One of them was doing a vet internship, and the other was a department store buyer.

"Grace is thirty-four, and April is twenty-six."

Thirty-four. Jesus. That made him feel old. But Noreen was only a year younger than him, and right now, she was the embodiment of young at heart.

She'd removed the scarf, fluffed her hair, and freshened her lipstick. Appreciating how photogenic she was, he took pictures while she mugged for the camera. Handing the phone back, he waited as she flipped through the photos to make sure there was one she wanted to send.

She grinned at him. "Fabulous. You actually made me look good, despite the sun on my face."

Didn't she know she looked good in any light? It had been true all those years ago, and time hadn't changed the fact.

St. Augustine had a cute touristy downtown, filled with artisan shops, quaint hotels, bed-and-breakfasts, and plenty of eateries, everything in fitting with the town's old-time roots. St. Augustine was founded in 1565 and the Castillo built in 1695.

She chose a restaurant with only a ten-minute wait. Cutter had never been fond of waiting for a meal, not that he dined out much. He hadn't felt like impressing a lady in a long time. Sure, he had female friends, or, using the more popular term of the day, friends with benefits.

The wait turned out to be more like fifteen minutes, but

he handled it well. Once they were seated, she ordered Eggs Benedict, while he got a regular breakfast with bacon, eggs, hash browns, and toast. He liked that she wasn't finicky about her weight, which she certainly didn't have to worry about.

She took out her phone while they waited for their meals to arrive.

"Okay, let's figure out where we'll stay tonight in Tallahassee."

"I thought you booked that last night."

"I'm winging it," she said, smiling. "Besides, didn't we only just decide on Tallahassee?"

She had a point. After a few minutes of phone scrolling, she gasped, her pleasure seeping through. "Oh my God." It wasn't just her tone or her gasp, it was the bright light in her eyes. "You won't believe what I just found."

He wanted to groan. It would probably be something horribly expensive, like a wellness spa where she'd make him take a mud bath.

"It's a train park."

He quirked one side of his mouth. "What the hell is a train park?"

"You sleep in a converted train car. How cool is that?"

"Sounds uncomfortable," he said drily.

She clucked her tongue. "They're all tricked out, with their own bathroom too. And this one has twin bunk beds." She rolled her shoulders with just a hint of embarrassment. "I mean, it might be the same room, but it's separate beds. And there's even a privacy curtain to pull over your bunk."

Okay. He could handle that. He wouldn't have to look at her sleeping. Except that he'd smell her perfume. And damn, she smelled good. Like sweet fruit.

But he'd be good, scout's honor, even if he'd been the furthest thing from a boy scout. No throwing himself at her. He'd respect her.

Even so, his, "Sounds great," came out a bit strangled.

She frowned. "You don't like it."

"No, it sounds..." He searched for the right word. "Interesting."

She waggled her eyebrows at him. "It even has its very own hot tub."

"Inside the train car?" he asked with animated surprise.

"There's a deck outside, with a barbecue and a table and chairs. And a hot tub."

They hadn't gotten around to using the hot tub last night. And in the bright light of morning, he suspected that was a good idea. But their own a private hot tub seemed infinitely worse than a public one at a resort.

He'd be alone with her. And they'd be wearing nothing more than bathing suits.

Maybe a mud bath at a wellness spa was a better bet.

But he was strong. Besides, he hated to dampen her enthusiasm this early on. "I mean it. It sounds great. Let's do it." Then he asked, "How much is it?"

"It's actually cheaper than some of the other places on here." She shrugged, drawing his attention to her shapely shoulders in the sleeveless blouse. "Maybe no one wants to sleep in a train car."

He laughed. "Yeah, go figure." But when she grimaced, he added, "Go on, book it."

Her fingers flew over the phone, and finally she smiled. "Done. Now let's find somewhere really cool to visit in Tallahassee."

Their food arrived, and she was forced to put her phone down, picking it up between bites, sometimes even scrolling while she ate. Then she waved at him, pointed at her phone screen, her eyes once again alight with excitement, and after swallowing, she burst out with, "Oh my God, I found the perfect place."

"Dare I ask?" he drawled.

She cross-eyed him. "Yes, you may ask. Because you'll love this. It's the Tallahassee Automobile Museum."

He gave her a disbelieving snort. "After touring the Speedway yesterday, you actually want to go to an automobile museum?"

She fluttered her eyelashes at him. "It's got all the Batmobiles."

"Wow!" He almost ruined it with a snicker.

"And for you, there're a ton of muscle cars."

"Amazing. Let's do it."

She huffed a sigh at him. "You said it was my choice. And here I thought you'd be terribly excited that I didn't pick something like the Erotic Museum."

He damn near snorted out his coffee. "I'm not sure, but that might've proven quite interesting."

Her eyes twinkled. "You'd have hated it. Cars are more your style."

He wouldn't have hated it at all, not with her by his side and the blushes that were sure to creep up her face. "Is there really an Erotic Museum in Tallahassee?"

She batted her eyelashes, grinning wickedly. "You'll just have to look it up yourself."

It was suddenly way too hot in the café's window seat.

It was hot, and Noreen finally had to ask Cutter to pull over and put the top up. So much for driving top down all the way to California, but she was frying in the sun. After that, they drove with the windows open, the air blowing through the car. It was lovely.

Though it was four hours to Tallahassee, with Cutter driving, they made it in record time, even though they took the bypass around Jacksonville. As they rolled into town, Noreen looked up the directions to the museum on her phone's GPS.

Okay, the parking lot was nowhere near full when they arrived. That might be a bad sign. But then she saw the statue of Elvis strumming his guitar by his tricked-out pink Cadillac, and she knew the place was perfect.

Jumping out of the car after Cutter parked, she handed her phone over. "More pictures, please. The girls will love this one." They'd texted back after breakfast with oohs and aahs over the Castillo pictures. But Elvis would be even better. Though they'd probably roll their eyes at her.

She practically grabbed the phone from him. "Oh my God, this one is absolutely perfect." Cutter knew just how to make her look good. Almost popping in close to kiss his cheek, she thought better of it just in time.

Inside the museum, she realized the status of the parking lot was indeed an omen, but actually a good one. After buying their tickets, hardly anyone roamed the rooms inside, almost as if they had the place to themselves.

She dragged him to the Batmobiles first and made him take more pictures. "Aren't they cool?"

He raised a sardonic brow. "Yeah, really cool."

Maybe he was just playing with her, or mollifying her. But there was a glint in his eyes, as if he might actually enjoy what he saw.

They strolled through the muscle cars, and he stopped to read the signs, sometimes smiling, sometimes snorting, as if the descriptions were wrong. They found the Corvettes and his comment was, "The XB-70 far surpasses any of these cars."

She had to agree. Her Corvette was a stunning beauty well worth a place in a museum. But though it was called an automobile museum, the place featured more than just cars, including collections of matchbox cars, old cash registers, boat engines, and one-of-a-kind pianos. They even had the horse-drawn carriage that conveyed Abraham Lincoln's body after his assassination.

"I don't think that's the real thing, just a replica," Cutter said.

"Why not?"

"I'm pretty sure they paraded Kennedy's body in the same carriage. And that it's in the Smithsonian. Or they still use it or something."

She harrumphed, narrowing her gaze on him. "Let's look it up." She quickly found a picture of Kennedy's funeral procession. "Okay, you're wrong." Now, why did she enjoy that so much? She pointed at the photo, holding it out to him. "Kennedy's carriage was a flatbed they call a caisson. It's just two big wheels with his casket sitting on top." She pointed at Lincoln's hearse, a big carriage with windows through which Lincoln's casket could be viewed.

Cutter snorted, but she could swear a smile lurked as well. "Still doesn't mean this is Lincoln's hearse and that they didn't use Kennedy's caisson."

She gave him a mock growl. "All right, let me find pictures of Lincoln's funeral." It was far easier than she'd imagined, images popping up right away, and she held up the phone to him again, tapping the screen. "See there? It's a carriage, not a caisson."

"Yeah, I see," he grumbled.

Then he took her phone and opened another link, standing close to her so they could both read the article.

God, he smelled good. He'd always smelled good, even after he'd been working on cars. She'd never minded that hint of oil and manly sweat. It made her think of how well he worked with his hands, made her remember all the things he could do with those powerful hands. Maybe it was just him, his sexy pheromones, because honestly, she couldn't detect even a hint of grease and oil, not at all, just Cutter, all male.

But she needed to concentrate on the controversy at hand.

"See here," he said. "Lincoln's body toured the country for two weeks, and they used sixteen different horse-drawn hearses."

She wrinkled her nose. "Two weeks, a hundred and fifty years ago?"

"They had embalming even back then."

"Yes, but..." She left the rest unsaid.

He chuckled, probably thinking the same. "I guess you're right."

She put her hands on her hips. "You *guess*?"

He made a face. "You're right. It's not the same carriage as Kennedy's."

She punched the air. "I win."

"However—" He pointed at the museum's hearse. "We still don't know if this was one of the sixteen hearses." He drew his finger beneath a line on the signage. "They don't actually have provenance authenticating that it's one of those carriages."

"Okay, so you're saying we're both right?"

"Yes, we can safely say we're both right."

She actually enjoyed arguing with him. It was just too fun.

Then he linked his arm with hers and pulled her along. "Since you picked the place where we're staying tonight and the tourist attraction we visited, I'm choosing the restaurant."

The moment he spoke, her stomach rumbled.

"And I guess we're just about ready." He looked pointedly down at her stomach, and she quickly covered it with her hand.

Yet there was something in his look, maybe a spark, maybe just a tiny gleam, that set her pulse racing.

SHE SNORTED WHEN THEY PULLED UP IN FRONT OF HIS restaurant choice. "The Aphrodisiac Oyster Shack?" Now *that* was a loaded question.

He simply raised one eyebrow. "I did my own checking. And this place has the best oysters in town." He didn't comment on the word *aphrodisiac*.

It was early, at least for the usual dinner crowd, but they still had to wait a short time for a table. Once seated, she couldn't help asking, "Remember the oysters we used to eat as kids?" They hadn't been kids, but teenagers, then almost adults. Doing adult things.

His smile was wide. "They were the best."

She primly pursed her lips. "They were gross and slimy. I didn't like them even then."

He pulled back as if she'd shocked him. "You didn't tell me that."

She hadn't wanted to tell him his choice sucked. It was only later in the summer that she learned to say what she really wanted, their Corvette summer, when she told him all the things she wanted him to do to her.

She looked down her nose imperiously. "I'm telling you now. I don't like the slimy kind."

He rattled his plastic menu. "All right, fine, we won't get anything slimy."

She shuddered. "I don't have to get what you get."

He sighed. "These aren't single plates. They're for sharing." He pointed at the menu.

She realized you ordered by the number of people in the party. "Okay. Just don't get anything slimy."

He shot her a mild look. "You already told me that."

She huffed. But she enjoyed nattering with him, like they had in the museum.

When the server arrived, Cutter ordered. "We'd like the baked oysters."

"What size would you like?"

Cutter chose the largest, enough to feed an army. Then he ordered beer for them both, looking at her after the waiter left. "You can't have froufrou drinks with oysters."

She merely shrugged. "I like beer." Only sometimes, she thought. But it would probably go well with the oysters.

"The baked ones are like Oysters Rockefeller, with bread-crumbs on top," he explained. "You'll like them."

He was right. When they arrived, they were cooked, not raw and slimy, and covered in yummy-looking ingredients. She ate the first one, and it was so good, she couldn't stop herself from having another, and another. "You're right about the beer too."

Everything was good, really good, especially sharing it all with Cutter. And though she hadn't believed they could eat the entire lot, the oysters were going fast off the platter.

"I must have been wrong about oysters when I was a kid," she said with a sigh of immeasurable pleasure. "These are amazing."

"You had oysters the night you asked me to teach you how to kiss."

His words gave her a shiver she tried to hide.

Maybe he was right. She'd arrived on the island a couple of days before that night. She hadn't seen him for an entire school year, and whether he'd changed or she'd changed, she couldn't say, but he was so darn hot. Especially when he took her out in her uncle's car, first for oysters, which she hadn't liked but eaten anyway. That was probably why he thought she liked them, because she'd pretended, wanting to please him.

They'd gone for a drive that night, stopping at a beach just before the Seven Mile Bridge. Standing beside the car, looking at the subtle undulations of the water, she spoke without looking at him. Even now, she remembered her nerves as she'd summoned her courage. "I only need one thing from you this summer," she'd told him, trying to keep the tremble out of her voice. "You have to teach me how to kiss."

He'd snorted a laugh. "Is this a joke?"

"No," she'd said with an exaggerated teenage drawl. "I absolutely cannot go back to California for my senior year without knowing how to kiss?"

"What happened?" He tipped his head, looking at her with a compassion that made her want to cry. "Someone made fun of you?"

"I kissed a boy. And he said I wasn't very good. He told all my friends, and they all laughed at me."

"He was an asshole. And they weren't your friends."

"I know that. But I still need to learn how to kiss."

He reared back from her then. "Well, I sure as hell can't do it. You're jailbait."

"I'm seventeen."

"And I'm eighteen. That makes you jailbait."

"It's just kissing. I can't be jailbait if all you do is kiss me."

He gazed at her with wide-eyed skepticism. "Yeah, but once I teach you how to kiss, you'll want to learn other stuff. And then you'll be jailbait."

She'd fisted her hands in his T-shirt, went up on her toes, and pulled him down for a kiss, a deliciously long kiss that made her toes tingle.

She wasn't sure, but he might have been breathing hard.

Then he'd said, "Okay, maybe you need a few lessons in kissing."

Oh God. Just thinking about it now made her want it. Badly. As badly as she wanted it all those years ago.

Or maybe it was all the aphrodisiac oysters she'd eaten.

☙ 10 ❧

After a long day of driving, touring, and eating, then stopping at a liquor store for champagne—one simply couldn't sit in a hot tub without champagne —the sun was already setting by the time they arrived at the night's stop. What Noreen thought was a train park was actually an RV recreation area on the outskirts of town. And there were only two cabooses, one of which she'd rented.

That didn't dampen her mood in the least. "It's fabulous, don't you think?" Especially since theirs was the only site with a private hot tub.

Cutter glanced around as if he couldn't care less. "Looks decent."

His lack of enthusiasm didn't faze her. A typical male never showed visible signs of excitement.

They entered the car from the rear, climbing onto a small platform and crossing the threshold into a wide sitting area with a couch, two chairs, and even a flatscreen TV. A coffee maker and microwave sat on a sideboard, with a small refrigerator under the counter. Through a doorway covered only by curtains, they found the bunk beds, two on either side. The caboose could fit a family of four, ladders affixed to the sides of the bunks allowing access to the top beds. The bathroom at the end, not huge, but serviceable, had a stall shower, sink, and toilet.

"I just like the fact that it's a caboose." It didn't bother her that the accommodations weren't luxurious. "The guy at reception said the hot tub is ready to go. You want to take a dip?"

He shrugged nonchalantly. "Sure."

A few tingles popped up in goosebumps on her arms as she thought of sitting in a hot tub with Cutter and wearing nothing but a swimsuit.

After pouring herself a glass of champagne, she changed in the bathroom while Cutter closed the curtains and donned his trunks in the front room. He was already in the tub by the time she stepped out, the skimpy bath towel wrapped around her. It was deep twilight, the sun sinking below the horizon, yet light enough for her to feel self-conscious in her one-piece bathing suit.

She was fifty-seven, not seventeen. He would have memories of the girl she'd been, not the menopausal woman she was now.

Then again, she weighed no more than she had during her university days, despite her two pregnancies. She walked, hiked, as well as Pilates with Tammy twice a week.

And now she threw her towel over a chair defiantly.

"Oh my God, that's so good." Setting her champagne glass on the rim next to Cutter's, she sank below the water. It was warm, but not too warm considering the temperature outside. It was almost refreshing.

"It's only ninety-nine," he said. "We don't want it much hotter. Not like you probably need out in foggy San Francisco."

"I'm not right *in* San Francisco." She swished her hands in the water, then reached for her glass to sip the bubbly. "I live in Belmont. It's a suburb on the Peninsula, about twenty minutes south of San Francisco." Her home had a lovely view of the Santa Cruz Mountains to the west. "But even in May, I want my hot tub at a hundred and two."

He laughed. "So you have a hot tub. I should have known."

She smiled, not taking offense. "I love my hot tub. So do my girls."

His lips parted, as if he was about to say something he suddenly thought better of. And after a moment, he asked, "They live with you?"

She shook her head. "I wish. But Grace is up in San Francisco, and April's out in Santa Cruz on the coast."

"I know where Santa Cruz is. Great surfing. So tell me more about your girls."

She loved to talk about her daughters. She was so proud of them. "I told you Grace is thirty-four." She couldn't remember everything she'd told him and decided not to worry about repeating. That's what old people did anyway, right? "She works for a very prestigious department store, one of their specialty buyers. She has long, beautiful blond hair, but she always wears it up. She's so pretty when it's down." God. She sounded like her mother. *You'd be so pretty if...* Which translated to *you're not pretty the way you are.* "Not that Grace isn't gorgeous any way she wears her hair." She was digging the hole deeper.

"And April is twenty-six," she went on, ignoring herself. "She works in one of those mountain towns just outside of Santa Cruz. She's a vet, and she's doing what I'd guess you'd call an internship, you know, like doctors do residencies. Just like her sister, she's very smart. But she doesn't look like me at all. She takes after her father with all these gorgeous glossy dark curls and amazing olive skin."

He was looking at her oddly, his head tipped. "So how can Grace be blond if her father was dark? Isn't there something about recessive genes?"

She realized her mistake in revealing too much, and she had to admit the truth. "They have different fathers. My first and second husband."

He raised an inquiring brow. "First and second husband?"

She had foot-in-mouth disease. "Yes, well." Why not just admit the truth? Then she wouldn't have to watch everything she said. Besides, she didn't have to hide anything. He was just her mechanic, right? "Actually, I've been married four times."

"Holy hell," he said, eyes suddenly wide as if he couldn't believe it.

Sometimes even she couldn't believe she'd exercised that much poor judgment. But she shrugged. "I'm a four-time loser."

"Maybe they're the losers, not you," he said matter-of-factly, without sounding all judgy, as her daughters would say.

She laughed then. "That is absolutely true. Although none of them would ever admit it. I married my first husband when I was twenty-two and only recently out of college. Larry was a surgeon and ten years older than me."

"Wow. A doctor." He chuckled, but she wasn't sure it was humorous. "Doesn't every mother want their daughter to marry a doctor?"

"Yes. And my mother actually drooled over him. But I wanted to marry him too. And he wanted to start a family quickly, which we did."

She sighed, thought about shutting her mouth and leaving it at that. Maybe it was the champagne. Maybe it was the falling darkness. But she didn't shut her mouth. "There's that old saying about acting in haste and repenting in sorrow. Anyway, I didn't know him well enough. I'd wanted to be a

New York editor, but after we married—" She laughed softly at her naivete, or maybe it was stupidity. "He said he couldn't move, that his practice was in San Francisco. So I got a job as an editor at a small press in the city. And when Grace was born, he said I should stay home with her. So I did freelance editing." Freelancing and Grace were the two good things she got out of the marriage. "The first time he hit me, I thought it was a one-off." She looked deep into the water, not wanting to see Cutter's eyes. "I guess you think that's what all battered wives say. 'He said he was sorry,'" she imitated in falsetto. "'And that he'd never do it again.'" She dropped to her own tone. "But that's what I thought. He was sorry and he wouldn't do it again. I'm a cliché." She looked at him then, couldn't help herself, and his eyes were dark and unreadable as twilight turned to full dark. "But of course, he did it again. So I took my bruises and my daughter and walked out."

"I'm sorry." She thought he sighed, sadly. Maybe compassionately. "I don't wish that on anyone."

She shrugged. "At least I had a mother who would take me in. So many women don't have anywhere to go."

"I admire you for acting so quickly."

She breathed in his praise, feeling the genuineness of it in his soft tone. Her mother had been livid, believing Noreen made up the story. It was only when Larry paid out the humongous divorce settlement that Mom was finally mollified.

"And then there was marriage number two," he prompted, as if he actually wanted to know her history.

She pushed aside her humiliation. After all, she'd already told him she was a four-time loser. "Then I met Javier, and I thought he was fabulous. He was a chef, and he owned his own restaurant, which was written up in gourmet magazines and doing really well. And he loved Grace. He was so good with her." She smiled at the memory. His sweetness with her daughter was a big part of what she fell in love with. "Then we had April, and he was the most devoted father to both my girls, even if Grace wasn't his biologically." She took a long, cool drink of her champagne.

Cutter leaned his head back against the rim of the tub and put his glass to his lips too. Then he said drily, "Sounds all sunshine and lollipops."

She laughed. "I know. I was all starry-eyed. The only problem was that Javier didn't think monogamy was a marital requirement. He said the women meant nothing to him." She took a breath, her chest suddenly tight. "But they meant something to me. I planned to leave him. I just wanted all my ducks in a row, as they say. But then he died in a fire at his restaurant."

"Holy shit." Cutter sat up quickly, sloshing champagne out of his glass.

"Hoisted with his own petard," she quipped, even though it had been devastating. "He'd been having sex with his new sous-chef when a grease fire got out of control."

"So if he'd been paying attention to his stove instead of his sous-chef," Cutter said.

And she finished. "Neither he nor his sous-chef would have died of smoke inhalation."

He looked at her a long moment. "It's not funny. It's *really* not funny. But—" He gave her a cheeky little smile. "But talk about hoisted with your own petard."

If it had been anyone else, she'd be appalled by his smile. But she got it, completely, and she actually laughed, saying through it, "It's not funny."

He covered his mouth as if he was still smiling. "Tell me about husband number three."

She sagged back into the water. "Rodney was my financial advisor." She didn't need to tell him she'd done quite well out of her divorce. And there was Javier's life insurance. She'd opened trusts for the girls, which had paid for their college educations.

"I feel something bad coming," he said, and his teeth gleamed against the dark in an obvious smile.

She gave him a tinkling laugh, because she hadn't been the proverbial stupid blond that time around. "Once Rodney and I got engaged, my lawyer recommended I switch financial advisors, and to protect the girls, she suggested I get a prenup." Rodney had been angry, saying she didn't trust him, but she went ahead with her plans. And now she simply said, "I found another financial advisor, so we didn't have to fight about money."

"But you fought about it anyway?" he asked, trying to figure out what happened.

He'd never guess. "No. We rarely fought at all. We had a very nice life, fabulous trips to the Caribbean and Hawaii and the south of France." She smiled at the memory. She'd loved Saint-Tropez and Saint Bart's and Maui. "And then he was arrested for embezzling his clients' funds, and they sent him to one of those club fed places."

Cutter laughed outright. "Jesus, you have the worst luck."

"I like to take credit for my own actions," she said almost snootily, covering up how idiotic she'd felt. "And say that I have the worst taste in men. Luckily, I'd kept all my assets separate. I'd never even sold my house, just rented it out."

"So what did husband number four do? Turn out to be a serial killer?"

She laughed with him, finding the humor in her pathetic history in a way no one else had ever helped her see. "Not quite that bad. Everett was fine." She sighed. She was sighing a lot tonight. "He wasn't an ax murderer or a thief or a bone breaker for the mob. He was just..." How to describe Everett? "Controlling. He didn't like my wardrobe or my friends or my spa weekends with my best friend or my sister or my girls."

She didn't mention that she suspected he'd been tracking her phone. He knew places she'd been during the day, always saying a "friend" saw her somewhere. Admitting that, though, might make her sound paranoid.

"Seems Everett didn't like a lot of things," Cutter drawled.

So true. "But the proverbial straw that broke the camel's back—" She used another cliché on him. "—was when he decided he didn't like me flying to France to visit my mother without him." She looked at Cutter a moment. "Did I tell you my mother remarried after my father died and moved to Paris?" Cutter merely shrugged in answer. "Anyway, Everett said it didn't look right if I left him for an entire month every year and that he'd put up with it long enough, and it simply couldn't happen again."

"What a dick." Cutter let out a disgusted laugh. "But what do you expect from a guy named Everett? Sounds hoity-toity."

She giggled at his description. Maybe the champagne was getting to her. "My thoughts exactly." And she waved her hand in the air. "So I wished him away."

"Into the cornfield?"

She got it immediately. The old *Twilight Zone* episode where Billy Mumy wishes everyone he didn't like into the cornfield. "Oh, if only I could've wished him into the cornfield," she said wistfully. "Then he wouldn't keep popping up periodically to check on me."

"You mean like a stalker?"

She shook her head and sighed out a soft laugh. "It's more like he wants to remind me of what a mistake I made in leaving him." Suddenly, she felt the weight of all her bad decisions. "I guess you think I'm terribly picky."

He shook his head, the water lapping at his wide shoulders as he moved. "I can't look down on you for trying to make marriage work, when I never even tried at all."

"I thought you just couldn't find a woman who wanted to live on Key West."

Silent a long moment, he finally said, "I could have compromised. When my girlfriend said she wanted be with more than a mechanic who wanted to live on an island that was miles from civilization and a shopping mall, instead of trying to see her side, I got mad and told her she should find someone who had far better money-making potential."

She felt his words like an uppercut to the jaw, knocking her head back to rest on the tub's edge. For a moment, all she saw were stars. That's the woman she was. The woman who'd never considered him boyfriend material, not because he lived in Key West and she lived on the West Coast, but because he was a mechanic and she'd wanted a surgeon. It was horrible to realize she truly was a classist. Tammy had said it laughingly, but with Cutter's words echoing in her ears, Noreen saw it now in a way she never had.

She asked weakly, "Wasn't there ever anyone else?"

He was once again quiet, almost too long. "After her, not really. Some women want you for the man you are, and some want you for the man they think they can turn you into. I was never the type a woman thought she could turn into something she wanted."

She shuddered with guilt, but kept it below the water. "You were certainly never the moldable type."

Would she have wanted to mold him? Sadly, the answer was yes. She would have wanted him to be ambitious, a go-getter, like Everett, but without the control issues. But that was forty years ago. Now she knew the kind of man she wanted couldn't be molded. And the men she chose were deeply flawed. She couldn't trust herself to see a man for who he really was.

Except Cutter.

Cutter was like her uncle. He didn't have huge material

needs for which he had to make large sums of money. More than things, he valued his freedom to do what he wanted when he wanted. Honestly, that was probably the reason he'd never married. Not because women wanted to mold him, but because he valued his freedom more. And that was fine. If he hadn't valued his freedom, she wouldn't have gotten him to come along on this ride.

Then he asked, his eyes twinkling in the starlight that had descended upon them, "So tell me, was I the best of them all?"

She laughed. "Yes, you were. But don't let it go to your head."

He was still smiling when he asked, "Which one?"

To him, she appeared as lithe as she had at seventeen.

He'd watched as she descended into the water, the lines of her black one-piece bathing suit clinging to all her delicious curves. Back then, she'd been almost boyish. But now, her breasts begged for his touch. Round and sweet. Not that she hadn't been sweet then, only that perhaps she was a little sweeter now.

He wondered how men could have made so many mistakes with her, how they could have let her slip through their fingers. Just as he'd let her slip through his fingers. Though it was obvious he'd never had a chance. She'd never said the words, but he'd known just the same that she could never have lived with a mere mechanic. Wasn't that why he'd applied for that college scholarship? Because he had something to prove after she left? Noreen Kincaid had a lot to do with that decision. But the life hadn't worked for him. He'd hated the job, the career, and the path he'd chosen. So he'd left it all behind. And she could never have lived with a man like him, even the man he was now. She was a woman with standards, and he would never live up to them.

There was only one thing he'd ever excelled at, and that was the pleasure he gave her in her uncle's Corvette.

He puffed up his chest and hit her with a mocking tone he didn't feel. "I'm delighted to know I was the best."

And he let it go to his head, both of them.

Noreen lay awake for too long. There'd been some sort of invitation between them in the hot tub. She felt it, even yearned for it, but she hadn't taken him up on it. Or perhaps he hadn't taken her up on it.

They slept in their separate bunks on either side of the caboose, the curtains pulled across for privacy, Cutter with his feet sticking out. Maybe the caboose and two bunk beds weren't the best idea.

He didn't snore. Three of her husband's had snored. But not Everett. He was too controlled to allow himself to snore.

She had no idea when she fell asleep, but she woke to the morning sun. Cutter was up and out, putting the car's top down and packing up his stuff. He even left coffee for her in the pot.

When she left the caboose, bag in hand, Cutter smiled. "Good morning. You wanna drive today?"

"Absolutely," she told him.

He didn't seem at all phased by the night's intimate conversation. Maybe because she had done all the revealing, admitting her mistakes. She should probably regret it. But she was too old for regrets. She'd told him, and they'd commiserated over their pasts, and that was that.

Scrolling through her phone last night and studying her map app, Noreen had decided on Mobile, Alabama for their next stop, and Cutter agreed.

She loved the feel of the Corvette on the road. The car didn't handle as easily as her Lexus, but it didn't matter. The lady had power. They both did.

Before they'd made it out of town, Cutter pointed to the right. "Pull in here."

She made the turn into another repair shop before asking, "Is something wrong?"

"The XB-70 isn't used to driving so many miles in just a couple of days. I want to check a few things, make sure she's okay. Especially the water pump."

She patted the perspiration off her brow. "Is this what I need to do every time I take her for a drive?"

He shrugged. "If you want to keep her in good running order."

"Even if I'm not driving two hundred and fifty miles every day?"

He clucked his tongue like an old maid. "She can be temperamental."

She shot him a glare after she'd parked. "Is that why you call the car a she?"

"No, she's as *she* because she's a beauty." He climbed out of the car, leaned on the door frame, and looked down at her in the driver's seat. "But she is high maintenance, and if that scares you, you've got a willing buyer right here." He tapped his chest with his fist. "Anytime, just name a price."

The Corvette was priceless. "She's not for sale," she singsonged at him.

She suspected he was being overly cautious. Over time, she would learn the Corvette's ticks and noises, learn to figure out when something was unusual. And right now, she didn't hear a thing wrong.

Stepping away from the car, he waved a hand. "Pull into that bay right there."

The doors were open over four bays, three of them full. "Don't we have to check in with them first?" She pointed at the office.

"I know these guys. Besides, I called ahead while you were in the bathroom this morning." He said it as if she'd taken forever, which she hadn't.

Had she misjudged the camaraderie they seemed to have developed last night? He sounded testy now.

She recognized the sign over the garage as she rolled into an empty bay. Budget Auto Repair. "This is the same chain as Zeke's. And the one you work for."

"Yeah," he punctuated with a nod. "They're all over Florida."

Of course they'd squeeze him in. He probably knew them all.

A mechanic in his early thirties, his long hair pulled back in a man bun, laid down his wrench and wiped his hands on a rag. "Hey dude."

He and Cutter performed a complicated handshake. "I heard you had troubles with the water pump." The name tag on his pocket read Brody.

"News travels fast," Cutter said, then waved a hand. "This is Noreen, Mortimer's niece."

Brody grabbed a clean rag from a stack and wiped his hands again. "Nice to meet you."

"You too." She shook his big hand, which didn't feel greasy at all. Did all mechanics have big hands?

Except that Brody's hands were nothing like Cutter's. A heat wave rolled over her as she imagined all the things Cutter's hands were capable of.

She really needed to stop the way her mind trailed off into thoughts she shouldn't have.

Since it was early in the day, Brody's overalls were relatively clean, as was the shop, with a shiny checkerboard floor and tool chests in each bay.

Brody waved a hand at the car. "You need some help here?"

"I'm just checking the hoses and stuff. I'll be fine."

Jutting his chin at the mechanic stooped over the car they'd both been working on, Brody said, "Darrell's fine on his own. He's a good kid, learns quick." Three other mechanics were working on cars in the other bays, all of them with their heads buried beneath the hoods. One guy stretched out on the floor beneath an engine, only his feet sticking out.

Clapping his hands, Brody said, "Let's check this baby out."

Cutter popped the hood while Brody patted a stool. "You can sit here, if you'd like," he said to Noreen. "No worries, it's clean." He grinned, his teeth white in his handsome face.

"Thank you." She perched on the stool until Cutter called her over.

"You should know more about he," he said.

It was nice to be invited. "I'd love to learn." Not that she'd be able to fix anything.

The engine was remarkably clean, but Cutter had been the Corvette's mechanic for years. He probably used a cotton swab dipped in rubbing alcohol to clean all her crevices.

"She's a beauty, all right." Brody turned a sheepish gaze on Noreen. "Sorry about your uncle. He was a good guy."

"Thank you. He was a sweetheart."

"Yeah, he came up here with Cutter a few times." He elbowed Cutter. "For a joy ride."

She appreciated that Cutter had taken her uncle on trips,

even if only to Tallahassee. Though it left a stab of guilt that she'd never taken her uncle anywhere when he got older.

Cutter started his rundown for her benefit. "You check the oil here. This is the dipstick." He pulled it out.

"I know what a dipstick is," she said dryly.

He stopped still for one second. Then he smiled. "Of course, you do." And he winked.

Brody didn't seem to notice the byplay. It was definitely sexual, and the same kernel of heat she'd felt last night blossomed once again.

"She likes to eat oil," Cutter went on explaining. "So check her regularly." He jammed a nozzle in a can he'd pulled off the shelf behind him. "I'll just top her off, but she's nowhere near empty."

"And if she runs out of oil," Brody said, tapping the radiator cap. "You'll blow the whole motor."

"What about filling up the water?"

Brody shrugged. "Closed system. Shouldn't have to unless she overheats. And your mechanic should check the coolant levels when he does an oil change."

Cutter tipped his head to look at her from his position over the engine. "Just watch the temperature gauge."

"I was watching it. But I was under the impression my mechanic had checked over the car before I left." She smiled sweetly.

He smiled back. And it was anything but sweet.

Yet it made her hot.

"The temperature should run about one-ninety." Cutter pointed to the spot on the gauge. "And the oil gauge should be around fifty-five psi."

He showed her the hoses and told her what to look for, and she watched the way his hands moved. Muscular hands, and she remembered how they'd touched her, caressed her.

Darn, if she didn't pay attention to what he said instead of what his hands could do, she wouldn't remember a thing. She catalogued everything, but the best thing she could do for the Corvette when she got back home was to look for a good mechanic.

Finally, the two men wiped their hands on rags, and Cutter closed the Corvette's hood with a thunk.

"She's looking good, dude," Brody said, nodding.

"Thanks for the help, man." The two shook hands, this time without the complicated movements.

"Everything good here at the shop?" Cutter asked.

Brody grinned. "Fan-fu—" he cut himself off just like Zeke had. "Fantastic."

And Noreen asked, "Can I run across the street and grab you guys some coffee or snacks?"

"That's real nice of you." He jutted his chin at the office. "But we got a pot in there. And the boss buys premium coffee too." He laughed and punched Cutter's shoulder. "Thanks for letting me tinker with the XB-70. It's a privilege and an honor."

"It's probably the last time." Cutter pointed at Noreen. "The car is Noreen's now. She's driving her back home."

Brody's eyebrows shot up. "You take good care of her now." He shook his finger like an old grandpa. "Or your Uncle Mortimer's coming back to haunt you."

She smiled with a slight pinch. "I absolutely know he will."

Cutter thanked Brody again, and after rolling the Corvette out of the garage, he checked in with the other mechanics, saying hi, shaking hands.

Brody watched as she climbed into the passenger seat. "Well, that's something special, because nobody drives the XB-70 but Cutter. Toward the end, Mortimer made him do all the driving." He ran a hand along the door. "Cutter sure is going to miss her."

She laughed. "Did he put you up to saying that?"

Brody chuckled. "Just stating the facts."

"That's why I'm letting him come along on this cross-country trip. So he can say his goodbyes. And so he'll know I'll take very good care of her."

She was truly starting to think that Uncle Mortimer should have left the car to Cutter, not her. But, God only knew why, he hadn't. And the thought didn't stop her from wanting the car herself.

Cutter climbed in beside her. "Learn a lot?" he asked, as she pulled away from the garage, waving at Brody.

"I did. Thank you for the lesson."

He and Brody hadn't been condescending but informative and interested. "I promise," she said, her tone solemn. "I will take the very best care of her." She looked at him, smiled. "I'll even send you pictures if you like."

That made him toss his head back and laugh. It was a beautiful sight.

Out on the open road, she tore off her scarf, stuffing it under her thigh so it wouldn't blow away. She wanted to feel the wind in her hair as she navigated the highway. It was a glorious day, and she was on a glorious trip. The sun and the wind and the feel of the steering wheel beneath her hands was a sensual, almost sexual feeling, akin to the tingling sensations of last night when they'd flirted with a bit of sex talk, and she'd remembered that summer.

God, she missed good sex. It wasn't that she'd *never* had good sex with any of her husbands, but life got in the way. There was work and babies and the inevitable arguments that came with living with someone else. Life seemed to subjugate all those sexual feelings, turning them into duty rather than desire. How many times had she thought, please, God, not tonight? In the end, it was hard to remember if the sex had been as good as anything she'd done with Cutter.

With him, it had all been so different. They weren't negotiating a relationship. They were experimenting, learning each other's bodies, each other's likes, the things that made them crazy. There was no jealousy. They were best buddies. Cutter hadn't been dating anyone that summer, nor any of the summers she was on Key West, so it was easy to sneak off. It was the best time of her life. There were no ties, no fighting, no emotions getting in the way of good, hot sex.

Cutter taught her everything she wanted to know.

He'd taught her all the things she still craved.

And her thoughts turned her jittery with desire.

They stopped for an early lunch, having skipped breakfast. And she wanted to touch him, to renew the taste of him. It was crazy, the frenetic feeling of that summer, wanting to get him alone, begging him to show her the next new thing. It was supposed to be only kissing, but that hadn't lasted long. She'd felt all the sexual energy beneath their smiles and laughter.

And she felt it now, as if the thrum of the Corvette's motor had revved them both up.

Or maybe it was just her feeling it. She had no idea about Cutter.

And she wasn't about to bring it up.

Diving into her phone as soon as the waitress left, she searched for the next perfect place to stay. It had become a challenge to find something unusual, and she gasped with delight when she found it. "This will blow you away." She flipped the phone for him to see.

"What the hell is it?" he asked, leaning in, then looking at her, his brows drawn together.

"It's a treehouse. It even has a bathroom with a shower."

He barked out a short, sarcastic laugh. "In a tree?"

She shrugged. "Don't ask me how they do it. They just do."

The waitress slid their meals onto the table right then, and Noreen pulled her phone back. She'd ordered a shrimp po' boy, because having a plain old hamburger for her first time crossing the Florida Panhandle just didn't seem right.

And the first bite was utterly delicious.

But she wasn't letting the po' boy distract her. "There's even a separate bedroom and a pullout sofa in the living room."

He gazed at her over his plain old hamburger. "In a tree?" Sarcasm dripped from his words.

"The pictures look fabulous." Then she gave him the cream on top. "And there's our own private hot tub down below."

"You have a thing for hot tubs," he said noncommittally.

"Don't you?" She eyed him when he didn't answer. "You enjoyed it last night."

Something she couldn't read flickered in his eyes.

Maybe it was a hint of the same things she'd been thinking all morning.

She grabbed her phone. "I'm booking it. It's perfect."

"Who has to sleep on the sofa bed?"

She used the same trick on him that she'd pulled in Daytona Beach. "I'll pay for the room if you agree to take the sofa bed."

He gazed at her a moment longer. And then he said, completely without expression, "Deal."

THE WOMAN COULD TALK HIM INTO ANYTHING. A RESORT, a caboose, and now a treehouse. He'd slept fine on the train last night. He was used to roughing it, having slept on a boat, in a car, on the floor, on the ground, sometimes heading out to the beach and sleeping there all night. Sleeping under the stars was a beautiful thing. Going to the races, he often slept in his car. He could sleep anywhere. And the bunk hadn't been all that bad after he'd stuck his feet over the side.

But he was dubious about the treehouse. Could it possibly be big enough for the two of them?

The pictures were probably taken with one of those wide-angle lenses that made everything look bigger than it really was. And instead of a spacious apartment, they'd find a cramped box up in a tree.

But she was excited. And the private hot tub sounded good.

Another soak with her in that one-piece bathing suit sounded even better.

She'd consumed his thoughts the entire morning. Her scent wafting past him, the wind in her hair, the smile of pleasure on her pretty lips.

But still, she was untouchable.

She ate and somehow scrolled through her phone at the same time. Gasping, she gave him that wide-eyed, slightly open-mouthed look, light dancing in her gaze.

The sound and her laughing eyes set him off, as if she were about to ask him to teach her how to kiss the way she had all those years ago. Then she'd turned him into her slave, getting him to do anything, everything.

And he said, as mildly as possible, "What?"

"The RV park with the treehouse is right near the Gator Boardwalk."

He gave her his customary, "Wow," without inflection.

"There's all these boardwalks where you walk out over the water and you can see alligators and birds and all sorts of stuff."

She brimmed with so much excitement it was almost sexual. But that part might be all about him.

"You've seen gators before," he scoffed.

She set her phone down and looked at him with all the sadness in the world. "That was forty years ago. I hardly remember it."

He huffed even though his heart was racing, dying to keep up with her. "If you really wanted to see gators, I could've taken you out to Blue Hole at Big Pine Key."

"I didn't think about that," she said snootily, sitting straight. "But I'm thinking about it now. And we'll be so close." She eyed him, a pretty pout on her lips. "You got the Automobile Museum and the Speedway."

"You chose the museum."

"I chose it for you."

"You said you chose it for the Batmobiles."

"I just said that to make you feel good."

Christ. Why did she have to say that? He wanted her to make him feel good. He wanted it bad.

"Okay." He gave in so she wouldn't keep saying things that made him so freaking hot and bothered. "We'll go to the Gator Boardwalk."

She clapped her hands in delight, having won the battle.

He wondered who would win the war. And exactly what the war was about.

They drove the bridge over Escambia Bay into Pensacola.

"Let's take a drive through the town," she said.

And Cutter directed her to Emanuel Point, then into downtown Pensacola, past the Basilica of St. Michael the Archangel, and down to Fort Barrancas and the Pensacola Lighthouse. It was a pretty town, with arbors of trees to pass under. This close to the water, the air felt steamy and sultry.

After the driving tour, Cutter asked, "You want me to tell you how to get back to the freeway?"

Noreen smiled. "Can you find something that's a little more backroadsy? I don't care if it takes a little longer."

He found a route that took them straight out to Mobile Bay, then almost paralleled the water into Mobile. It was a lovely drive, better than the freeway.

And finally she took the bridge over the water, past the USS Alabama right on the edge of the bay, the massive warship tourists could ramble through. And she did the same thing as they'd done in Pensacola, driving through town to see a few sites. Using the Bankhead Tunnel to get into downtown, they came out right by the History Museum, which sat across from Mardi Gras Park, two harlequins marking the entrance like other city parks might have lions.

"Do you mind if I tool around just to see a few things?" Without the rush of the wind, she could hear herself.

Cutter shook his head. "Just tell me where you want me to direct you."

They looped around to see Colonial Fort Condé, which was only a replica but still impressive, then past Christ Church Cathedral and back up to the main street they'd come in on. She drove past the Mobile Carnival Museum. It, too, had life-size harlequins in front.

"I've heard that Mobile is actually the home of Mardi Gras," Cutter said drily.

She laughed. "I bet New Orleans wants to fight them on that." But the harlequins at the park and the museum might be a testament.

"Turn right here, and we should find the Cathedral Basilica of the Immaculate Conception."

The street came up so quickly, she almost missed it, turning with a slight squeal of the tires. "I thought it could be either a cathedral or a basilica, but not both."

He shrugged, quirked his mouth. "I'm just reading the map."

It looked more like a government building with its massive Doric columns at the entrance, though the two towers on either side made it appear more like a church. A pretty park sat across the street from which tourists could sit and gaze at the facade.

Turning again, she drove down Dauphin Street with restaurants and bars and shops and street artists. The brightly colored buildings and wrought iron balconies reminded her of New Orleans.

"Well, that was fun," she said, smiling. "So how do we get to the Gator Boardwalk?"

"Uh," he started as she idled at a stoplight. "We have to go back through the tunnel."

"You're kidding. We're backtracking?" She hadn't put the Boardwalk or the RV Park into the GPS when she'd booked the treehouse. She'd asked for rentals around Mobile, and the treehouse was just so awesome.

"It's no big deal, just ten miles."

"Grrr," she growled, her stomach turning over.

"I'm not bothered if you're not."

"I should have checked."

"Then you'd have missed beautiful downtown Mobile."

"But we could have done that tomorrow on the way out."

He looked at her. "It's okay. You don't have to beat yourself up."

And she realized that's what she'd done since Everett came into her life. When she'd worried about doing something wrong and upsetting him. He'd been so good at the silent treatment, and she'd hated it.

She puffed out a pent-up breath. "You're right. It's only ten miles."

He smiled. "And we have gators and a treehouse to look forward to. And—" He waggled his eyebrows as if anticipating something lascivious. "This time we can drive through the George Wallace Tunnel, getting two tunnels for the price of one."

She laughed out loud as the light changed. "You know, I like the way you think. It's called looking on the bright side."

He snorted. "That's me, a bright side kind of guy."

The return trip took only twenty minutes. Like Cutter said, no big deal, even though the Gator Boardwalk was all the way on the other side of the bay.

Everett would have been livid.

But she wasn't with Everett. And she never would be again.

It wasn't the Okefenokee Swamp, but more in the middle of the small town, a hotel right across the street. As they pulled into a nearby parking lot, the scent of grilling meat permeated the air.

"Gator dogs," Cutter told her when she wrinkled her nose.

"Ick," she answered, grimacing. "And isn't it kind of rude to be cooking gator dogs right outside a gator sanctuary?"

She thought he barely resisted rolling his eyes at her.

"This is amazing," she said as they wandered the board-walks. Gators swam lazily through the water or sunned them-selves on the rocky banks. Amid the constant buzz and drone of insects, herons and egrets stalked the waters, flying into the air with a whoosh of wings if an alligator got too close.

"Those birds are boat-tailed grackles," Cutter said, reading a sign filled with bird photos and pointing to the black birds with long tails.

A gator suddenly snapped at something in the water, though Noreen couldn't see what or even if the gator caught what it was after.

"I certainly wouldn't want to be gator food," Cutter leaned close to whisper.

Noreen shivered. It could have been the thought of those big gator jaws. Or it could have been Cutter's scent filling her head.

They wandered through the boardwalks and trails for more than an hour, stopping for pictures or to sit quietly by the water and watch the wildlife. It was beautiful, relaxing, and she didn't even feel the humidity.

"It's lovely here."

"It's muggy," he said.

"I was just thinking that it doesn't bother me at all. I must be acclimating to the south."

He laughed. "You ain't seen nothing yet."

"I saw it every summer when I came out to visit Uncle Mortimer."

"Yeah, but you always wore a bikini top and shorts."

She snorted a laugh at him. "You didn't seem to mind the bikini top."

He looked at her, a grin spreading across his face. "Those ties were so easy to undo," he drawled, then waved a hand at the blousy sleeveless top she wore over a strappy tank. "That thing has way too many buttons."

She went hot and cold with chills of pleasure as she imagined him undoing every single one. "I don't undo the buttons. I pull it over my head," she said in the same dry tone he'd used.

He shrugged. "Easy, I guess, but the bikini was easier." Then he smiled so widely his white teeth showed. "And you were so much easier back then too."

She gasped. "I was not easy."

"Oh, please, Cutter, please do this to me," he imitated her in a high voice.

She swatted at him. "You certainly didn't seem to struggle getting the job done."

She liked the sexual banter. It ratcheted up all the sensations she'd had on the drive.

Maybe she should say it all again, just the way she had forty years ago when she'd begged him to teach her how to kiss.

Please, Cutter, please.

She could almost hear her long ago voice whispering the words to him on sultry nights in her uncle's Corvette.

He stood suddenly, as if, despite their laughter, he needed to break the sexual tension between them. He held out his hand. "You know what it's time for?"

She shook her head, still bemused by the banter, still thinking about the past, about him, about his touch.

"We need a gator dog."

He pulled her to her feet even as she gaped at him. "You've got to be kidding. The smell was..." She wrinkled her nose the way she had when they'd first pulled into the parking lot.

He shook his head slowly, a glint in his eye. "You're at a gator park. You absolutely need a gator dog."

"Isn't this some sort of protected place? They wouldn't kill their own gators."

He laughed outright. "You saw the food truck on the other side of the parking lot, right?"

"Yes." The scent of grilling meat and grease had filled the air. "I don't think I can eat a gator."

Cutter began pulling her back along the boardwalk. "Oh yeah, you can. And you'll love it. Just like you loved the oysters."

Because he was pulling her, they walked hand in hand. And she liked it, the feeling of being together, of wanting contact, of connection with another human being. Connection with *him*.

Her stomach rumbled with the offer of food. They hadn't eaten since late morning, skipping lunch until later in the afternoon. The rumble grew louder as they left the boardwalk and stepped into the lot, where the food truck's scent was overpowering.

Cutter ordered two gator dogs and two beers, without asking her what she wanted to drink. And when she looked at the bottle he handed her, he simply said, "You must have beer with a gator dog."

She looked at the dog he handed her, its silver foil already open, looking like a sausage, brownish gray speckled with spices. "What do you put on a gator dog?"

He headed to the condiments on the other side of the truck. "Whatever you put on a regular hot dog."

She added mustard and relish, while he slathered his with ketchup and mustard. Then he led her to one of the picnic benches beneath the trees.

They weren't the only gator-dog eaters. Three couples had joined the line behind them, most of them with kids in tow, and other groups, a few families and couples just like them, sat on the picnic benches.

Cutter bit heartily into his dog, and said, even with his mouth full, "Come on, eat up."

And Noreen did. The meat was spicy with herbs. It didn't taste like an alligator, not that she knew what an alligator tasted like. This was a little greasier than a sausage, but with so much spice she couldn't detect the real flavor.

"What do you think?"

She wrinkled her nose. "It's so greasy."

He handed her the beer bottle. "Here, this helps cut the grease."

And it did as she took two big swallows. She ate the whole dog, swigging the beer to wash out the grease taste. As she wiped her fingers on a napkin, he waited expectantly for her decree.

"It wasn't terrible," she admitted. "But it was awfully spicy and really greasy."

He grinned. "They're supposed to stick with you all day. But I've got a cure." He jumped off the seat, getting in line at the food truck. Returning five minutes later, he held out the treat. "Ice cream will do the trick."

He handed her a jumbo drumstick covered in chocolate and nuts. She gobbled it down before it could melt, taking sips of beer too. "Oh God, that's good."

Just as he'd done out on the park bench in the Gator Boardwalk, he stood and held out his hand. "Let's get some drinks and snacks for the night. You can't live in a treehouse without snacks."

When was the last time she'd eaten like this, greasy dogs, beer, ice cream, and the promise of snacks?

He drove this time, finding a gas station mini-mart close by. As they stood in the aisle of chips and snacks, he asked, "What's your favorite?"

"I don't have a favorite. I never eat this kind of stuff."

He rolled his eyes and snorted softly. "It's not a road trip without snacks."

The need rolled off her tongue. "Cheese puffs." She hadn't eaten cheese puffs in years.

He punched the air. "You go, girl." He grabbed a big bag.

"What's your favorite?"

In answer, he added a bag of Oreos.

"Ah, a sweet tooth," she said.

"Dessert."

"We had ice cream for dessert."

"That wasn't dessert. It was just to cleanse your palate after the gator dog."

She laughed. "I had to cleanse my palate so I could eat cheese puffs and cookies?"

"You can't have the gator dog messing with the taste of your chips."

"You are something." She laughed, feeling wonderful.

He buffed his fingernails on his shirt. "That's what they all say."

He added a bottle of champagne to their bounty, and not knowing what amenities would be in their treehouse, she added plastic champagne flutes and a pack of plastic bowls, as well as napkins.

"We could eat out of the bag," he said, laughing at her.

She gave him a purse-lipped glare. Yet she felt like a

teenager on a road trip, eating greasy food, drinking beer, munching on snacks, and topping it off with champagne.

The RV park was only half full. Motorhomes dotted the complex, people sitting beneath the trees, their barbecues spewing smoke and the scent of sizzling meat in the air.

Their treehouse was on the outer reaches and they received appreciative stares as the Corvette rolled by, as well as a few thumbs up. The attendant had given her the key and directed them to their treehouse buried in the forest, the platform probably fifteen, maybe even twenty feet off the ground.

"Oh my God." She pointed, wanting to hop around in delight. "Look at that glorious hot tub." A round wooden style, it would be a tight squeeze for four, but plenty of room for the two of them.

Cutter grunted his approval, grabbing the bags out of the trunk. She slung her computer case over her shoulder, but he wouldn't let her take her own duffel. Instead, she carried the snacks and champagne, plus her shoes.

"At least we don't have to climb a rope ladder," he said.

It was a sprawling tree with a thick trunk and massive branches stretching wide.

Sturdy, weather-faded stairs climbed to a wrap-around, screened-in platform holding two padded deck chairs with a view through the trees. All Noreen could say when she opened the door was, "Wow." She sounded like Cutter, but she totally meant the word.

Cutter bumped into her back, and she stepped fully inside to allow him entry as well. He didn't echo her, but she felt his awe.

There was one word to describe it. Amazing. A comfortable leather sofa with two matching chairs sat on a colorful Persian rug laid across the plank floor. The living room lacked a TV, but that was fine with her. A small table and two chairs nestled next to a sideboard with a microwave, coffee maker, and a small fridge. Plates, bowls, mugs, glasses, even wine-glasses and champagne flutes, covered a shelf above, and beside the coffee maker a basket overflowed with packaged coffee, creamer, teas, and sugar like in any hotel room.

Dropping the duffels on the floor, Cutter strode to the bedroom, Noreen following. Four pillows and a thick duvet draped the high double bed. An old-fashioned pitcher and basin sat on the side table and a low bureau ran the length of one waist-high wooden wall. The screened porch kept the bugs out since there were no windows, and they could close the wooden shutters at night.

"Will you look at this?" Cutter called from an open door-way, his first words since they'd entered.

She'd seen the pictures, but the bathroom had to be seen to be believed. The rain shower and the double sink made the room big enough for two, with the toilet hidden behind a screen.

"How did they get the plumbing up here?" Cutter marveled.

It was unanswerable. And she wanted it to remain a mystery. "And there's Wi-Fi," she said with awe, then looked at him. "Did I do good?"

He grabbed her shoulders and leaned in for a quick, miraculous kiss that stunned her. It wasn't sexual, just friendly, but he'd shocked her.

"Yeah, you did real good." Back in the living room, he threw himself on the sofa, stacking his hands beneath his head. "And the couch is comfortable. I don't even need to pull out the sofa bed." He grinned like a cheeky boy. He was endearing. And the sight was so sexy.

Before actually flinging herself on him, she said, "I say we break out the snacks and champagne, and get into our bathing suits to enjoy the hot tub."

He bounced back up. "Never have I heard a better idea." He winked.

And her heart fluttered in a way she absolutely shouldn't let it. Especially not with him.

13

Grabbing her duffel off the floor, Cutter stalked to the bedroom, throwing it on the bed. Coming back, he unzipped his own, rummaged inside for his swim trunks, and headed to the bathroom to change. When he was done, she followed suit, and by the time she returned to the front room, he'd already filled bowls with their snacks. She'd found two fluffy towels in the bureau and wrapped herself in one, laying the second one on the table for him while he poured the champagne.

"We'll have to drink the whole bottle tonight because I didn't think to buy a cork," he told her as he handed her a glass.

She raised her flute. "It's only two glasses a piece. We can handle it."

Then, carrying a bowl of cheese puffs and her champagne, her towel clutched around her, she marched down the stairs. At the bottom, she saw the plumbing encased in a big wooden box following the line of the tree trunk, which was wide enough to hide the sight from the hot tub on the other side.

The tub was secluded under the branches of the enormous tree, with shrubbery shielding them from other campers. Setting her flute and snack bowl on the tub's wooden rim, she kicked off her thongs and climbed the steps, perching on the edge to swing her legs around.

"Oh God, that is so good." The water was warmer than the air, and its delicious caress tingled along her calves. She sank down, sliding along the seat to give Cutter room to get in. Much as she was tempted, she didn't watch him enter the water, turning instead to grab her champagne. After that kiss up in the treehouse, he was too beautiful to look at without losing her breath.

She was safe once he slid beneath the water, covering his distracting chest but leaving his shoulders in the open air. Leaning over, he tapped his champagne flute to hers. "Here's to another good travel day. We're making good time. Where to next?"

His mouth against the glass as he sipped made her imagine his lips on hers.

They were making enough good time. After too many days and nights like this with him—drinking champagne and lounging in a hot tub—she would be a goner. Through no fault of his, he was too hard to resist. She couldn't shut off her memories of all the things they'd done. She couldn't stop counting how long it had been since she'd had really good sex. She couldn't stop remembering that he truly had been the best.

And she couldn't stop wondering if they could do it all over again. Another Corvette summer. Even if it was only two weeks on a cross-country trek.

Praying that none of those thoughts would accidentally pop out of her mouth, she said, "I suggest either New Orleans or Baton Rouge."

He tipped his head back against the rim of the tub,

savoring the bubbly. "Baton Rouge. Everyone talks about New Orleans. We should do something different."

"Have you ever been to New Orleans?" She was terribly curious about him. He was still so much a mystery after all these years.

He nodded. "Yeah. I even went to Mardi Gras. It was insane. Excellent but insane." Then he asked, "Have you ever been there?"

She nodded with the lovely memories. "April wanted New Orleans as her graduation trip. We had a fabulous time. We toured all the old homes in the Garden District. And ate beignets at that famous place."

"Café Du Monde."

"That's it." She pointed at him. "And for Grace's graduation trip, we went to New York. She wanted to visit all the fashion houses. I told you she's a buyer for a big chain store, right?"

"Yeah. And April is a vet."

"God, I'm repeating myself like an old lady." She laughed at herself, but she was pleased he remembered. Some men just let a woman's words go in one ear and out the other.

"Then, since we've both seen New Orleans, Baton Rouge, it is." He raised his glass to her again. "We need to visit the capitol building. I've heard it's got that old Louisiana style."

"It's a plan. Once we're back in the treehouse, I'll find a nice place."

He gazed at her steadily. "I hear you can book rooms on old steamboats."

"I thought they'd turned them all into gambling casinos." She was surprised he'd even think of steamboats.

He shook his head, his lips in an upside-down smile that didn't quite become a frown. "I'm sure there's gambling on them too. But some are floating hotels. Let's stay there."

"Deal." She loved that he chose where they stayed next. He might actually be excited about the trip.

As he drank from his champagne flute again, she let her gaze follow the line of his Adam's apple as it bobbed up and down. Then to his chest, a few stray hairs peeking above the water.

"Christ, it's getting hot." He hauled himself onto the rim, water sluicing down his body.

Oh God.

He was beautiful, silver gray whirls of chest hair dusting his pecs, then a darker line sliding down his abdomen and into his swim trunks.

Why did she have to look?

He stretched, as if he were preening, swiping his hands back through his hair, even though he hadn't dipped beneath the water.

He was a Roman statue, all taut muscles and tawny skin.

She wondered if he knew what he did to her. She wondered if he did it on purpose.

Then he looked at her. "Aren't you overheated yet?"

Oh yeah, she was. In more ways than one. But she couldn't let him see everything on display. Even if the one-piece suit covered all the essentials.

"It's not like it's one-oh-two in the water," she said drily, mostly because her throat was parched from the sight of him. "I wouldn't do any less, especially in the wintertime. Although," she left off, as if she was truly considering her answer. "In the summer, when it's getting close to a hundred outside, it's refreshing to turn it down to ninety-five."

"The water's refreshing after you get really hot and sweaty." There was something in his eyes, a burning, as if they were talking about far more than the heat of her hot tub.

And she was getting hotter; in fact, she was hot hot hot. It wasn't the water. It was all him. His chest, his six-pack abs, his thick biceps. Did he work out at the gym? Or was it all work on his cars? The six-pack abs, how did he get those from leaning over the engine of a car? Maybe it was swimming. It could be surfing.

It could have been just the way he was made. Perfection.

Then he slid down into the water again and grabbed the bowl of cheese puffs, moving closer, holding out the bowl to her.

She fished out one, crunched, cheesy deliciousness filling her mouth. "Now I know why I don't eat cheese puffs. Because I can't stop."

"Come on," he cajoled. "You can't have just one."

She'd had only one kiss, and she wondered if he was thinking about that too.

She took another cheese puff. Then he reached around her, his chest touching her arm, sweeping her flesh with goosebumps, and he grabbed her champagne, handing it to her. "I'm getting way ahead of you. Drink up."

She drank, looking at him, the slide of his gaze down her throat.

He was melting her with just a look and the flame in his eyes. She had to fumble the glass back onto the tub rim, almost toppling it into the water. When she turned back, he hadn't moved away. Her heart beat hard in her ears, her pulse racing, her breath fast.

And he was looking at her lips.

That was when she lost it. He'd grinned like that when she was seventeen. And she wanted it all now as badly as she'd wanted it back then. It was a compulsion, a tidal wave of need, unstoppable.

And without thinking about what a bad idea it was, she pulled him down by the ears. "I need one thing from you on this trip," she echoed the words of her youth. "You have to teach me how to have good sex again."

His grin split the night. "That's two things. You want me to fix the car as well."

"You're right, two things."

"You're still too young for me." His eyes were dark and hot.

"I'm not jailbait anymore."

"But you're just as dangerous."

"You're far more dangerous," she whispered.

He opened his mouth to say something else, but she pulled him down. "Stop talking."

She kissed him. It wasn't like that first kiss with him, the first best kiss of her youth, untutored, frightened, nervous, yet so delicious. She wasn't that young girl anymore.

And now she straddled the man, kissing him hard, taking his tongue, throwing her arms around his neck and her legs around his hips.

That's when she knew he was just as affected as she was. His heat between her legs, only their suits separating them, he put his hands on her hips, pulling her down, grinding against her.

She thought she might come right then.

"This is a bad idea," he said when she left him a moment to breathe.

"Why?" She didn't want him to echo her thoughts, and she kissed him again before he could answer, taking his lips, his mouth, his tongue, going deep. And her body screamed for how good an idea this was, his hands on her back, her sides, her thighs, his fingers dipping beneath the elastic of her suit. His hands weren't thinking it was a bad idea at all.

"Complications," he said.

"No complications," she said. They didn't even speak in complete sentences.

They didn't need complete sentences. The only communication needed was on this most basic level, the touch of skin, the shush of their breaths, the taste of each other in their mouths. He held her down, his body heaving up against hers, setting off a wave of tingles inside her.

She managed a full sentence. "There's only one question." She took a break from the kiss. "Are you up to teaching me?" She squeezed her thighs around him. "How good sex can be?"

She allowed him a breather. Yet he didn't answer for several moments. Until finally he said, "We just don't need any expectations coming out of this."

She leaned down and sucked on the skin of his throat. Then she whispered, "Were there expectations last time?"

And again he was quiet a long moment before saying, "You didn't put any expectations on me."

She boldly reached down between them and cupped him in her hand, squeezing lightly, feeling the surge of his blood. She owned her power. After years of disappointment, after four failed marriages, after Everett told her how to dress and what to do and who to be friends with, she relished the power of not having a single expectation.

Power flowed through her as she said, "You just have to ask yourself if you want it now. Because we both have the freedom to stop. You can say no. I can say no. But right now, I'm saying yes." She held his gaze, his eyes dark against the deep twilight. "What do you say?"

He groaned, pulled her tight against him, held her down where there was no doubt what his body wanted.

Just before he took her mouth, he muttered against her lips. "Hell yes."

NEED ROARED THROUGH HIM. HE'D NEVER WANTED anything so much in his life, except maybe that summer with her. When they'd both been young, and there'd been no expectations because she was a summer girl.

All his expectations had come later, at the end of the summer, when it was time for her to leave.

He pulled at the neat bow tied at her nape, and the bodice of her suit fell down, revealing her luscious breasts. Bigger, sweeter than before, and he leaned her back to feast on her nipples, ripe and sweet as berries.

She wasn't perfect, but he didn't want or need perfect. Perfect was something for a man in his youth. Or a man trying to get back there.

She moaned, clinging to his shoulders as her head tipped back, her legs parting around him. She smelled sweet, like Florida oranges, and need pounded through him. How long it had been since he'd gone to Miami, where a friend answered his needs? But it had never been like this. Not for years.

Not since Noreen left Key West.

An arm around her back, he used his other to wander her skin, dipping down to the heat between her legs.

She squirmed in pleasure, gasped.

He'd always wondered if it was raging teenage hormones that had made that summer what it was. When they'd broken the first barrier between them, and then neither of them could get enough. Yet it was the same now, the heat rushing along his skin like fire, his muscles rigid, his blood racing through his veins, turning him so hard he thought he'd burst wide open.

He'd only ever felt like this with her.

His mind galloped with the need to taste her. She'd always been so damn sweet.

Rising, taking her with him, he turned to set her on the rim of the tub, and pulled her suit over her hips, letting it hang off one knee as he bent to the richness between her thighs.

Christ, she tasted as sweet as he remembered. Her moans were like music ringing in his ears. He'd taught her to love this. He'd been the first, all those years ago, spreading a blanket on the ground beside the Corvette, then spreading her open to this, even as she'd whispered, "Oh my God, this is embarrassing." And he told her, "No, you're beautiful."

He'd devoured her until she cried out her pleasure. Night after night, she begged him for it. And he'd been on top of the world.

Just like he was now. He pushed her to the edge so fast, she quaked and quivered while he held her down as he lapped her sweet juices. Biting her lip to stifle her cries in the night, she bucked beneath him like a wild animal. Until she pushed him off and slipped down into the water, pulling him down for a kiss, sweet with the taste of her still on his tongue. Her hands all over his chest, she tweaked his nipples, then reached down to the tie of his trunks, pushing them over his hips, taking him in her hand.

He'd taught her how to squeeze him, how to pump him. They'd taught each other exactly how they liked it, the moves that felt best, hitting all the sensitive spots.

And she found all of his now.

"Stand up," she demanded.

Once he was above her, she went down deep in the water, letting it cover her shoulders, and took him in her mouth as he leaned back against the rim of the tub.

It was glorious. It was like going to heaven. It was like forty years melting away, with her mouth on him, sucking him just the way he needed. They'd learned each other's bodies, each other's needs. She took him now in the way only she had ever done, with the perfect rhythm, the perfect squeeze of her hand, the perfect slide of her tongue around him. His legs quaked with need, threatening to collapse beneath him.

He would have come if she hadn't pulled away. She knelt

there, looking up at him, her face beautiful in the dappled moonlight.

He wanted to beg her not to stop, but he didn't have breath for even a word.

Then she spoke, stealing that last breath he had. "I want you to do me in the car like you did the very first time."

He still had one brain cell left. "I don't have any condoms."

She laughed, her lips moist with drops of his need. "Well, I'm certainly not worried about getting pregnant. And I haven't been with anyone since I left my husband a year ago."

She squeezed him. He thought he'd die.

"I have a friend I sometimes see, but we're always careful. And it's been a while." Months.

She raised one eyebrow, her hand a mind-blowing vice around him. "A girlfriend? Because I'm not a poacher."

"Just a friend. She agrees about that too."

She dipped down, taking him in her mouth once more, the gentle lap of her tongue making him crazy. And he was so damn glad he was clean, that he'd always insisted on protection. Because he wanted her. More than he'd ever wanted any other woman.

And if he'd had to wait to find a condom, it would be the death of him.

SHE ROSE SLOWLY, TEASING HIM, THE WATER RUNNING OFF her body almost like his fingertips trailing her skin. Her swimsuit floated away in the water, and she didn't care. All she cared about was that he wanted her. As much as she wanted him.

That's all she'd cared about when she was seventeen and nothing had changed. It was supposed to be just kissing. But once it started, neither of them could stop. Not until they'd done everything.

Her gaze steady on him, she reached for her towel, dried her upper body, her arms, her throat, loving the way his eyes traced her movements. Her skin tingled and her body turned electric.

She wrapped the towel around her and sat on the rim of the tub, swinging her legs to the stairs. Lifting a foot to dry it with the edge of her towel, she gave him a glimpse of thigh. Then she dried the other foot and finally stepped down into her flip-flops.

Here beneath the trees, the twilight had burst into full night, sealing them away beneath the canopy of trees and shrubbery.

Turning, she watched him as he towel-dried. And he watched her as she backed toward the Corvette.

She wanted him in the car first, so she could climb on top of him, just like she had all those years ago.

Was she trying to relive the past? With a mental no, she shook her head. She wanted to create new memories, wanted to feel alive again. And he was the perfect man for it. She opened the passenger door, waited for him.

Towel wrapped around his waist, he stepped into his flip-flops and padded to her, gorgeous in the dappled light.

She hoped she looked as good in moonlight.

As he rounded the open door, she stepped aside to let him slide down into the seat. He kicked off his flops before putting his feet inside.

She wanted to laugh. They were both so careful not to dirty up the Corvette.

But oh God, how she wanted to get dirty with him.

He patted his lap. "Come here."

She wondered if it was a conscious reminder of the past. Then she didn't care, hiking the towel higher so she could straddle him. Leaving the door open to give them more room, she settled on top of him, her hands on his shoulders.

"This is exactly what I need," she murmured, not worrying whether the timbre of her voice seduced him. He was already oh-so-seduced beneath her.

All those years ago, they had fumbled with her clothing, tearing her shorts, ripping her panties, but now she was already naked, and she pulled aside the towel around his waist, revealing all his glory.

Was he bigger, thicker, harder?

She couldn't make the comparison. He was simply beautiful, as beautiful as her memory. Taking him lightly in her hand, she stroked until he groaned. Then she shifted, touching his tip to her core.

She'd taken care of herself when she'd been on her own. After all, a woman needed release just as much as a man.

But this, God, this was so much more. "I want you inside me," she whispered.

She slid down, barely taking him inside, yet the feel of him filling her was like nothing she could ever remember. Not even that first time.

"Do it," he begged, his voice hoarse.

She did, allowing herself slow, short strokes over that hard, heated spot inside her. Only he had ever done it this way, going slow, so slow, giving her pleasure before he took his own. It stoked her fire, turned it into a blaze, and she braced herself on his shoulders, using her thighs to slowly rise and fall.

"It's never been like this with anyone but you." She didn't care what it revealed. She wanted him to know.

He gripped her hips, his nails digging in just short of pain. "The best ever."

"Oh my God, yes, the best." She let her held head fall

back, her arms stretching out, and then he put his finger on her, stroked her in time with her body's movements.

"I always liked it that way," he murmured. "Your body tight around me, squeezing me, making me crazy."

She loved to talk. She couldn't remember if they'd talked back then. Except when she told him how she wanted it. *Lick me this way, stroke me that way.* And he'd done the same, taking her head in his hands, guiding her, words falling from his lips. *Yeah, just like that, slow, all around me.*

The words could have been his now, just as easily as they could have been the past.

The tremors began in her legs, traveled up her body. "Is this what you like?" She moaned. "The way I tense around you."

"Christ, yes."

Her breaths came faster, the sensations inside building, intensifying. Finger on her center as she rocked on him, he helped her keep the rhythm that would shoot her to the peak. Then it was as if every feeling in her body shot deep down inside her, hitting her right where they joined, then exploding.

She cried out, couldn't help it, even though they were outside where she knew she should be quiet.

He took control then, pulling her down, slamming into her, the friction forcing the sensations to expand like the universe, like the trees and the stars and the moon above her. The pleasure went on and on until she heard his gasp, felt his quakes, his deep surge inside her.

She came again, this time with him as he gave her everything she'd been looking for, everything she hadn't known she wanted.

Everything she'd waited for.

14

Christ, it was good. So good. Too good.

Hadn't he been thinking just the other day that women his own age weren't interested in sex anymore? It sure as hell wasn't true for Noreen. She'd always been different from any other woman he'd ever known.

The night creatures chattered outside the treehouse. What had started in the car carried right up into the bedroom, and now Noreen lay sprawled across his body, asleep. Cutter liked the weight of her on him way too much. His body felt exquisitely sated, perfectly relaxed. He hadn't experienced sex like that in a long, long time.

Maybe not for forty years.

If you think about something for forty years, reality either ruins the fantasy forever. Or makes it way better than the memory. They'd just created a fantasy to last another forty years.

Christ. He'd be dead by then.

He ran his fingers along her arm, feeling the smooth skin, their sex still scenting the air. They'd do it again. Tomorrow night. The night after that. And he'd want it just as badly.

When was the last time he'd wanted a woman twice in one night? Not that his sex drive wasn't still healthy. It was just that no one had excited him like this in a long time.

And that was a bad sign. That meant things could get complicated. What if she wanted more than just a couple of weeks on a road trip?

Worse, what if *he* wanted more?

It wouldn't be like driving up to Miami to satisfy an itch. He and Noreen lived a continent apart. What if there were expectations?

Expectations were a crazy thing. They took over your life.

He'd learned the lesson that last best summer with her, when he'd wanted things she couldn't give.

And he would never leave Key West. He tried it once, and it hadn't worked. The Keys were in his blood, his DNA, his dreams. Whereas Noreen was a big city woman, so far from the life he lived in Key West.

She could never stay there.

Just like she hadn't stayed the last time.

Not that he'd asked. Or even hinted. Instead, he'd let her walk away, plaguing himself with some vague notion that he'd somehow prove he was good enough for her. All he'd proven was that he couldn't hack the big city career a woman like her wanted in a man.

So why didn't he just tell he'd become a success in his own way, doing something he loved?

He could. But it felt like cheating.

It was admitting he was only good enough for her if he had money.

She felt good. Amazingly good. Out-of-this-world good.

Noreen woke to an empty bed and the scent of coffee. She was already sitting up and scrolling through her phone when Cutter carried a mug to her. "Bless you, I need this," she said, smiling after that first sip.

She could need him too. Right now.

"What are you doing?" Mug in hand, he stood in cargo shorts and a bare chest, his hair wet from the shower.

Hadn't she been contemplating taking a shower with him?

God, he was beautiful.

So much more beautiful than he'd been at eighteen. She didn't know why some women craved younger men. A man like Cutter, in his prime, set her on fire.

But she didn't voice a single one of her thoughts. "I'm looking for a casino boat hotel on the water in Baton Rouge. I want to book it now before I forget." He'd wanted it, and so far she'd booked everything according to what she wanted. This was the first time he'd asked for anything.

"Sounds good." He sipped his coffee.

Then she had to ask, because she didn't want to assume and get slammed down. "Shall I book one or two rooms?"

She thought something flickered in his eyes, but she couldn't be sure. "What would you like?" he asked.

Oh God. She didn't want to play the guessing game. Couldn't he just say what they did was great and he wanted it again, even needed it? She didn't want to be forced to say it first.

But then wanting him to be first was a game too.

After another swallow of coffee, as if he'd heard her thoughts, he said, "Two rooms would be a waste." And his eyes darkened. "Because you know we're gonna do this again."

Then she saw what she wanted, a flare of fire in his eyes.

And suddenly it was no longer about the road trip. It was about him. It was about the nights, not the sites they would see. It was about the sexy things they'd do to each other, not the car or the miles. Just like it had been that summer. Even though she'd known she'd leave in the end, that summer had been all about *them*.

And now this drive would be all about them.

Even though he'd leave when it was over.

❀

IT WAS CUTTER'S TURN TO DRIVE, AND NOREEN LOVED flying down the road, her scarf holding her hair down and her sunglasses blocking the sun. And she could look at him.

Cutter had always been a sight to behold. But somehow, this morning, he was so much more than she'd ever remembered. And she'd remembered a lot.

It was warm and humid along the Gulf Coast, but she didn't care. The wind over her was like the caress of Cutter's fingers last night. She never been a twice-in-a-night woman. Or maybe it was just that her husbands had never been twice-in-a-night men. But with Cutter, it was glorious.

Doing it in the car had been like reliving the best memory of her life.

After Cutter taught her to kiss, he'd taught her to touch and lick and so much more. She'd begged him to. And then she'd begged him to take her virginity. He'd told her she shouldn't waste it on a guy like him. Then he'd reminded her about accidental pregnancy. The next day, she'd screwed up her courage and gone to a drugstore. No one cared these days, but back then, even though it was the eighties, she felt as if every eye was on her, as if she had a scarlet letter tattooed on her chest.

But it hadn't stopped her.

And that night, she'd pulled out a condom and shut down all his objections. He hadn't *taken* her virginity in the Corvette. She'd gifted it to him. And she was glad. In the passenger seat, she could be on top, in control. He let her do it her way, slowly, easing down, and somehow the slowness made it better. Or at least she'd thought it had since she had no comparison.

And she never regretted it. She'd been a nervous, mortified, humiliated girl when she left home at the end of the school year. Cutter sent her back a confident woman.

Even if there were times she didn't believe she'd ever again find the pure beauty of that summer.

After four divorces, she could definitely say she hadn't.

As they passed through Biloxi, Noreen searched for a place to have an early lunch, finding a restaurant along the waterfront that had great online reviews. They'd poured the rest of the morning coffee in to-go cups and stopped for a croissant they'd shared along the way. Though Cutter was horrified she'd drop a crumb in the car.

"It's my car," she'd singsonged at him. "I can have it vacuumed."

He'd grumbled anyway. "This car needs someone who won't drop crumbs in the first place."

"You mean like you?" She laughed at him when he dropped a crumb.

They rolled up to the restaurant an hour before the lunch rush and got a seat right away.

Looking over her menu, she said, "I want to order every weird thing they serve."

He looked over the options. "What's weird on here?"

"Beach balls."

He read the description aloud. "Fried mashed potatoes filled with cheese and bacon bits. What's so weird about that?"

She rolled her eyes at him. "And fried pickles." Dill pickle chips, breaded and fried and served with ranch dressing.

"Why don't you get the gator bites then?"

She shuddered. "I've already tried that weirdness. I want new weirdness. And I definitely want the fried green tomatoes. I saw the movie, but I've never tried them."

"Wow," he said. "That's a lot of fried and battered stuff for a Californian. Don't you people out there clog all your arteries if you even touch fried food?"

She scowled at him and didn't dignify that with an answer. "And we're going to top it off with a bucket of royal reds." The name sounded so good, she had to try the royal shrimp.

"We can't possibly eat a whole bucket along with beach balls, fried pickles, and fried green tomatoes," he said as if they'd suddenly switched roles.

"We'll get some ice and put the leftovers in that little cooler I have." He'd squeezed it into the trunk every morning, filled with drinks for the road trip. She smiled. "We can eat them for dinner, along with the rest of our snacks."

"Then we'll need more snacks. You finished all your cheese puffs."

"You mean *we* did." And they'd broken out his Oreos, eating them in bed.

The beach balls were amazing, the pickles were just *meh*, but the fried green tomatoes were everything they were cracked up to be, crunchy and tangy. The royal reds capped it all and were to die for.

"They're just carriers for the cocktail sauce," Cutter said, loading it on.

She batted his arm, then popped a shrimp in her mouth without a lick of sauce. "Yum."

With all the appetizers, they made it less than halfway through the shrimp, leaving plenty for the evening. The waitress gave them extra cocktail sauce, a bag of ice for the cooler, and conned them into taking a slice of Mississippi mud pie that looked decadently chocolaty.

"See, we've already got dinner and dessert." She stroked

his arm as he shut the lid on the cooler. "We can eat it on our room's veranda overlooking the river while we watch the sunset."

He looked at her, a smile curving half his mouth. "Do you realize how excited you get about food?"

She couldn't resist, as if he was asking for it. "There are a lot of other things I get excited about too."

He grinned. "That's the real dessert."

THEY PASSED INTO LOUISIANA AND DROVE THROUGH Slidell. It was a pretty town, especially with that old-town vibe of years long gone. Stately homes sat on tree-lined streets, and the old town, with its ancient town hall and jail-turned-museum, sported old-fashioned brick buildings with columns and balconies along with rows of cutesy shops selling antiques, vintage clothing, and local art.

Even with the stops in Biloxi and Slidell, they arrived in Baton Rouge long before check-in, most of the afternoon playing out before them.

"What shall we do first?" she asked him.

"I thought you had our itinerary all planned."

She smiled. Her criminal husband, Rodney, said she was OCD because she always planned everything. Maybe there was a bit of truth to that. But she'd loved winging it on this trip, deciding their next move almost on the spur of the moment. Okay, maybe a day ahead.

"Let's start at the new capitol, which is the tallest capitol building in the United States, so we have to go up to the observation deck, where we'll see almost all of Louisiana. Then we can head to the old state capitol that you talked about, and from there to the Magnolia Mound Plantation." She widened her smile. "We can even walk. It's only three miles from the capitol to the plantation. What do you think?"

His expression remained deadpan for a moment, then a grin spread across his face like a sunbeam stretching over the horizon. "Get your walking shoes on, ma'am."

Parking near the Louisiana State Capitol, they headed straight for the elevator to the observation deck on the twenty-seventh floor. The view was everything the website said it would be. On such a clear day, all of Baton Rouge lay before them, and even far beyond, the Mississippi River, the wide spans of its bridges, and below them stretched the capitol gardens. From up here, the geometric shapes of the pathways were easily discernable along with the sparkling green of its lawns. Everything was green in Baton Rouge.

"It's like taking a helicopter ride over the city."

"Let me get a picture of you with the view in the background so you can send it to your girls."

How sweet. She handed him her phone, and he held it high as she posed, snapping the picture from above to get as much of the view as possible.

Taking the phone back, she waggled her fingers at him. "Let's get a selfie. Come here."

She wouldn't send it to the girls, and not Tammy or her sister either. They would totally freak out that she was on a cross-country trip with a man she barely knew.

Except that she knew Cutter. She'd hung out with him four summers in a row. Her uncle had trusted him. She trusted him. She'd given him her virginity, for God's sake.

She knew they'd all say that he could have changed in the past forty years, turning into a monster.

But Cutter was the furthest thing from a monster. He was kind and thoughtful. He never pushed, he made her laugh, and she loved bantering with him, both sexual and non-sexual. He might be a mechanic, but he was far more deferential than any of her husbands had ever been.

"You take it," she said. "Your arms are longer."

He grinned. "So now I'm your selfie stick?"

She made a face at him, and just as she turned, he leaned down, kissed her. It was sweet and lingering. She forgot the crowd in the tower. There was just his lips on hers, his arm around her, his body warm against the length of hers. She was still in a dream state when he handed her phone back after snapping a couple of selfies.

She left the observation deck totally bemused, and they skipped the tour of the capitol building. "I'd rather spend more time in the old State House," Cutter said.

They passed through the beautifully manicured capitol gardens they'd seen from the observation deck. It was warm, though not stifling, but she'd added another layer of sunblock to her shoulders, arms, and the back of her neck.

Cutter never seemed to need sunscreen, as if his skin had grown used to the rays.

The Old Louisiana State Capitol, also called the State House, was worth the walk. From the front, it resembled a medieval castle.

Cutter took her phone again. "Stand on the steps and I'll get another picture. For your girls," he added.

She wondered how she would explain to the girls who had taken the photos. She could tell them strangers in Louisiana were friendly, and she always took their pictures for them too.

Even as she had the thought, a couple approached them. "We'll take your picture if you take ours," the woman said in the sweet, high voice of a twenty-something.

Cutter handed over the phone. "Thanks, that'd be great."

There would be more pictures of the two of them on the camera roll. She'd have to download everything to her computer, then delete the photos out of the cloud before showing her trip album to the girls when she got home.

But then Cutter was putting his arm around her, pulling her close, and she forgot everything but the feel of him against her. His body mesmerized her. His scent entranced her. His kiss made her lose herself.

But she didn't forget that tonight all the seduction was planned, unlike last night where it had been spontaneous. Still, she fully intended to have her wicked way with him. Over and over. Until this trip was over.

She wanted all the erotic memories of really good sex that she could store up.

There was nothing wrong with that, right? She'd sworn off relationships—because she totally sucked at them—but she hadn't sworn off sex. And Cutter seemed very willing.

He took the steps down two at a time, while she followed him more slowly, enjoying his rear view. The other couple took their position on the stairs, smiling at her, and Cutter snapped pictures of them, horizontal, vertical, then close-up, and she muttered to him under her breath, "You're such a tourist."

He laughed, and his eyes crinkled charmingly at the corners. "They're the tourists. I just want them to enjoy their experience." Then he bounded back up the steps with all the energy of a sleek, powerful jungle cat.

He swept Noreen along with his enthusiasm.

"We have to see the most important thing, the capitol dome." He took her hand, and she liked the feel of his fingers wrapped around hers, the heat of his palm on her skin, as if they were a happy couple other tourists felt comfortable asking to swap picture-taking.

She just plain liked being with Cutter. She always had.

Standing at the bottom of the spiral staircase, the stained

glass dome glittered with sunlight, a glowing spectacle above them.

"It was added during a restoration in the eighteen-eighties." He spoke in an oddly reverent voice she wouldn't have expected from him.

But she was in awe of the dome's beauty right along with him as the sun shot prisms of light over the stairs, the floor, and Cutter. When she held out her arms, her skin gleamed with color. It was breathtaking, as marvelous as the view from the top of the new capitol building.

They wandered the exhibits and the assembly rooms, which were set up as if the state assembly was about to open session.

"I would never have thought of you as a museum man."

He cocked his head, shrugging. "I like the old architecture."

Though interesting, nothing they saw was as dazzling as the dome. She could only hope her pictures did it justice, especially the one she'd taken of Cutter in the dappled light.

They left the building hand in hand, and she realized she could like these touches far too much. That she might start wishing they'd never stop. But that was impossible. He was east, she was west. And neither of them wanted a new relationship.

"On to the Magnolia Plantation?" she asked. Suddenly, maybe it was her thoughts as her hand lay in his, but she felt strangely shy, almost having to force a smile.

"Lead on" Cutter said, swinging their clasped hands, walking fast, while Noreen kept pace.

The old State House was about halfway between the plantation and the new capitol, but she wasn't tired, feeling as if she had the same boundless energy he did.

It might have been the exhilaration of his touch.

The plantation house wasn't the big colonnaded antebellum home she'd seen in *Gone with the Wind*. In the Creole style, it was a long bungalow with a pitched roof that ended in a peak along the center. The wraparound porch stood on brick supports, long wooden steps leading up to it. Originally, the house comprised only a couple of rooms, then expanding many times during the years.

The history was fascinating, the plight of the slaves horrifying. They toured the old shacks, read all the interpretive signs describing the vast disparity between the lives of the slaves and those of their masters.

And yet she couldn't help admiring the breathtaking beauty of the house, the grounds, the trees, the flowers.

"Ready to go back?" Cutter asked as they gave the house a last admiring look.

Glancing at her watch, she realized it was long past check-in time. Not that it mattered, since she'd already paid for the room.

He gave her a wide grin. "I can jog to the car and drive back to get you."

She gaped at him. "Do I look like some sort of weenie? It's only three miles. I can make that in less than an hour."

He chuckled evilly, and she knew a challenge was coming. But she was up for it.

"Don't say I didn't offer." Still holding her hand, he took off at a fast clip.

"No fair," she said, hanging onto his hand and letting him pull her along. "Your legs are longer."

"Then you set the pace."

Not wanting him to show her up, she set a faster pace than her normal. She was used to fast walks, often heading out on trails by the house or driving to a nearby regional park.

Following the levee path along the river with its view of the traffic streaming over the Horace Wilkinson Bridge, they passed the USS Kidd on the water and a Navy jet on display outside the Veterans Museum. It was only a forty-five-minute walk, but she was winded and sticky by the time they made it back to the car parked at the capitol.

Not that she'd admit that to Cutter.

She wanted him to think she was in the best shape of her life. Especially at her age.

Especially in the bedroom.

15

They headed out to the river and their floating hotel. The day had felt very touristy, like they were a couple taking a vacation. They'd held hands for much of it, Cutter sometimes pulling her beneath his arm as they studied an interpretive sign.

Those sweet, seemingly unconscious touches showed Noreen how much she missed being the other half of a couple. It felt like a new romance, especially knowing what they'd do tonight.

But she couldn't let herself think like that. He'd turn around and fly away once they got to San Francisco. They weren't a couple. They were just... friends with benefits. And that was good. It was totally hot. But it certainly wasn't romance.

She didn't want romance. She'd had too many bad romances to believe in them anymore.

She'd imagined that cabins on a boat would be small, even a casino boat that never left the shore. Booking a suite had occurred to her, but it was only one night. Yet this place was as spacious as a good hotel room. They could both fit in the bathroom at the same time. In addition to the queen-size bed, a sofa with an end table and two chairs sat by the balcony doors, with a small refrigerator tucked into a cabinet.

Sliding open the glass door, she stepped onto the verandah, with two chairs and a small table set out to enjoy the view. The Mississippi wasn't clear, which was why they called it the muddy Mississippi, but it flowed freely, unencumbered by refuse or debris. Barges floated down the river, and amid the greenery on the opposite shore, factory smoke stacks billowed out plumes of steam. The view and the water's gentle *shoosh* were beautiful, even calming.

Cutter came to stand in the doorway behind her, his body pressed close to hers, igniting delicious explosions along her skin.

"We need a glass of champagne, don't you think?"

She turned her head slightly, his lips almost touching her cheek. "I thought you were a beer kind of guy."

"But you're a champagne kind of woman."

She laughed, softly, seductively. "I do love my champagne."

"But you loved your special Key West punch when you were seventeen."

Smiling, she said softly, "I thought that was a special Cutter Sorensen punch."

He wrapped his arm around her waist. "It was. And guaranteed to lower all the inhibitions."

"I don't recall you needing to get me drunk to have your wicked way with me."

His chuckle vibrated through her. "I was talking about me. *You* got me drunk so you could have your wicked way."

"So true." She moved sinuously against him. "Just like I had my wicked way with you last night."

"And tonight," he murmured close to her ear, sending

tingles to every part of her body. "It'll be my turn to do some very naughty things to you."

She shivered just imagining it. What if she let him take complete control?

A knock on the stateroom door interrupted them.

Cutter answered, and she heard the murmur of voices, his deeper, the other higher, probably a teenager. While he was occupied, she slipped out of her walking shoes and put on sandals to ease the ache of her feet.

After the snick of the closing door, Cutter returned to the coffee bar. Setting down two glasses, he looked at her, a cheeky smile curving his mouth. "I ordered champagne glasses because those plastic things we bought just won't do." He winked. "And the young gentleman brought ice as well." Retrieving a bottle of champagne from the liquor store bag, he shoved it down in the ice bucket. "It shouldn't take too long to cool."

The ice in the cooler had kept the shrimp fresh and delicious, and they feasted on barbecue potato chips, shrimp, and champagne. It was by no means a healthy meal, and Noreen promised herself a salad tomorrow.

They relaxed after the day in the car and all the walking, eating leisurely as barges and tugboats floated along the river, the occasional paddlewheel cruise ship steaming by. Eventually the sun set over the water, streaking the sky with tendrils of lemon and tangerine. It wasn't a Hawaiian sunset, but it had its own beauty. That's what she'd learned across three states, that every city had its own beauty, its own specialties.

On that thought, she dug the mud pie out of the cooler. "Ready to dive in?" She tugged the lid off the container and handed him a plastic fork.

He motioned for her to take the first bite, and she scooped up the rich chocolate and whipped cream, a chocolaty ambrosia on her tongue. "Oh my God."

Then Cutter rolled the delicious concoction around his mouth, his smile beatific, his eyes closed in reverence.

"Good?" she asked.

Without cracking a lid, he said, "I could live on Mississippi mud pie and key lime pie for the rest of my life."

She burst out a laugh, and he joined her. Then he winked. "And sex."

All day she'd thought about tonight, with equal parts anticipation and nerves. What if it was awkward? Last night had been a thing of the moment, unplanned. There hadn't been time to think, only to enjoy. But tonight, she'd booked one hotel room, and now she ruminated about how it would go. Would there be seduction? Or would they get in the bed like an old married couple and just do it?

Yet suddenly, with that devilish wink, he'd taken all the nerves out of it.

"It has to be really good sex," she said.

He demolished another big bite of mud pie. "Oh, definitely good sex. Great sex." He gave her that sexy, shit-eating grin. "Fantastic sex."

"Don't let it go to your head." Then she added before he could, "Either of them."

He laughed once more. "It already has."

He made it all so easy, made her so unselfconscious.

She speared the pie, coming up with a big forkful. "Finish the mud pie? Or sex?"

Holding her fork out to him, he wrapped his warm hand around her slender wrist and pulled the fork to his mouth. Eyes on hers, he took the bite of mud pie, and after he'd swallowed, he murmured, "There's no reason we can't have both."

Then he dug his fork in and fed her a bite. It was like foreplay, the way they fed each other.

The temperature rose, her breath quickened, her heart rat-a-tatted. Everything in her was primed.

Had it ever felt quite like this with any of her husbands? The race of her blood through her veins, the way his gaze on her ignited a fire deep inside, how her breasts ached for his touch, his lips. God, no, it had never been like this. This was being seventeen again, when all she could think about was the next ride with Cutter in her uncle's Corvette.

And this was why she had to have the Corvette. It represented the best times in her life, second only to her daughters' births.

They fed each other until the plastic container was empty. Sliding his finger through the chocolate and cookie crumbles, he raised the sweet leftovers to his mouth, sucking them off his finger. Then he did it once more, and this time she licked him clean, her tongue rolling around his finger, imitating things she'd done to him so long ago, things she'd done last night.

He stood, held out his hand, pulled her to her feet and into his chest, wrapping that big, warm hand around her nape and holding her still for a kiss that made her blood roar and her knees go weak.

She tasted of cookies and cream and chocolate. He wanted to eat her up, all of her. But they had all night, and no need to rush. Rushing this would be like jamming his face into the mud pie instead of savoring each individual bite.

"I need a shower." He walked backward into the room, her hand in his, leading her.

Last night, she'd been the one in control, and he'd enjoyed every moment. But tonight, he intended to make her scream five or six times before he took his own pleasure.

Forty years ago, he hadn't mastered the fine art of

multiple orgasms. But tonight, he intended to show her just how good he really was when he wanted to be.

In the bathroom, he stripped her down slowly, undoing each button of her blousy sleeveless top. He kissed the line of tan along her shoulder, then tore his T-shirt over his head. Unclasping her bra, he rolled it down her arms, kissing the tip of her breast before sucking her into his mouth.

His belly burned with desire as she moaned for him, threading her fingers through his hair and holding him close.

He unsnapped her clam-digger pants, and she let them drop to the floor, stepping out of them and her sandals at the same time. Her skin smooth beneath his fingertips, he bent to kiss the faint lines of her pregnancies.

Then he shucked his shorts, his boxer briefs tight, highlighting his erection. She patted her hand on him tentatively, as if she were that seventeen-year-old girl who wasn't sure of what she was doing. If only she'd known that he hadn't needed to teach her anything at all. She'd been a natural. Or maybe there'd been something special between them, something he'd searched for but never found again.

His groan wasn't just for pleasure, it was for the perfection of her touch.

After stripping off her lacy panties, he shucked his briefs. Then he turned on the shower and pulled her beneath it even before the water heated.

She shrieked. "Holy crap."

He shut her up with a kiss that turned the water to scalding with its heat.

When they were both soaked beneath the rain shower, he grabbed one of the specialty shampoos in the shower niche, poured a daub on his hand, and rubbed it into her hair. Eyes closed, she let him massage her head, moaning with pleasure as if his hands were between her legs. He kissed her again as he pushed her beneath the spray and washed away the shampoo. Then he applied the conditioner, and while it sat on her hair, she washed him, giving him a scalp massage as delicious as a slice of key lime pie. Or a taste of her.

Then he soaped her up with the shower gel, caressing all her nooks and crannies, making her gasp with a long, sweet touch between her legs. Rinsing her off the same way, water spilling over her body as he delved into those same nooks to caress and wash the soap away.

But she wasn't letting him off the hook, soaping him up, stroking him, turning him hard and aching, making him near crazy as she washed it all off again, cradling his erection, squeezing, teasing, tantalizing.

He could have hauled her up his body, shoved her against the shower wall and taken her right then.

But he had bigger plans.

Wrapping her tight, he let her feel the pulse of him against her stomach. Then, as water rained over them, he kissed his way down. First her throat, his lips on her throbbing pulse, then the sweet line of her shoulders, the swell of her breasts, and the tight bead of her nipple. He squeezed a bud between his fingers, then looked up at her as he sucked her into his mouth, working her until her breath came in gasps and moans. He kissed his way down her abdomen, the slight roundness of her stomach, his tongue in her belly button, making her laugh and groan. Then, going to his knees, he spread her legs, touching his tongue to her center, making her shudder and quake as he steeped himself in the scent and taste of her, drinking in the sounds of her pleasure.

Shoving her fingers through his hair, she tried to pull him off. "I can't, I can't, not when I'm standing."

But she could. He would make her. He wouldn't stop. Because this was only the first. He had a week or more to show her how much pleasure she could take.

Then she came for him, her voice a low wail. He held her

there, his fingers inside her, his mouth on her, his head pressed between her legs, until finally he let her push him away.

Her body flushed pink with far more than the heat of the water, her breath came fast, her chest rising and falling, her lids at a sexy half-mast. And before she could slide down the wall, her knees giving out, he held her up, gently drying her off, rubbing the water out of her hair.

And he whispered, "I'm not done yet."

OH GOD, HE ABSOLUTELY WASN'T DONE YET. SHE NEEDED more, so much more.

Noreen didn't care that her hair needed to be styled after it got wet or that her makeup had probably smeared under her eyes or that she needed moisturizer on her face. There were only his hands and his lips and his tongue on her.

He dried her off, then hauled her up until she wrapped her legs around him. Her breasts brushed his chest tantalizingly as he smacked off the bathroom light and carried her to the bed.

Though the curtains were open, the room was dark, and she didn't care if someone saw. She was too drugged with desire to care about anything but the feel of him against her.

Her wet hair was soaking the pillow, and she wriggled her legs, kicking the covers to the bottom of the bed.

Then he was on her again, just like in the shower, nuzzling, licking, suckling, his magic fingers inside her, making her cry out, dazzling her. If someone on the other side of the wall heard her cries, they could just enjoy.

"Do it now," she gasped, needing, praying for him to be inside her.

He crawled up her body, sucking a nipple into his mouth,

then kissing her with the taste of herself on his lips and his tongue. All the while, his fingers were on her, gliding inside, back out, all around, and climax followed climax, almost as if they were all one, never-ending.

His mouth against hers, he whispered, "Two more. I need to get six out of you."

She groaned. "Oh my God. It's enough. I can't take another." But she did. And it was glorious.

Then finally, God, *finally*, he fell between her legs, spreading her so he could rub the crown of his erection against her. He kept the buzz going, heightened the sensitivity of her skin and the tremble of her limbs. And just when she thought, no, she *knew* she could squeeze out another orgasm, pleasure rolled through her like a perfect surfing wave. She arched, and he filled her, pounding into her, hard and so very good. She grabbed his butt cheeks, hauled him in, directed him, begging for his hard thrust inside her. The hammer of his body against her forced the sensations on and on.

Until he reached his limit too, and she felt the quake of his body deep inside, his groans rumbling against her. He was so close, and she let herself go, taking him with her, relishing every deep plunge, until he arched, went rigid with his orgasm, his throat stretched, his head thrown back, his beauty overwhelming.

HE STAYED DEEP INSIDE HER, ROLLING WITH HER, UNTIL she straddled him. He didn't want to let her go yet. This was too good, too perfect.

"I'm pretty sure that was six," he said, his mouth buried in her hair.

"It was probably seven, but who's counting."

He wanted to chuckle, but he didn't have the strength. She'd sapped everything out of him, and now there was just this sated lethargy. How could he ever have thought a woman her age was past the desire for sex? She changed all his assumptions. Noreen Kincaid was in her prime.

Christ, he loved the weight of her on top of him, the heat of her surrounding him. It had taken every ounce of willpower to hold back until the last moment.

And then he was a goner.

She hummed lightly against his ear. "Oh my God. That was good, so good." She pulled back to look at him. "Was it that good way back when?"

"It was damn good." He puffed out a laugh. "But not this good. We've come a long way since then." He reared up for a fast kiss, a quick taste. "And we still have a long way to go. Maybe I can stretch it out ten orgasms in a row."

She laughed, then groaned. "I don't think I can handle ten. I don't even know how I handled seven."

"Maybe I can give you a rest in between."

"I might die if you don't." Then she bit her lip, her eyes shining. "So where the heck did you learn all that?"

He liked the sexy banter.

They'd been too shy for banter all those years ago, too virginal. Even though she hadn't been his first, it wasn't as if he knew everything the way she'd thought he did.

And he could admit now that she'd taught him a few things too. "A lot of what I know I learned from you."

She reared back on her hands, her arms taut. "You were the teacher."

He slowly shook his head. "Don't you remember telling me you liked it this way or that way? 'Do it like this, Cutter, do it like that,'" he imitated.

She shook her head, her hair falling over her face. "I don't remember saying anything at all. I just soaked up all that pleasure."

He nodded slowly, once up, once down. "Oh, you were verbal. You let me know when it was good or when I was just off the mark or when you were close. And if I stopped doing whatever thing was getting you there, you made me do it all again. 'Just like that, Cutter, don't stop,'" he couldn't resist adding.

She was silent a long moment, her eyes unreadable in the fall of her hair. "It was a two-way street."

"Oh yeah, it went both ways. I liked the way you let me guide you. How you wanted me to tell you exactly how I liked your mouth and tongue on me."

She laughed softly. "And telling me not to use my teeth."

He laughed with her and, unimaginably, felt himself growing hard inside her.

"Wanna do it again?" His smile grew until it was a shit-eating grin he could feel across his face.

"Me on top?"

"You on top. Where I can touch you when you're riding me."

She sat up straight and began a slow, mesmerizing bob on top of him. He put his finger to the tight bead between her legs, and it didn't take long to send her into orbit again. When she blasted off, she hauled him into heaven right along with her.

At his age, it might actually have been a miracle.

THEY WERE ON A ROAD TRIP, THEY WERE IN BATON ROUGE, and they should have gotten out of bed for a late evening stroll. They should have at least gone to a show since they were on a casino boat.

But Noreen lay in his arms, so lusciously replete that she couldn't move. Didn't *want* to move. She'd missed good sex. She'd missed a man's arms around her, missed walking hand in hand, missed companionship and having someone to talk to, to share thoughts with, to drink coffee with late in the mornings. Someone who didn't nitpick her, who didn't check up on her, who let her go for a dinner, or a day or a weekend, and welcomed her back with open arms.

She missed the ease of a man like Cutter.

"Where to next?" His voice rumbled pleasantly against her ear as she lay on his chest.

Where to next? It could mean so many things.

"I was thinking somewhere like Austin. I've heard it's a college town and very hip. And after that, I think Santa Fe and Sedona."

His chuckle vibrated against her cheek. Maybe it was that 1960s word, *hip*. "Don't forget Las Vegas." He breathed out a sigh. "Austin is a longer drive than we've been doing, six and a half, maybe seven hours."

She tipped her head to look at him. A slice of moonlight illuminated his face, and she shivered with how beautiful he was. "Will the car make it?"

He snorted. "Of course she will. The XB-70 has stamina." Every morning, Cutter checked her hoses, pipes, feeding her oil or any other fluid if she needed it.

"Then let's do it." She smiled against his chest. "And this time, I want a luxury hotel."

"What happened to glamping?"

She shrugged sinuously against him. "For one night, I want a massive bathtub." She glanced up at him. "Big enough for two."

Then she fell asleep to the rhythm of his breathing against her ear.

She woke in the middle of the night, alone in the bed, and

for just a moment, her entire body froze. He was gone. He'd picked up his duffel and left. Noreen rolled in the bed, pulling the covers over her shoulders as if the room had suddenly gone cold.

Then she saw him, a dark form sitting on the balcony. She was about to call out to him, tell him to come back to bed, but the words didn't make it. They shouldn't make it. He'd come back when he was ready. This was just a fling, a two-week interlude in their regular lives.

Despite all the things she missed about being one half of a couple, she remembered all the things she didn't miss. The telling looks, the arguments, the disappointments.

She didn't want all that with Cutter. She didn't want to ruin this beautiful interlude. She wanted to enjoy every moment of the now.

Because they couldn't fit into each other's lives anywhere but on the road.

❧ 16 ❧

With a long drive ahead of them, they didn't linger the next morning. Noreen grabbed to-go coffee and a couple of pastries while he checked the car. He'd gotten over the whole eating-in-the-car thing. First of all, he had to admit she was fastidious, and second, the XB-70 could be cleaned. After he checked the fluids levels, he cleaned her up, wiping bugs off the windscreen, the bumpers, the headlights.

"Wanna drive?" he asked.

She shook her head, the big lenses of her sunglasses hiding her eyes. "You drive. I want to check for a place to stay."

"Let me take care of that this time."

Her brow wrinkled and her lips thinned, and he thought she'd put up a fight. But then she said airily, "Okay. Sounds good," and settled into the passenger seat.

More and more, she let him drive. She wasn't afraid of driving the car, actually loved it, evidenced by the blissed-out smile on her lips when she had the wheel beneath her hands.

He supposed she was letting him get his fill of the car before he had to say goodbye.

Why did that feel like a metaphor for their relationship? Not that they had a relationship. They were just driving and having sex. That wasn't a relationship.

The problem was that he didn't think he'd get his fill of her during this jaunt across the country, not just the XB-70, and especially not Noreen.

She'd worked her way under his skin, just like she had forty years ago. There'd been times long ago when he'd thought about flying out to California to see her. He'd had visions of looking her up, showing up on her doorstep, handing her his university diploma, emblazoned with its grad-uated-with-honors stamp. And he'd say something like, "See, I'm not a loser."

But those were fantasies. When Mortimer told him he was flying out to the California for her wedding, he'd invited Cutter along. Cutter hadn't gone, and neither had Mortimer, as if he were afraid that once he left the island, he might never come back.

And Cutter put away all the fantasies. Except then he'd started looking for women like her. Maybe that was why he'd never found the right woman. He'd done too much comparing.

And dammit, all he wanted out of her now was great sex and the XB-70.

Anything else was just a pipe dream.

HE STOPPED IN A SMALL TOWN THAT BOASTED THE BEST barbecue in Texas. Old trucks and ancient sedans filled the dusty main street's parking spaces. The town lacked the gentrification of vegan restaurants and stylish boutiques, and more power to them for that. A mom-and-pop hardware store, an old five-and-dime, and an appliance parts store bracketed the Best Barbecue in Texas diner.

"Oh my God," she said, rattling the paper menu. "They actually have crackling."

"You mean pork fat," he said dryly.

She rustled her menu again. "My mother used to make the best crackling." She tipped her head, thinking back. "We didn't call it crackling though. I don't even remember what we called it. But she always made a pork roast for Christmas."

"Pork roast? Not turkey?"

She shook her head. "Pork roast. Before she cooked it, she scored lines in the fat, making sure not to cut through to the meat. Then she slow-roasted, and by the end, little squares of crispy deliciousness covered the whole thing. My sister and I fought over every bite."

"Then I guess you have to order crackling."

She sighed and clucked her tongue. "It won't be as good as Mom's. I don't want to ruin the memory. Did you always have turkey on Christmas?"

Cutter looked at his menu, not her. "We had whatever my dad caught that day." He laid the menu flat as if he'd decided. "But my mom, she always did the fish up special for Christmas. And it was good."

Somehow, her question cast a pall over the table. She'd always known he hadn't come from a rich family. But nor had they been a caricature, the wife beater or the drunkard. His parents were solid, his dad a fisherman, his mom a waitress at a local restaurant. Mortimer had told her that Cutter's dad died of cancer, and his mom from a brain tumor. They'd both been gone a long time now. But maybe being poor left a stain Cutter didn't want to remember.

"You want to get beef ribs and I'll get pork ribs and we'll share?" she asked to break the tension.

He drummed his fingers on the table. "Yeah, that sounds great."

When the waitress took their orders, Noreen added a Mexican corn salad, especially since she'd told herself she'd have a salad after yesterday's indulgences.

"Oh my God, this really is the best barbecue," she said on the first bite.

Cutter nodded his agreement. She ate with her fingers, not bothering with a knife and fork the way her mother would. Cutter did the same. With each rib she tossed on the plate, she licked her fingers clean and downed a couple of forkfuls of the corn salad. "This is good. I could make it at home."

Then he said, as if he hadn't been thinking about anything else, "Have you thought any more about selling the XB-70?" Before she could answer, he added, "She's running like a dream now, but she needs constant maintenance. You can't let the maintenance go, or she'll fall apart."

She thought he was overstating. Since the water pump and the work he'd done in Tallahassee, there hadn't been a single problem. "I told you I'd find a good mechanic."

"But you can't run her over to a mechanic every time you want to go out for a drive."

She countered with, "Do you really need to check her so fastidiously every morning?"

He raked his gaze over her as if she'd gone crazy. "Yes, I absolutely do."

"But only because we're driving two or three hundred miles a day."

"She needs to be taken care of properly," he said emphatically, stopping just short of slamming his hand on the table.

Why was he bringing this up now? Other than vague references, they hadn't talked about selling the car since Florida. At least she thought the last time was Florida. "You don't trust me to take care of her, do you?"

"I just want to make sure you understand the logistics involved."

"You've already explained them to me. And I've already told you I'll find someone good."

"All right, fine," he said on a huff. "But you need to send me the guy's name so I can check him out."

She snorted a disbelieving laugh. "What, is there some sort of mechanics registry where you can check someone out all the way across the country?"

"I'll make some calls."

She sat back, drummed her fingers on the table just the way he had. "You're over the top."

"She just means a lot to me." He paused an overly long moment, then finally added, "I rebuilt a Mach Three once."

It sounded like a total non sequitur. "What's a Mach Three?"

"A motorcycle. A two-stroke Kawasaki." Whatever a two-stroke was. Noreen didn't interrupt to ask. "I replaced everything on her. She was a beauty, a veritable fiend on the road. She had so much power, she damn near knocked my socks off." He paused. "Then I sold her to a summer kid."

"If you loved her so much, why'd you sell her?"

"I needed the money," he said, without additional explanation.

She would have said she was sorry he had to give up the bike, but he went on. "A week later, the kid crashed her, trashed her completely." He raised his hand before she could ask. "Oh yeah, he was fine, but the bike." He shook his head sadly.

"That's not me." She didn't ask if he'd rebuilt the bike again. "I won't crash the XB-70. I'll take excellent care of her. Otherwise, Uncle Mortimer will come back to haunt me."

She smiled, trying to take the bite out of the conversation. "And I know you'll haunt me too."

"I'll absolutely haunt you. I promise you that," he said, his voice intense, his brows pulled together.

For a moment, she felt as if he was talking about something else entirely. But then he added almost mildly, "Just remember to call me when you decide to sell her."

"Of course I will."

They would always have that between them, that she could call him whenever she decided to sell.

Except that she never would.

HE COULD ONLY HOPE HE HAUNTED HER. BUT JUST LIKE HE hadn't haunted her after that summer, he doubted he would when their cross-country trek was over.

She was like the kid and the Mach III, who got his kicks while it lasted, then walked away after he crashed the bike. The kid had never looked back, and neither had she.

Maybe it was a new realization, or maybe it had been simmering below the surface since he'd rescued in her in Florida City, but he saw clearly that he should never have come on this drive. If he'd stayed on his island where he belonged, he would have been able to keep on telling himself he was long since over the summer girl, that she was just a dream he'd had forty years ago.

But here he was. And thinking about the differences in their upbringings brought it all back to him. He'd wanted her then, and he wanted her more now.

And yet she was even more unattainable than the XB-70.

But since he couldn't have her, he would damn well keep asking her to sell him the Corvette.

THEY FINISHED THEIR MEALS, HAVING SHARED LITTLE, AND Cutter paid the bill. They'd fallen into a pattern. She booked and paid for the accommodations, and he bought their meals. It wasn't exactly what she'd planned when they first started, but it was good enough.

Out by the car, she said, "I'd like to drive."

She'd almost asked if she could drive, as if she needed his permission. That just wouldn't do. It was her car. And maybe she only wanted to drive now to assert her authority over the car.

He didn't acknowledge her with words, just went to the passenger door. Behind the wheel, she tied her scarf over her hair, and, on impulse, fished her phone out of her purse. "Would you take a picture of me? I want to send it to the girls."

She couldn't remember if she'd taken one of her behind the wheel. If she had, she certainly didn't think she'd sent it.

He took the phone, again without a word, snapped a picture, handed the cell back. Slipping it into her purse, she slid the bag down between the seats.

Then the engine roared to life beneath her touch.

Cutter settled back, playing on his phone. As she pulled the car onto the road, he said, "I'll find a place for us to stay."

Her jaw ticked, words jumping to get out. She'd agreed earlier to letting him make the booking for tonight, but finding accommodations was her job, and suddenly she didn't want to give up that bit of control she had, especially not after the strange conversation about the car.

Yet her feelings made her shudder.

She didn't want to be like Everett, who had to control everything. She could let Cutter drive and pick out the place herself. Or she could just give it up and let him make tonight's booking.

Why the hell should it matter who picked the place?

And she forced herself to say, "I can't wait to see what you find."

In her periphery, she saw him scroll, read, type, scroll again. And then he grinned, more to himself than to her. Had he found something? He'd barely looked.

Growling under her breath so he wouldn't hear, she told herself to stop the madness. She absolutely wasn't a control freak like Everett. It was just that conversation about the car. It had an angry tinge to it, as if last night's intimacy had never happened. As if they hadn't walked hand in hand through Baton Rouge.

As if the only reason he came along on this trip, the only reason he had sex with her, was to get his hands on the car.

Then he said, loudly, over the roar of the engine and the rush of the wind, "I found it. You wanted luxury, and this is luxury."

"Where?"

He replied smugly, "You'll see when we get there."

It pricked a nerve when it shouldn't have. She was being touchy, and she didn't like it. It was silly to get worked up over a conversation that was no different from the other conversations about the car. It was just that *this* conversation had come *after* they'd had sex.

But really, it was no different. Get over it, she told herself.

"What shall we visit in Austin?" she asked.

He was silent a long moment. Or maybe he'd spoken, and she couldn't hear over the car noise.

But then he scrolled on his phone again. "Austin's a big music venue. They've got concerts and festivals going all the time, and live music all over the city, in clubs and bars and restaurants. Let's find some music."

"Perfect."

And she let him look for the best music venue while the miles rolled away beneath the tires, the warm air and the rumble of the engine soothing her. They never talked much in the car anyway. With the top down, they had to shout. And she found that when she let herself go, the car calmed her. It was almost like meditation. She could stop ruminating, her mind free.

He'd find the perfect spot for the night, they'd have a fabulous evening, then he'd take her to bed, and everything would be okay.

It was only when he spoke again that she thought how much the conversation in her head sounded like one's she had with herself over Everett, over all of her husbands, in fact. *If I just do this, he won't get angry with me. If I just do that, he won't cheat on me.*

"Okay, I found it," he called out over the drone of the engine and the thoughts in her head.

"What?"

"It's a surprise, but I guarantee you're gonna love it."

It made her itchy not to know. She wished she hadn't chosen such a long drive for today.

When she pulled off to use the restroom at a fast-food restaurant, she gave the wheel to him. He took over like a teenager driving his daddy's expensive sports car on a prom date.

And she went to sleep.

HE'D ACTED LIKE AN ASS, GRILLING HER ABOUT THE CAR. IT was just that he'd woken in the middle of the night with a bunch of stupid thoughts running through his head. About the past, about why the hell he was falling into her bed like a lovesick idiot, about what it would feel like when she dropped him off at the San Francisco airport. Or maybe she'd tell him to take a cab.

Then she'd brought up his family. They hadn't been rich. His parents did their best, but they'd never had the luxuries she was used to. She was a summer girl, slumming with the local kids, then flitting back to her better life. Maybe that's why he told her about the Mach III and the summer kid who'd crashed it. So she could see the comparison. But she hadn't. All she'd asked was why he'd sold it. Because he'd needed the damn money for college. A scholarship didn't pay for everything. But then she'd never worried about where the money would come from to pay her college tuition and living expenses.

But they were a teenage kid's thoughts, not a man's. They were the thoughts of someone who felt sorry for himself, and Cutter didn't. He'd made a good life and helped his parents, though they'd both died too early.

And Mortimer had made his decision. The XB-70 was hers. Cutter was over it. Just like he'd gotten over her leaving all those years ago. And what they were doing now was just good, hot fun. With her sleeping in the passenger seat, he could remember last night. It was good, so damn good, and he'd enjoy every goddamn remaining night with her, no idiotic ruminations allowed. He was used to relationships ending. This wasn't even a relationship. It was a business deal that had morphed into hot sex. And he wasn't a teenager who ruminated about a thing long enough to ruin it.

He'd found the perfect place for the night, as well as the perfect music. She would love it, guaranteed.

He'd already put the address into his phone, and the map app herded him toward a wooded area on the outskirts of Austin. A pretty college town, they could explore it after they'd settled in. She'd wanted luxury, an enormous bathtub, and he'd found a tub that would dazzle her.

She woke up when he pulled into the long, tree-lined drive. Stretching, she yawned and pulled off her sunglasses to rub her eyes. "Where are we?"

"We've arrived at our accommodations for the night," he said, waiting for her reaction.

As the house came into view, she gasped in awe.

Two stories with four columns along the front, the wicker furniture surrounding a glass table on the wide front porch beckoned visitors. In the photos, an inviting picture of iced lemonade sat in the middle of the coffee table. A balcony with a set of French doors ran along the upper floor. Though the well-appointed house wasn't a mansion, it was more than enough for the two of them.

He pulled to a stop in front. "What do you think?"

"I'm speechless."

His heart was beating harder than he wanted it to, as if he needed her approval. "It's not a luxury hotel."

"It looks like a palace." She gazed at it, mesmerized.

"It's not as big as you might think, just two bedrooms and an open concept living area downstairs."

"It looks like one of those magnificent antebellum homes." She turned to him. "I love it."

He was pleased because she was pleased. He wouldn't tell her how much it cost. It was only one night, and he didn't care. He'd taken the opportunity to order a few supplies, a service the property manager offered for an extra fee. He wouldn't mention how much did that cost either. She'd probably try to pay for something anyway.

He wouldn't let her. This night was his, and he wanted to steep her in luxury, even if she was already used to luxury.

She climbed out, still looking up, pulling off her sunglasses and dragging her scarf from her hair. While he opened the app to check the front door code, she climbed the five steps to the wraparound porch.

"It's so cool under here with that lovely breeze," she called out to him, holding up her hands as if she needed to feel the wind against her skin.

She seemed dazed by his choice, and he liked it that way.

Unlocking the door, he stepped aside for her to enter. He knew what to expect after scrolling through the photos on the site, but once again, she gasped.

In the wide living room, sofas and chairs grouped around a massive fireplace and floor-to-ceiling windows opened along the back. French doors led to a sunporch, the screen so thin it was almost invisible, providing a view of a lap pool, green lawn, and woods beyond.

She put her hands to her mouth as she turned to the massive kitchen on the other side of the dining table. Separated from the main room by a long bar with tall stools, the kitchen gleamed with stainless steel appliances, white cabinets, marble countertops, and a state-of-the-art range in a center island. His supplies sat on the counter, boxes of crackers, bottles of Perrier, a bowl of bananas and grapes. The rest would be in the refrigerator.

"It's amazing." She turned full circle, stopping to look at him. "You're amazing."

"And you haven't even seen the upstairs yet."

"Show me."

He felt the seductive timbre of her voice all the way down to his belly.

Upstairs, the front bedroom had its own bathroom, bunk beds, and a queen Murphy bed.

But it was the master bedroom at that back that he'd chosen just for her.

C utter wanted to see her reaction. He wanted to please her. It was only for another week, then this whole thing would be over. Never one for brooding too long, he expunged all the negative thoughts that had run through his head last night and into the morning light. And now he told himself he was fine with how it would end, just like he'd been fine the last time she left.

And for now, he wanted to enjoy her.

Walking into the master bathroom, she damn near squealed. "The tub, it's crazy." Her hands once again covered her mouth with surprise.

"Crazy good?" he asked.

"So crazy good, it's the best ever."

Yeah, she made his blood pump faster. The woman could get excited about damn near anything. But it was an amazing tub.

Two steps up and set into a big marble platform, its white porcelain gleamed. The view out into the woods behind would make her feel as if she were in a forest. Candles ringed the rim, and a big, leafy philodendron hung from the high ceiling overhead.

"How did you find this place so fast? You were only scrolling for a little while."

"I woke up in the middle of the night," he told her. "I didn't want to wake you, and I sat on the balcony for a while."

Maybe it was ridiculous to feel so pleased with himself, yet her pleasure gave him a pathetic glow inside.

"I can't wait to see what you picked for the music venue." She went up on her toes and hugged him.

He wanted to grab her up right then, carry her to bed, forget about the music, and spend all night making her come.

The days to California were counting down, and he intended to make the most of every single one.

WHILE HE PREPARED A FEAST OF THE DELICACIES NOREEN was sure he'd ordered, Cutter sent her to the screened-in porch overlooking the pool, the cicadas creating a symphony outside.

She didn't ask how much the house cost. It was probably a fortune to him, and yet he'd done it for her. Telling him she wanted to pay for at least half would be a slap in his face. So she sucked it up and enjoyed the pleasure of his gift.

The house was perfect, better than any luxury hotel, private and elegant, and best of all, completely theirs. Screw the music venue, she wanted to get him upstairs and into that tub. But for now, she sat on the sofa with the gorgeous view of the trees before her, so relaxed her bones felt as if they were melting. Dropping her sandals to the floor, she propped her feet on the table.

Her mouth felt dry after falling asleep in the car, and she popped a couple of mints from her purse. But she was still sleepy, and she closed her eyes, just to rest them until Cutter brought his surprise.

She might actually have fallen asleep again if her phone hadn't rung.

Grace's name and number filled her screen, and she answered with, "Hey, sweetie."

"Hi, Mom. Looks like you're having a fabulous time on your trip."

"I'm so glad you're enjoying the pictures I've sent." She snuggled deeper into the sofa, leaning her head back.

"Yeah, about the pictures. Who's the guy?"

Her blood slowed to sludge in her veins, and her stomach pitched like she was floating on stormy seas.

"What guy?" She hadn't sent any pictures of Cutter, yet her immediate reaction was to put her phone on speaker so she could flip through the photos she'd sent.

"The really hot older guy." Was that an edge in Grace's voice?

There were no pictures of Cutter in anything she'd texted. "What you talking about?" Her voice came across completely mystified, the way she felt.

"The one in all those pictures on your cloud."

Her cloud? Her head felt as if *it* was in the clouds because she didn't get Grace at all.

"Yeah, your album? You didn't send a bunch of pics, so I went into our shared album."

She got it then. What an idiot. She hadn't even remembered that she'd shared her photo album with the girls. All her pictures went in there because she never found the time, or the energy, to separate them into named albums. And it was too late now to download all those photos of Cutter and save them to her computer's hard drive.

"Love the one of him kissing you in that tower," Grace drawled.

Yeah, way too late. Cutter had obviously clicked the camera button on the selfie right as he kissed her.

God help her, she wanted to see the photo now, wanted to feel his lips on her again. But...

"Who is he, Mom?"

Her daughter said Mom as if she were the mother and Noreen was the daughter who'd missed her curfew.

And she'd resent looking those pictures of her and Cutter and hearing her daughter's reproach.

"Mom, do not tell me you picked up some guy on this cross-country trek of yours," Grace said as Noreen fumbled for a decent excuse.

"I mean, I don't care about your love life," Grace went on. "But that's just plain dangerous. Even at your age, you can't just hop in the sack with any old guy."

Noreen bristled. "At my age?" she snapped.

But Grace steamrolled right over her. "The world isn't a safe place, Mom. It's not like it was when you were young. There are predators out there."

Predators? "He's not a predator."

Grace burst out in a disgusted laugh. "How do you know if you just met him? This is crazy, Mom. Was he a hitchhiker or something?"

Grace had said Mom one too many times, and Noreen's temper flared. "Oh, please, like I'd really pick up a hitchhiker. He's just my mechanic, for God's sake. You know, like James Dean always took his mechanic along?"

"Who the hell is James Dean?"

Noreen puffed out a sigh. "Never mind. The guy I'm with was Uncle Mortimer's mechanic for years. And I asked him along to take care of the car in case anything goes wrong."

"If he's just a mechanic, why was he kissing you?"

She thought fast. "That was a fluke. We were taking a

selfie when we both happened to turn our faces at the same time."

Grace snorted. "So he's just some mechanic your Uncle Mortimer knew?"

"Are you grilling me?"

"No, I'm not grilling you, Mom." There it was again. *Mom.* Said in that patronizing tone. "I'm worried about you. You're all alone out there. Anything could happen. And don't tell me you wouldn't feel the same way if it was me driving all the way across the country on my own."

Grace had her there. Noreen would absolutely freak out. "Well, you can stop worrying. I'm taking care of myself. And he helps with the driving."

She thought about telling Grace that she'd known Cutter forty years ago, but she was pretty sure that would make her daughter even more frantic. "Look, I'll send you more selfies. At least twice a day. Then you'll know I'm okay."

"I want phone calls, Mom, not just texts and pictures. I mean, it could be him sending them from your phone."

"Stop being ridiculous." But it actually made her feel good that her daughter cared enough to read her the riot act. Lots of mothers couldn't even get a phone call once a week. "You'll see the pictures in the cloud in real time." Now she had Grace dead to rights. "But I will call, I promise. It is just that you girls always like texts instead of phone calls." That was how she learned about what happened in Grace's life. And April was even worse. But they were the cell phone and social media generation. "So stop worrying. I'm doing great, and this trip is the best thing I've done in years. And right now, I'm in Austin."

"All right, Mom, but you know you have the worst taste in men."

Oh my, how the tables had turned. Now her daughters were dispensing advice instead of the other way round.

"I love you, Grace, but I'm hanging up now."

"I didn't mean to throw your mistakes in your face."

Oh, yes, she did. Grace had been the first to say there was something wrong with Rodney the criminal and that Everett was too controlling. April was soon to echo her sister's thoughts. And Valerie wasn't far behind. Only her best friend Tammy knew better than to say anything.

Of course, Noreen hadn't listened. She was a fool.

"Do not go blabbing to your sister or your aunt."

"I will if you don't check in on time. I knew letting you go on this trip all by yourself was a bad idea."

Noreen laughed. "Since when have I ever listened to any of you?"

"Never," her daughter groused.

"You're too much, sweetheart. So much worrying will give you a migraine."

"Love you, Mom. Gotta go."

In the moment of dead air after Grace hung up, Noreen didn't know whether to laugh or cry. Did the fact that her daughter knew about Cutter change everything? Because Grace certainly didn't believe the kiss had been an accident or that Cutter was *just* her mechanic.

"So, I'm *just* a mechanic."

Noreen jumped to her feet, the phone clattering to the floor.

Cutter stood in the open French doors, two flutes of champagne balanced between the fingers of one hand, a platter of appetizers in the other.

Oh God. He'd heard the whole thing because she'd had Grace on speakerphone while she scrolled through her texts to see what pictures she'd actually sent.

She waved a hand in the air as if she could dismiss every-thing she'd said. But exactly how much had he heard? She decided to tough it out. "I couldn't very well tell her you're my friend with benefits on this trip. Daughters don't want to hear about their mom's sex life."

He rounded the sofa and set everything down on the table.

Then, quick as a flash, he hauled her against him, and muttered, "I guess I better take care of my duties then."

His mouth crushed hers in a sizzling, no-holds-barred kiss. He banded his arm across her back and shoved his fingers through her hair, holding her tight as he plundered her mouth like a pirate.

It was too good for words, too good even for the moan that trembled up her throat.

What fifty-seven-year-old woman didn't want to be plundered like this?

He pushed the rattan sofa back with his foot, giving them more room, and slipped her down on it, falling on top of her. Buttons popped, and zippers rasped. Then his mouth was on her breast, the peak already bursting. He sucked, and she groaned. Nothing had ever felt so good, not even those old times with him.

This was fast, primal, animalistic. Perfect.

CHRIST, SHE TASTED GOOD. HE COULDN'T GET ENOUGH of her.

He'd stood on the threshold listening to her explain him away, even if her daughter wasn't buying it. His big head had wanted to get hot under the collar, but his little head was already growing, wanting, needing.

He'd let his little head take over because sex with her was so freaking good.

And it was the best way to show her he was way more than *just* her mechanic.

She tasted slightly of the sweat of the day, of the sun on her skin as they drove. She smelled of the lotion she'd put on this morning, the scent that mesmerized him as he watched her slather it on her legs and arms, something fruity, definitely tantalizing. Even the sunblock hadn't washed away the sweet aroma.

He relished the moan that rose up her throat as he pleasured her. She was so easy, and he loved that. He only had to kiss her or touch her, or even whisper naughty words in her ear, and she got hot for him. He'd never asked for more in a woman. Yet he'd never found it exactly like this, not with anyone but her.

Trailing his hot fingers down her body, her skin twitched, her flesh quivered, and he glided inside her pants, then her panties, finding the wet heat of her. He stroked her slowly, each agonizing movement designed to make her crazy. She seemed to flood his hand with her moisture, so wet, so ready. But he kept at her, sucking one nipple and rubbing the other peak to a diamond chip.

Until she couldn't take anymore. Scrabbling her pants off, she shoved at his, the zipper already open, the shorts sliding over his hips. He'd gotten only one leg out before she grabbed his butt, pulling him up.

Her eyes glazed with need and desire, "Please, please," puffed from her lips, then a series of unintelligible words.

He was sure he heard his name in there, and he was so hard now, he couldn't wait, couldn't bring her to her first orgasm before plunging deep. She cried out, spasming around him as the climax rolled through. He knew her body so well, and pounding into her, he pushed her higher, kept her going. She tossed her head on the cushions, her eyes squeezed tightly shut, her lips open and ruby red.

Then he let himself go, falling off the peak and hurtling down right along with her. His orgasm hit him like an avalanche high in the mountains, burying him deep as her body gripped him tightly, owned him. She pulled him down, opened her mouth, took him in, kissing him until he lost his mind. There was nothing but the feel of her skin against his, the heat of her body surrounding him, the taste of her lips, and the sweetness of her mouth.

The years melted away, and they were kids again, doing what they'd loved best, making each other feel better than good.

He melted into those years he couldn't stop dreaming about and couldn't help longing for, melted into the woman he'd never forgotten.

The woman he had to admit he'd never be able to forget.

HIS WEIGHT WAS BEAUTIFUL AND HEAVY ON HER. SHE could stay this way forever, with him buried deep inside her, still twitching, still wanting.

But he pulled away with a groan, scraping a hand through his deliciously thick hair. Sitting up, he hitched his shorts back over his hips before he slumped against the sofa. She had no choice but to pull her clothes in place when all she really wanted was to tear them off and go at him again.

She should write a self-help book for women over fifty-five. *How to Have the Best Sex of Your Life*. First ingredient, the right man. Second ingredient, a healthy desire. Third ingredient, let all your inhibitions go.

It would be a bestseller. Oprah would invite her on her show. She'd do the talk show circuit. Women would clamor to hear all her secrets.

She was afraid the only secret was Cutter Sorensen and that Corvette summer forty years ago.

Leaning forward, he picked up both champagne glasses,

handed her one, and tapped his to hers. "So, I'm just your mechanic."

His eyes were half lidded, his hair a sexy mess, and the scent of sex on them was an aphrodisiac, far better than the oysters in Tallahassee's Aphrodisiac Oyster Shack.

"Well," she started primly, "I think you're a bit more." She spider-walked her fingers down his arm. "I think you're the best sex I've ever had."

He laughed. "Yuh *think*?"

"Well," she said again, this time with a seductive drawl. "There was this guy a long time ago on Key West. And I have to say he was pretty good. I'd do him again. Over and over."

He winked, sipped his drink, and said, "You've already done him several times over." Then he wrapped his hand around her nape, pulled her in for one of those deep, delicious kisses he was so good at. "And we've got Santa Fe, New Mexico, Sedona, Arizona, and Las Vegas, Nevada to go."

She grinned. "I knew I should leave all the trip planning to you. You have the absolute best ideas."

He slumped back against the sofa once more, champagne glass in his hand. "Best trip planner, best mechanic, and best..." He let the sentence hang.

When he smiled like that, he made her gooey inside. "Best friend with benefits."

Something she couldn't translate flashed in his eyes. And he murmured, "Best ever booty call."

She waved a hand over the platter of appetizers he'd brought to the table. Pepper crackers, brie, grapes, bananas, pâté, red pepper hummus, mixed nuts. "Best ever host."

"Best driver."

She laughed. "Second best driver. I'm the best."

He snorted and leaned forward, setting his glass down, and slathering pâté on a cracker. "In your dreams, baby." Then he powered down the cracker, prepared another, feeding this one to her.

She thought he'd be angry about her conversation with Grace. She'd thought the sex had been a strange sort of punishment, or his desire to show her that he was way more than just her mechanic. But now he'd turned fun-loving and playful. As if what he'd overheard meant nothing. And that was good. She didn't have to explain that she hadn't wanted to invite Grace's comments about her sex life. That was all. It was no big deal. What she'd said meant nothing.

But the food and the banter and the laughter, and most especially the sex, were starting to mean more than she wanted to think about.

IT DIDN'T MEAN A THING. HE WAS JUST HER MECHANIC, and yet he'd enjoyed showing her just how much more he truly was. And there was a lot more *showing* to be done by the end of this trip. She'd tell her daughters, her sister, and her friends that he was the best ever at everything. Not that *he* needed her to tell anyone.

He just didn't like the denial. He didn't like being relegated to a grease monkey. As if that was all he could ever be.

But Jesus, he was almost sixty years old. What the hell did he care anyway?

They were enjoying the hell out of each other and that's all that mattered. Just like they'd enjoyed the hell out of each other forty years ago. He'd long since stopped being that teenage kid with titanic expectations. And he didn't have to prove a damn thing by telling her the Budget Auto Repair shops were *his* franchises.

This time she fixed a cracker, handed to him, and before he ate it, he said, "We need to talk about tomorrow's drive."

She made another cracker for herself. "What?" Then she popped a couple of grapes in her mouth too.

He munched, swallowed. "Like, where do we want to stop between here and Santa Fe?"

She brought the map app up on her phone. "Lubbock's about halfway between. Since it's Buddy Holly's hometown, there's a lot to see."

He'd looked over the route last night as he sat sleepless on the balcony ruminating about her and this trip and... Well, hell, he was about to ruminate again. "We could also split the drive up with Abilene or Amarillo. But both of those mean a shorter drive tomorrow and longer the day after."

"How long to get to Santa Fe?"

"Eleven hours."

She nibbled on her cracker like a rabbit. Christ, he even liked that, the way she concentrated, the way she savored. It was akin to the look she wore when she took him in her mouth.

Noreen Kincaid had always savored him in a way no other woman ever had.

There he went, ruminating again.

"Can the XB-70 make it?" she asked.

He liked that she called the car by her name. "She's never gone seven hundred miles in her life."

"But *could* she do it?" She concentrated on preparing a cracker with brie.

"Hell yes," was the only answer.

"Well," she said, drawing out the sound. "We could get up early and go all the way to Santa Fe, share the driving, then stay two nights there and take a whole day to see the sights."

He thought about it. After the water pump incident, the XB-70 had performed superbly. He checked her every morning. She wasn't eating oil, all her fluids were good, and she drove like a dream, as if she'd been waiting all her life for him to let her have her head. Maybe it was time to loosen the reins.

He grinned as Noreen handed him the cracker with brie, a grape plopped on top.

"Deal."

And her eyes sparkled with promise.

❧ 18 ❧

Noreen lounged on one end of the oversized tub, a plate of crackers already prepared with cheese, pâté, or hummus, grapes and banana slices for toppers. She'd also refilled her champagne glass.

There was plenty of time to relax before heading out to the music venue Cutter had chosen, which he was still holding as a surprise. Her body felt tender and achy and satisfied after what he'd done to her on the couch. She'd missed the spontaneity.

Everett had been anything but spontaneous. He'd controlled everything, even their lovemaking. She always knew he wanted sex when he went upstairs early in the evening to take a shower. That was her signal to clean up too, although not in the shower with him. Everett was fastidious. He would never have sex without showering after a long day. Never hoist her up on the kitchen counter and just take her, never pull her pants down in the middle of a long, sweaty, dusty hike on a secluded trail even though no one was likely to come upon them. None of her husbands had been spontaneous. Well, except Javier when he'd been with other women.

Although spontaneous sex in his kitchen had turned out to be a very bad idea. She'd wished a lot of bad things on him, but that hadn't been one of them.

Why had she chosen men so different from Cutter when what they'd done that summer was so good? When she continued to crave the kind of sex Cutter had taught her to love?

It was one of those unanswerable questions.

As if her thoughts had conjured him, Cutter stepped into the bathroom.

She was glad the bubble bath she poured into the water covered all her flaws. She wasn't seventeen anymore, and though she was in good shape, she was fifty-seven years old.

Then Cutter stripped down and stole her breath.

He was so unselfconscious, as if he wasn't even aware of how beautiful he was, like a Greek God with bronzed skin, a taut stomach, and hard muscles. Her hand went reflexively to her stomach, which hadn't known the meaning of taut since she'd birthed her daughters.

He leaned over her to set his glass of champagne beside hers on the marble tile, and she smelled the sexy tang of male, a hint of clean sweat, and the muskiness of their earlier sex. She wanted to lick the sweat off him, taste the saltiness, savor his flavors on her tongue.

But he was already sliding down into the water opposite her, his legs spread, her toes slipping just under his butt. "I found a great place in Santa Fe."

"Something new and fabulous?" she asked.

"Even better. It'll be a bit of a drive to get into town, but that doesn't matter since we'll have a full day to tour around."

"I'm so excited." The word sounded flippant, but she meant it. His choice for tonight was amazing, not to mention the champagne and appetizers. When she let Cutter

Sorensen have his choice, he created magic. She didn't have a single qualm about letting him do it again.

He pulled her foot onto his thigh, the hard muscle beneath her heel, and began massaging the arch of her foot.

She groaned. "You even give good massage," she said without thinking, her eyes closed, her head on the tub's rim.

"I'm good at a lot of things."

She'd asked for that, and she cracked an eyelid, smirked at him. "Don't let it go to your head." Then she added too quickly for him to answer, "And don't ask me which one."

Moving her foot down, he pressed her sole against him. "Too late. You've already gone to this head."

He rubbed her foot against the hard length, and she thought about all the things they hadn't done downstairs.

Turning, she pulled her legs up, tucked them beneath her, and crawled between his legs. "Well, if you're already up."

She wrapped her fingers around him, and oh yes, he was hard again. He amazed her. How did he do that at his age? He was like a young stallion, always ready to go.

Stroking him, she watched as his pupils widened, as if that was another signal his body gave.

"You shouldn't do that." He gave her a slow blink, a grin spreading across his face. "Unless you plan to take care of it."

"I definitely plan to take care of it." She swirled her thumb around his crown, then slipped down to squeeze him."

His shit-eating grin died, and he groaned.

"Stand up," she ordered.

He rose more gracefully than she ever could, the water sluicing down his beautiful body. God, he was perfection. He always had been. He was more so now.

"Brace yourself," she whispered before she took him in her mouth.

He put one hand on the wall, his head falling back as she took him deep. He'd taught her how to do this in the front seat of her uncle's car, showing her exactly what he liked.

In the beginning, it was supposed to be just a kiss. But there had been so many kisses. And touches, hands giving each other pleasure. And there had been this, her mouth on him. Then his mouth on her. Until they taught each other the ultimate.

And she knew exactly how to send him over the edge.

HE'D TAUGHT HER THIS. THEY'D LEARNED HOW TO PLEASE each other, how to wring out every drop of pleasure.

Now she was using it against him, enslaving him.

Christ, how he wanted to be her slave in this moment. She'd always been the best, because he'd told her all the secrets to making him fall under her spell.

She licked and stroked and rubbed and squeezed until all his plans for her pleasure blasted right out of his head. She was so silky smooth around him, so wet, so picture-perfect down there on her knees. He was eighteen again, in her thrall, and all he wanted was to bury himself inside her. Yet he needed this, craved her mouth on him, and she found every single one of his sensitive spots, hitting him just under the ridge, squeezing him in her palm, pushing him to the limit. He wanted to beg, but he didn't have a voice. All he could do was shove his fingers into her hair, guide her, even though she already knew the perfect rhythm.

How many others had she done this for? How many others had begged her? How many others had she loved doing it to?

The thoughts, instead of knocking him off his stride, only shot him higher.

And he let it all go, a groan rising from his gut, his legs

trembling, his head exploding, his hands in her hair, the scent of her sex clouding his mind and pulling him down down down, right into her.

Then he lost time, finding himself beneath the scented bubbles of her bath, Noreen in his arms.

She kissed him when he opened his eyes. He savored the taste of her, his climax still on her tongue. Christ, he wanted her in a way he'd wanted no other woman but her.

"That was nice." He tried to sound nonchalant, but his voice cracked in the middle.

She smiled, like the proverbial cat that ate the cream. And that made him laugh because, in this case, the old saying was so apt.

He didn't tell her how good she felt nestled into him. Everything about her felt good, the heat of her skin against his body, the weight of her in his arms, the fragrant scent of her hair.

"Just nice?" She swirled her finger in his chest hair.

"Pretty damn good."

She scoffed in her throat. "Don't you mean the best ever?"

Christ, she made him smile. "All right, yeah, best ever. But don't let it go to your head."

"Which one?"

"*You* only have one." He chuckled, the sensation vibrating through both their bodies.

"But you know women can do a lot more with one head than men can do with two."

He flipped her over suddenly, sloshing water and surprising a squeal out of her as he rolled her beneath him. "Maybe we need to put that to the test." He kissed her, deep and sweet.

But when he let her up for air, she asked, "What time is it?" He reached for his watch on the side of the tub, held it up to her. "Oh my God," she gasped. "We need to get ready or we'll be late for the music."

He didn't give a damn about the music, wanted nothing more than to stay here with her, pour more champagne, run more hot water, and lay with her in his arms, lazy and satisfied.

Then carry her off to bed.

But she was already pushing him off and climbing out of the tub.

All he could do was lay there a long moment, falling for her long lines and her curves and her splendor.

Until she called out, laughing, "Come on, lazybones."

And he rose to do her bidding.

"YOU'RE KIDDING. YOU ACTUALLY CHOSE CLASSICAL guitar?" Noreen covered her mouth in surprise and delight.

Cutter had brought her to an old sixties-style basement club down a side street with concrete floors, café tables, wooden chairs, a long wood bar on one wall, no food on offer, just drinks, and the stage as the focal point.

"Yeah, classical guitar is cool."

She'd thought he'd make her listen to a heavy metal band. Or old Elvis songs. He'd always loved Elvis, even though the King was dead by then. "Since when did you listen to classical?"

He shook his head, smiling. "I like a lot of different stuff. I'm an eclectic guy."

She laughed at the word and admitted, "I don't listen to music much. I love audiobooks."

"That's seems like part of your work," he said with a nod, as if he was thinking about her life back home.

"It is." She looked at him with admiration. "When I'm

editing, I always think of how something will sound in audio. Like, can you tell which person is talking? And can you tell when someone says something versus just having a thought? Audiobooks are a performance. But I still don't get the classical guitar."

He shrugged. "You remember that cuchi-chuchi girl. What the hell was her name? She was a Spanish comedian who always acted like the ditzy girl, on stuff like *Fantasy Island* and *The Love Boat*."

"Oh my God," she gasped. "You watched *Fantasy Island* and *The Love Boat*?"

He rolled his eyes. "My mom did. Anyway, this woman." He snapped his fingers. "Charo. That was her name. And when she performed her music, she played a mean flamenco guitar."

She vaguely remembered who he was talking about, but when she was with him, they'd listened to old Elvis songs, The Doors, The Who, The Rolling Stones.

"You're going to like this," he guaranteed.

She would, the way she'd enjoyed everything he chose. The way she enjoyed him.

Her body was still buzzing from champagne and sex. After they climbed out of the tub, though they were running late, he had to show her again that he was the best, hauling her up on the bathroom counter, then pulling over the vanity stool and turning her body into a feast, leaving her a quivering mass all over again. Though still weak-kneed even now, her mind and body were deliciously relaxed.

The lights grew brighter on the stage, and a lone middle-aged man walked to the center. Sitting on the single tall stool, he propped his foot on a rung and his guitar on his thigh. Without an introduction, without saying anything at all, he strummed the opening bars of *Classical Gas*, a song made famous in the late sixties and still played on oldies radio stations.

She sat back, mesmerized.

This was the Austin music scene, where you could find anything, from jazz to pop to rock to heavy metal to big band to *Classical Gas*.

The guitarist played with his eyes closed, without a word, as if he didn't care whether or not he had an audience, loving his music and nothing more. As he played, the years melted from his face, his hair beneath the lights turned blond instead of gray. She didn't recognize all the pieces he played, but they were vibrant and heart thumping, several with a Spanish flare she associated with flamenco.

Then a young man rushed onto the stage, handed the musician a new instrument, as he set his guitar on a stand next to his stool.

Once he'd settled the instrument on his knee, he was once again alone on the stage, and he spoke for the first time. "This is an old mandolin concerto from the eighteenth century."

And now she recognized the deep-bowled instrument from a movie she'd seen. Maybe it was *Romeo and Juliet*, but she couldn't be sure. The music was amazing, lilting, rising, filling her, filling the club.

Cutter reached for her hand, then squeezed, pulling her over to whisper in her ear. "Like it?" As if he needed approval. As if he actually cared whether she enjoyed it or not.

She nodded, leaned close, her lips grazing his ear. "I love it."

His smile lit up the room, like a spotlight shining on him instead of the stage. She couldn't remember ever being with a man who got so much enjoyment out of simply pleasing her. Larry, her first husband, had wanted a young wife he could parade on his arm. Javier simply wanted a notch on his belt, another woman who would fall for him completely. Rodney, her third husband, wanted her money, even though he never got his hands on it. And Everett had only ever wanted her obedience.

But Cutter enjoyed pleasing her, not in a subservient, obsequious way, but because her pleasure gave him pleasure.

Maybe money, education, status, and career potential meant nothing at all.

Maybe the only thing that mattered was the way a man treated a woman.

AFTER THE SHOW, THEY WALKED HAND IN HAND THROUGH the bustling Austin streets. Music flowed out of every door. People stopped on the sidewalks, listened, and decided if this place was where they wanted to stay. Music of every type, for every generation, saturated the air.

She hooked her arm through Cutter's elbow, leaned close. "I like what you chose best."

"It was perfect for the moment." Then he pulled her toward a coffee bar. "Want a latte?"

"A latte would be fabulous."

Wanted the night to go on and on, she didn't remind him they had to be up early tomorrow for the long drive. She'd need only a catnap while he took the wheel and vice versa. After the delicious interlude in the bathroom, he'd dressed quickly, and gone out to check the car while she readied herself for the evening. He'd declared the hoses, the oil, the fluids were all good. She hadn't unpacked, and it would take only a few minutes in the morning to throw everything in the car.

They could afford these few extra enchanting minutes.

Of course music blasted, even in a coffee shop, a young

woman belting out country songs, everything from Patsy Cline to Dolly Parton to Shania Twain.

The decaf latte was tasty. She allowed herself regular coffee earlier in the day—she loved that first jolt in the morning—but stuck to decaf after three in the afternoon.

"Little known fact," she told Cutter as the girl sang an old Merle Haggard song about hungry eyes. "There's this old place up in my very own state of California called the Preston School of Industry. It was a reform school for wayward boys. Before it was built, they actually used to put these kids in San Quentin, but some nice governor or whoever decided the prison was too harsh for them. But the school was still a work camp. They even had this huge delousing pool they made the boys walk through. And Merle Haggard was sent there when he was a kid. I hear he hated it."

"I would to."

She leaned forward in her zeal. "If you strip away its history, it's really a cool building, like an old castle. They even nicknamed it Preston Castle. They're trying to restore it because a lot of the floors are caving in."

"I bet Merle Haggard didn't want to see it restored."

She nodded. "He didn't. Before he died, they asked him to perform a benefit concert to help with the restoration, and he didn't want to have anything to do with the old place."

"I can understand that. I prefer restoring old cars."

Suddenly she wanted to know more about what he'd been doing with his life, not some old building that hadn't seen many happy days. "Is that what you do in your spare time? Restore old cars like you restored the Mach Three?"

He nodded. "Yeah, I restore old cars, but then I like to pass them on. Or sometimes I get paid to do it. Most people don't crash the cars like that kid and the Mach Three."

"Don't you keep any of them?" She propped her hand on her chin, interested in every detail.

Grimacing, he said, "If I kept them all, my place would be an old junkyard. Besides, it's about the project, the work, the pleasure in seeing it completed, not so much about keeping it."

"Except the Corvette."

She probably shouldn't have said that. It was a sticking point between them.

He was silent a moment before saying, "Yeah, except the Corvette. The XB-70, she's different, even if she was Mortimer's car." He leaned close, his lips almost at her ear. "I'll make you a deal. You sell me the XB-70, and you can come out to visit her. I'll even service you like I did tonight." He sat back, his eyes glittering.

She laughed at him. "Are you bartering sex for the Corvette?"

Still with a gleam in his eye, he nodded. "Oh yeah. Is it working?"

She narrowed her eyes at him as if she were looking for the trick. "How often do I get to come out?"

His mouth twitched in half smile. "As often as you want."

Sitting back, she let a smile grow slowly on her lips. "I've got an even better deal. I keep the Corvette, and you can fly out to San Francisco to drive her. You can even work on her to your heart's content." She grinned at him. "And I'll let you service me at the same time." Then she added with a wink. "As often as you want."

They both laughed, but the idea intrigued her. Wouldn't that be the perfect way to have a man in her life? Someone who came every two or three months, worked on her car, and gave her a dose of very good sex. Then he left. Yeah, that could be perfect.

And Cutter gave very good car and very good sex.

19

The car was checked and packed, and they were on the road just as the sun rose. With bio breaks, they could make it to Santa Fe by six-thirty that night.

Texas was a lot of live oak and mesquite and cedar, some of its scenery dusty and dry, some of it hilly. The Corvette was a gas guzzler, the term coming out of the seventies and the oil shortage. She remembered gas station lines snaking around the corner, her father waiting patiently, her mother drumming her fingers on the steering wheel petulantly.

But she wouldn't think about the gas charges on her credit card. She'd made good plans for this trip. And everything was going even better than she'd hoped.

She called Grace at nine, and her daughter said, "Where are you? It's so loud it sounds like a rocket taking off."

"It's the wind. We're on the road, and the top is down." She had to shout, but at least she didn't have to worry about saying *I* versus *we* anymore. "We plan on getting all the way to Santa Fe today."

"Are you talking hands free?" Grace had to shout too.

That's why Noreen had called right now, because the conversation would be short. "Yes, dear, I'm hands free." She didn't bother to mention that she wasn't driving. "I have my Bluetooth ear buds."

"No wonder it's so loud."

"I won't keep you. I just want to let you know I survived the night. I'm still alive." She looked at Cutter, who grinned and shook his head.

"Well, all right," Grace said. "Send pics of Santa Fe. I've always wanted to see the balloon festival."

Of course, Grace could look at the pictures in the cloud, but Noreen didn't point that out. "I will. Love you."

She hung up and turned to Cutter. "Duty done. Now she knows you didn't kill me in the night and bury my bones under a tree somewhere."

"It wouldn't have been your bones. It would have been your body parts. And I'd put those in the trunk, scattering them at different places along the way to Santa Fe."

"But if you'd already killed me, why would you bother going to Santa Fe when you could just head back to Key West?"

"Good point. But it would be a good idea to head up to Santa Fe first to make them think I was going west. Then double back on a different route."

"Very smart." She smiled inwardly at the ghoulish talk.

They stopped in Lubbock, the halfway point. The Corvette handled like a dream, but it was a sports car, and Noreen's bones felt rattled after six hours in the car, even with the rest stops they'd made. Six more hours lay ahead. But tomorrow they'd have the full day in Santa Fe to rest up. Not for the first time, she was glad she hadn't attempted this trip in full summer. In Texas, with the top down, the drive would have been a nightmare. And the car didn't have air conditioning.

They'd had that discussion, which went something like this:

Her: "When did Corvettes have air conditioning?"

Him: "It became factory-stock in sixty-three."

Her: "Don't they have air conditioning kits you could add to the car?"

Him: "Yes."

Her, waiting a couple of seconds: "Okay, so why didn't you and Uncle Mortimer put in air conditioning?"

Him: "You're joking, right? This is a stock car. You don't put a bunch of stuff on it that's not stock."

Her: "Yes, but air conditioning would soon become stock. And it's so hot on Key West in the summer."

Him: "And don't even think about having some grease monkey add air conditioning."

Her: "But it's my car."

Him: "It will always be Mortimer's car and he'd roll over in his grave."

End of discussion.

"Since we're in Lubbock," Cutter said, his arm hanging outside the car to cool off. "We need to visit Buddy Holly's grave."

Lubbock itself was an ode to Buddy Holly, Buddy Holly this and Buddy Holly that. The diner where they stopped to eat lunch was Buddy's.

"I'll get pictures," she said. "My friend Tammy loves Buddy Holly."

Tammy loved the oldies, as far back as Buddy Holly and The Big Bopper, all the way to Diana Ross and Donna Summer. After disco, though, she wasn't particularly interested in the music.

Flowers lay on Buddy Holly's grave as if someone tended it regularly. No one else was there now, but she imagined old music lovers made the pilgrimage. When her generation died out, would anyone remember Buddy Holly? Or the Beatles? Or even Elvis? She'd grown up on all their songs. But her music was really the late seventies, Fleetwood Mac, Journey, and Heart.

She had Cutter take a picture of her with a cardboard cut-out of Buddy Holly and sent it to Tammy, who immediately texted back. *So who's taking all these pictures of you?*

She wondered if Grace had called Tammy too. Or maybe Grace called her Aunt Valerie, who had then called Tammy, like an old-fashioned phone tree. And though she wasn't as adept at using her thumbs on the phone as her daughters were, she typed back quickly.

My hot mechanic and driver.

Tammy sent a series of emojis, from an exploding head to a fire-breathing dragon to a devil face. Then she added, *You better call me tonight or else.*

She had six hours or more to figure out exactly what she'd tell Tammy. Part of her wanted to keep Cutter all to herself, but she'd opened the door, and now she'd have to say something.

They left Lubbock, Cutter driving for two hours and she took over for two hours. The scenery became monotonous and the drive exhausting. The last two hours, as Cutter drove, she slept off and on, her head lolling on the seat until she snapped awake again with a neck jerk.

And finally, thank God, *finally*, a road sign proclaimed Santa Fe to be thirty miles ahead.

They drove right on through the eclectic, artsy downtown.

"Do you want to eat now before we go to the rental?" Cutter asked. "Then once we get there, we can just hang out and rest up after the drive."

Before she could even get out an answer, he made another

suggestion. "Or we can stop at a grocery store and buy some salmon. There's a barbecue at this place. And you know how good I am on the barbecue." He waggled his eyebrows, making her laugh.

She thought about him wearing an apron and nothing else. She wasn't too exhausted for that. "Your shrimp on the barbie was truly amazing."

He winked. "Then let's do it."

"Aren't you too tired to cook?"

"Barbecuing isn't cooking. I'll make it easy and we'll just have a salad to go with the fish. Right out of the bag."

"Does New Mexico even have salmon?"

He laughed. "They have grocery stores."

Suddenly, she wanted a meal barbecued by him more than anything. Well, more than *almost* anything. "All right, let's do it."

Of course, Santa Fe had grocery stores just like everywhere else. He bought a slab she didn't think they'd ever finish, but then he was a man, and he would eat more than she could. And the salad would just fill up the cracks, as her mother would say.

Cutter had done the house-hunting the last two nights, and he hadn't said a word about tonight's accommodations. She hadn't asked, liking the idea of a surprise.

But when they approached the rental he'd chosen, her heart fell all the way to the Corvette's floorboards. "What is that?"

He smiled. Actually *smiled*. "Shipping containers."

Yep, that's what they were. Three mammoth shipping containers, like something you'd see lined up on a train or stacked on a cargo ship, sitting out in the middle of the desert with nothing else around.

"This is a joke, right? We aren't actually going to sleep in shipping containers?" She wanted sleep. She wanted luxury. She wanted salmon. She *didn't* want cargo haulers.

Cutter grinned. "Oh ye of little faith. You ain't seen nothing like this, baby." He reached over to pat her knee.

As he drove closer, she realized that the containers at least had windows cut in them. And those might be pretty lace curtains over the windows.

But it was still a shipping container.

Then Cutter wheeled the Corvette around to the other side.

And suddenly they entered a fairyland. The three shipping containers were set in an L-shape, the long part of the L with two stacked containers, sliding glass doors cut into the lower ones, long windows in the upper. A bright blue awning extended out over a patio set with an outdoor kitchen, including a barbecue, counter, sink, and everything to prepare the best meal. Flowering cacti and desert plants decorated a rock garden and rope lights crisscrossed to the far corner, turning the container house and yard into a square.

When Cutter turned off the engine, she heard the pretty babble of a fountain and finally saw the hot tub standing on a raised stone platform.

"I told you to wait and see," Cutter said.

And he was so right.

She climbed out of the car, blinking in the fading sunlight as if she was looking at a mirage. Stepping through the opening in the low rock wall, she discovered the babbling water wasn't just a fountain but a stream meandering through the entire rock garden. Metalwork sculptures cavorted about the rocks, everything from butterflies to geckos to tarantulas. Rocks glued together created animal shapes, a fox, even an elephant, all amid garden statues, a gargoyle, a goddess, a Chinese pagoda. There was no particular theme to any of it, yet the effect was charming, serene, and relaxing. She didn't even care what the inside of the container house was like. She could sleep out here under the stars.

But Cutter, carrying the small cooler they'd put the salmon in, grabbed her hand. "You gotta see this place."

He punched a code into the box by the door, retrieved a key, and presented her with an airy space inside as enchanting as the garden was outside. Mid-century modern furniture in hues of teal and seafoam filled the long room of the container, and colorful carpets covered the travertine floors, along with a pot-bellied stove in the corner and animal print tapestries on the walls to give the place a sense of warmth.

It was uncannily spacious, with a sofa and four chairs, a coffee table, a card table, a bookshelf full of board games, card games, and books, everything they could possibly need except a TV. Not that she'd turned on a TV since she'd left home.

"Is there Wi-Fi?" she asked.

"Try it out on your phone."

She found the wireless network, while Cutter looked up the password. And the internet sprang to life.

The kitchen, along the lower half of the two-story containers, was a cook's dream, every appliance known to man, copper pots hanging from a center island, state-of-the-art gas range, double oven, microwave, even a stacked washer and dryer at one end. Sliding glass doors opened onto the outdoor kitchen, which included a small refrigerator under the counter.

Where the containers met, a half bath filled the corner, along with a spiral staircase made of wrought iron and polished wood that led to the upper container.

As she climbed the stairs, Cutter behind her, the bedroom came into view step by step, a massive king-size bed on a pedestal, two bureaus, a vanity, and a picture window overlooking the desert landscape. Up close, she had a view of the rock garden, the fairy lights, and the hot tub. At the far end of the container bedroom was a master bath with dual sinks, a separate shower tiled in a luminescent green, and a huge soaker tub with a gorgeous view of the desert.

She didn't have to worry about pulling the curtains because there was nothing for miles but scrub oak and mesquite and mountains.

"This—" She stopped to catch her breath. "It's absolutely amazing."

His eyes sparkled with pleasure, and once again, she felt as if he'd been waiting for her approval.

"Unpack your stuff." He backed toward the spiral staircase. "While I prepare your dinner."

He treated her like a goddess, and she loved it.

Since they were here for two nights, she did as he said, unpacking her duffel and setting her clothes in the bureau, as well as making a pile for laundry. She thought about unpacking his bag, but it felt like violating his privacy.

Feeling sticky after the long day in the car, she peeled off her shorts and top and stepped into the shower, the hot water luxurious on her skin.

By the time she navigated the spiral staircase, Cutter had the salad ready, the barbecue fired up, the salmon resting on a platter, and the champagne chilling in an ice bucket.

"You go sit outside and enjoy the sunset," he said. "I'll just grab a quick shower, then put on the salmon."

"You haven't left anything for me to help with."

He chuckled. "There's not much to opening a bag of salad and unwrapping the salmon."

"Okay. But I can at least do laundry. There's a pile of my stuff on the floor. Just add whatever you want washed."

He saluted, then bounded up the stairs.

The champagne was already cold, and she poured herself a glass. When she heard the shower running, she went up to gather the laundry, then started the washing machine, hoping it didn't screw with his water pressure.

Outside, she sat on the swing chair, rocking it softly with her foot. The heat of the day had dissipated with the sun falling to the horizon. Sipping her champagne, she gazed out over the cheerful rock garden with its eclectic menagerie as hues of ginger, scarlet, and gold spread their fingers across the sky.

Unlike her, Cutter was fast, back before the sun actually dipped completely behind the mountains in the distance. He brought out the ice bucket, poured himself a glass, and sat on the swing chair beside her.

"You did really good again." She clinked her glass with his.

Should she offer to pay for half, or even all? But she didn't say anything, afraid it might ruin the moment.

He winked at her and settled back for the sunset, the sky lit up like fire. She pulled her phone out of her pocket to snap a photo, but only one. She wanted to watch the glorious panorama rather than see it only on the screen.

The sun dipped lower, the colors morphed, darkened, and just as the sun disappeared, the garden's fairy lights flashed on.

It was stunning. More than she'd ever expected from a man, from him. When they were young, he'd been a mechanic, lacking a single romantic bone in his body. He was still a mechanic, still earned his living with his hands, still went to work every day, and yet he'd grown the most amazing romantic streak. And this place was the ultimate in romance.

Not that they needed romance. They weren't that kind of couple. They weren't even a couple. They were... just friends with benefits.

But, oh my God, what a friend with benefits. More benefits than she could ever imagine.

"What do you think?" he asked.

"I have no words. Except to say you've outdone yourself."

He grinned widely and pushed out of the rocking swing, sending it into a deeper rhythm. "Just wait until you taste my salmon."

The sliding door slammed shut, and he was back in a moment, carrying the platter. Raising the barbecue lid, he nodded, smiled. "Perfect." And he laid the salmon on the grill.

In only moments, she smelled the tantalizing scent of cooking fish.

Having already set the dining table, even using placemats and napkins, he went inside for the salad and dressing. "I put the clothes in the dryer," he said on the way out again.

Wow. "Thank you." What man ever thought of wet clothes in the washing machine? He was one in a million.

Back at the barbecue, he talked over his shoulder. "You oil the fish, not the grill. And you cook it skin side down, lid closed. Then flip it at the very end," he explained as if he was giving away the secrets of the kingdom.

When the fish was done, he was oh so right. The meat was tender and moist and flaky. They ate with the view of fairy lights, garden, and mountains, which were now just an outline in the deep twilight.

She couldn't help giving him what he deserved. "It's the best salmon I've ever tasted. You're a master chef. You should have your own TV show, like *The Salmon Chef*, or *The Grill Master*, because those shrimp were pretty darn good, too." He could own a restaurant like Javier.

He winked at her. "Little do you know, I already have a gig." He laughed, and she knew he was joking. Maybe salmon and shrimp were his only two specialties. But what specialties they were.

They didn't need dessert tonight. The fish had been tasty and the dressing tangy.

As the sky darkened and the stars winked on like beacons in the sky, they refilled their champagne glasses.

"Ready for the hot tub?" he asked.

She wondered what deliriously naughty things he would do to her tonight in that hot tub. Or maybe he'd wait until they climbed into the fluffy king-size bed.

She winked at him. "We don't even need our suits since there isn't a single person around."

She stood and peeled off her blouse, then wriggled out of her crops, and ran across the walkway to the hot tub. Climbing up the platform, in full view of him, she stripped off her bra and panties and slid down into the warm, relaxing water. As she closed her eyes and leaned back, the jets came on, a delicious beat against the small of her spine.

When Cutter climbed in, proudly and splendidly naked, he brought their champagne, and handed over her glass before he sank down into the water. Then he held his flute aloft.

She waited breathlessly for his toast, as if it would be something momentous.

"To the XB-70 and the best damn trip she's ever taken."

Her stomach fell. She'd been craving something more personal, maybe more about her. But then she thought about the man Cutter Sorensen was and realized his toast was actually the sexiest and most romantic he could have made. To him, the Corvette was everything. And that meant this trip was everything.

"And here's to it getting better and better," she finished for him.

He downed half the glass of champagne. As if the more he drank, the more her toast for the rest of the trip would come true.

"I specifically searched for a place with a hot tub," he said. "After driving twelve hours, I knew we'd need it."

Once again, he was so right. The jets pummeled her muscles, easing the aches of sitting for so long. Closing her eyes, she leaned back, her legs suspended in the water, her arms floating on the surface.

And then she felt him between her thighs.

20

"I know something else," he murmured, "that will ease all the aches and pains." Coming up between her thighs, he spread her legs. Part of her wanted to open her eyes and watch him. Another part wanted only the sensation.

He trailed his fingers up her legs, back down, then along her thighs, her flanks, her sides, to the hollow of her armpits, then across the upper swell of her breasts and down between, circling, circling. Until finally he latched onto her nipples, each between a thumb and forefinger. And he pinched.

The sensation was electric, flashing through her body like lightning and shooting down to her core.

She was wet instantly, and it wasn't the water. It was all him, his touch, his voice. "Do you want me to stop?" he asked softly, with an evil, teasing cast to his tone.

She didn't open her eyes, muttering, "Don't you dare stop."

Then he dove on her, taking one nipple in his mouth, licking her, sucking, then biting with another delicious thrill. Hands at her waist, he pushed her higher, her breasts bobbing on the water's surface as he squeezed tight between her legs.

Pushing her against the tub wall, he alternately used his fingers and his mouth on her breasts.

God, she'd waited for this all day.

He slipped his hand down her belly, caressed her, toyed with her belly button, then gliding lower, lower, he slid his fingers inside. And she was almost there, on the edge of a cataclysmic orgasm.

Instead of giving it to her, he shoved her onto the lip of the hot tub and spread her legs, where she braced herself with both feet on the bench seat.

Then he drove her utterly insane.

She gripped the sides of the tub, holding on for dear life, and let him do anything he wanted. Everything she'd dreamed about, everything she needed.

When the climax hit, she cried out, giving it all her voice. The cries made it better, made it last, going on and on and on.

Even before she was done, he pulled her down into the water, onto his lap, her legs still spread as he slid deftly inside her, seating himself high and deep. He kept her there without moving, her body contracting and rippling around him.

Until finally she opened her eyes. "Aren't you going to do it?" The words weren't elegant or romantic, but she didn't care.

He plastered a grin on his face. "I'm not sure I'm ready. I'd like to hold on to this high for a little while longer. Holding you right where you are. And then..." His eyes glittered in the fairy lights. "Then I'll carry you to bed and make you scream like that all night long."

Oh God, she couldn't wait, absolutely could not. She needed him now.

As if he could hear her thoughts, he swept her hair back from her face. "This can be way better if you wait." He flexed inside her, sending thrills through her body.

"It's going to be murder."

"Oh baby, you don't know how much I want to murder you with pleasure."

She suddenly knew the meaning of the old song *Killing Me Softly*.

❀

HE WAS SURE HE'D DIE IF HE DIDN'T THRUST DEEP AND KEEP going. But Cutter had promised her all night, and that's exactly what he'd give her.

Still buried inside her, still unmoving, he whispered, "Go upstairs and get in the bed."

"What are you going to do?"

"It's not what I'm going to do. Is what you're going to do."

She whispered back, a little frightened, a little wary, and wholly turned on, "Like what?"

"Pull the covers down all the way and touch yourself."

Her eyes widened, but she didn't speak.

"That's what I want to see when I walk up the stairs, you, spreadeagled, getting yourself ready for me."

"You're sick. You're a demon," she murmured.

He laughed. "Thank you very much. You can't know how good those compliments are."

But then she rushed to do his bidding, climbing off him, scrambling out of the tub, water streaming down her gorgeous body. She couldn't wait, whether it was to touch herself or to feel his tongue on her or to drag him deep inside her, he couldn't be sure. But she would get all three. And more.

He liked regular sex, he liked kinky sex, he liked all sex. And he liked it best with her.

He rose slowly out of the water, toweled off, took his time. Then, naked and hard, he climbed the spiral stairs.

First, he saw the bed, then he saw her bathed in moonlight, one arm flung up, her hand fisted in the pillow. She lay flat, her legs wide, her hand caressing, her fingers swirling. And he rounded the bed to stand at just the right angle so he didn't block the moonlight falling across her tempting body.

Her eyes were closed, her lips parted, her breath coming fast.

And he'd never wanted a woman so badly.

He was painfully hard, painfully ready, but instead of taking what he needed, he crawled onto the bed, between her legs, and fit his fingers inside her, finding the sweet spot, working it while she worked her hot button. Her limbs quivered, then her body quaked, and just before she exploded, he pushed her hand aside and took her with his mouth, licking, sucking, circling. He felt the orgasm race through her as her body clamped around his fingers, tensed and released, tensed and released.

She damn near wailed at how good it was. How good *he* was.

He could have taken her then, filled her up, made her ride the edge of that climax for long, glorious minutes. But he wasn't done.

Lifting his mouth a fraction, it was just enough for her to lose the peak. Just enough to make her crave more. Then he started all over again, working her, licking her, his fingers playing her. She was up there again in a split second. She squirmed and trembled and quaked and cried out. Then he felt it, that perfect moment, that ultimate detonation, and he rose up, thrusting inside her, hard, deep, his body riding all her sweet spots inside and out.

He could have lost it then. He probably should have. But he was fifty-eight years old, and he had long ago learned how to hold off until the right moment.

And they hadn't reached it yet.

He hauled back, still seated inside her, dragged her legs over his thighs, and thrust slowly, short strokes in and out.

"Touch yourself. Right there." He put her fingers on her hot button. "Make yourself feel good."

The sight of her fingers circling almost made him lose it.

And they climbed to the pinnacle all over again. She tossed her head on the pillow, her hair flying, her body quivering. Raising her butt off the bed, she changed the angle, showing him how to get it just right. And when her body clamped around him, when she cried out, he slammed deep and hard, dropping on her, his rhythm fast. Reaching around, she squeezed his sack, just the way he'd taught her all those years ago.

She hadn't forgotten.

Then he forgot everything, screaming into freefall, and taking her down with him.

SHE WAS WANDERING IN THE LAND BETWEEN WAKING AND sleeping, delicious fantasies of all the things she wanted Cutter to do to her.

Then her phone rang, jerking her awake, and she pounced on it on the bedside table to shut off the noise. With the phone still vibrating in her hand, she jumped off the bed, looking down at Cutter, where he seemed dead to the world.

She'd grabbed a robe and was already climbing down the spiral staircase when she answered, whispering harshly, "Why are you calling so late?"

"It's only nine o'clock," her sister said dryly.

"Which means it's ten o'clock here."

"Since when have you ever gone to bed at ten?"

"Since I had a twelve-hour drive," she snapped. To be

followed by the most amazing sex she'd ever had, which, of course, she didn't say.

"Your daughter is the one who made me call."

"Grace?"

"She's worried about you."

Noreen opened the sliding glass door and slipped down onto the chair swing. "Why is she worried?"

She let her sister answer, even though she knew very well. "Apparently you're shacking up with some guy you barely know. Why do you think she's worried?"

"First of all, he's not a stranger. He was our uncle's mechanic. And I knew him when we were kids."

"Not that Sutter guy?" her sister said with disdain.

"His name is Cutter, not Sutter. And yes, that guy. So Uncle Mortimer and I have known him forever. And he's certainly not a danger to anyone."

"Except that now you're shacking up with him."

Valerie could be acerbic. But Noreen knew it came from a good heart, and she just needed to bring her sister down off the ledge. "We're not shacking up." She couldn't say they weren't having sex, since that would be a complete lie. But sleeping in shipping containers didn't constitute shacking up.

All right, she was splitting hairs. "He's my mechanic. He's helping me get the car across the country. The car is old, and she needs a lot of attention." Not nearly as much attention as Noreen had thought it would after the water pump blew, but she didn't tell her sister that. "And he kindly offered to accompany me." After she'd bribed and begged him.

Valerie huffed out a long-suffering sigh. "We're just worried about you. You're all alone out there, and we don't know anything about this guy."

"I just told you all about him."

"Grace said you were supposed to send pictures, but she only got one this afternoon and nothing the rest of the day."

Noreen slapped her hand to her forehead. "I forgot when we got here." She'd been thinking about sex and food, and she'd been bowled over by the amazing container house. That's where she needed to start. "I'll send you guys pictures of this place. You won't believe it. It's shipping containers stacked on top of each other, but it's amazing. And it has the most beautiful rock garden and a hot tub and an outdoor kitchen."

"You're trying to distract me."

Busted. "No, I'm not."

"Yes, you are."

Noreen laughed. "Okay, I was trying to distract you. But that doesn't mean this isn't a really cool place. And I'll send pictures right now, so you know this is me and not some silly serial killer who stole my phone."

"I recognize your voice," her sister mocked. "But he could have a knife to your throat."

"I wouldn't be talking like this if he had a knife to my throat. You'd hear at least some sort of anxiety. Do you detect any anxiety?"

"No. But you were always a much better liar than I was."

Noreen snorted. "Will you just stop? I'm sending a picture." She snapped a couple of photos of the yard and all the fairy lights and statues, hoping her sister wouldn't pick up on the fact they were in the middle of nowhere.

"Wow," Valerie said on an awed breath. "That's totally amazing."

"I'll send these same pictures to Grace and April so they'll know I'm fine. There's no need to worry. You guys don't have to call me sixteen times a day."

"I love you. But they're worried because you're still recovering from Gilbert."

"Everett, not Gilbert," she corrected. Valerie hadn't liked

Everett and had never called him by his real name, always mixing it up.

"So where are you?"

"Santa Fe. We'll be here a couple of days, then Sedona and Las Vegas. So the trip is almost over."

Where did that ache around her heart come from? She'd known this was just a trip, not a lifetime.

Maybe Cutter would want to come out to California every few months. That would be fabulous.

"So you'll be home in three days?"

"Don't make me commit to three days, in case we want to stop somewhere along the way. It could be three or four or five days, depending on how I feel."

Valerie puffed out another disgusted breath. "You're always so difficult to deal with."

Noreen laughed. "Look who's talking, big sister, always ordering me around and telling me I couldn't hang out with you and your friends."

"Ancient history." Then Valerie got serious. "Honestly, you need to send more pictures to make the girls feel good. They do actually worry about their mother."

She didn't mention that Grace and April could go into her online photo album and see whatever they wanted. "I promise."

As soon as she hung up, she sent photos of the backyard with a lovely text to both April and Grace, explaining where she was and what her plans were.

The phone rang only a minute later. Obviously one of them checking up on her, but when she looked, it was Tammy. She answered with, "Please do not tell me you're checking up on me, girlfriend."

"You were supposed to call me tonight, and you failed miserably. Valerie just called and told me you're shacking up with some guy."

"Oh my God," Noreen said dramatically.

"So tell me about the hot mechanic. Is he good? I want every dirty detail."

That was the difference between Tammy and Valerie. One wanted dirty details, and the other wanted to rag on her. Not that her sister had ragged. It was kind of nice to be worried about. Sometimes. But did she dare admit the truth? "I can't believe my sister just called you."

"Of course she did. She's worried about you."

"Grace and April are worried about me. Valerie is worried about me. And now you call me. I am actually a grown woman capable of taking care of myself."

"I'm not worried about you. I just want to hear about this hot guy." Tammy dropped her voice seductively.

"He's just my uncle's mechanic. And he's only on this trip to make sure the car makes it the entire way."

"*Just* your uncle's mechanic? He's the total hottie you lost your virginity to in your uncle's car. You darn well remember telling me all about him."

She wished she'd never told Tammy about her Corvette summer. "That's him. But he's a mechanic, and it's forty years later, and you can figure that out."

Tammy groaned. "Oh my God, he's got plumber's crack and a huge beer belly."

She couldn't perpetuate that lie. There were all those pictures in her cloud. "He's still a hottie. But he's still my mechanic. And you know how sex, even really good sex, can get in the way of a business relationship."

"You're doing him. I know it, I feel it." Tammy groaned melodramatically. "But you probably don't want to tell me because he's lying next to you in the bed, and it would be bad form to reveal any secrets right now."

Noreen guffawed. "You have such a vivid imagination. For your information, he's upstairs, and I'm down on the patio.

So he can't overhear a word I say." Just to make sure, she glanced at the closed sliding glass door.

"You're disappointing me. I wanted a great story. You could've at least lied." Tammy made snuffling sounds as if she were crying.

Noreen smiled to herself, her body suddenly going hot all over. "All right, here's a story. Do with it what you will. The sex is amazing, he makes me come over and over, and his body is so hot, it makes me drool. And he's big, really big, and he knows how to use it all. In fact, I'm going back up there and climb on top of him and make him do it all over again."

Tammy laughed. "Oh my God, I love your stories, but they make me so hot. Where's my husband when I need him?"

She could hear Tammy fanning herself.

"I hope that's good enough for you. I'll try to think of another story for a later date."

She was pretty sure Tammy didn't believe her, although she'd told the truth with every word.

"All right, go to bed, safe driving. And if anything else happens, I want an immediate text with all the dirty details."

"I promise, Scouts' honor."

"You were never a Girl Scout."

"Neither were you, so it doesn't matter."

After a laughing goodbye, she climbed the spiral staircase once more and slipped quietly into bed next to Cutter, trying not to wake him.

Until his voice cut across the quiet. "So, it's the best sex and I give you amazing orgasms over and over. And I'm the biggest and best ever."

She shot up in bed. "How did you hear that?"

He pointed to the open window beneath which she'd been sitting.

Pulling her on top, he said, "I'm pretty sure we can do it

even better than amazing. How about awesome? Or spectacular. Or fantabulous."

Then he rolled her beneath him and took her lips with an awesome, spectacular, fantabulous kiss that stole her breath.

Another orgasm would be even better.

❀

CUTTER MADE HER BREAKFAST IN BED, THE SCENT OF coffee and frying bacon waking her. There'd also been eggs, toast, and freshly brewed coffee. He'd even folded the laundry.

After having woken very late, it was almost lunchtime once they made it into Santa Fe, but she wasn't hungry yet.

They drove into town and strolled through the boutiques of Canyon Road. There were art galleries and artsy shops and clothing stores, everything pricey, but of such good quality that her mouth watered.

"You need to buy something," Cutter said. "You haven't bought a single souvenir from the trip. And I don't think you'll find anything better than what you get here."

They'd entered a ceramics shop displaying Anasazi pottery styles, each piece a beauty. "But what am I going to do with it?"

"Are you saying you have every space in your house filled?"

He stood with his hands on his hips, legs slightly spread. She wasn't the only woman looking at the way his jeans gripped his butt and his T-shirt outlined his six-pack abs. Even the younger generation was in thrall.

"I like these." She pointed to a set of six decorated prep bowls.

"What the hell will you do with those? You can't even get a decent-sized bowl of cereal in there."

She looked at him and said as dryly as Valerie would,

"They're prep bowls for cooking. You know, you dice up the green onions and put them in this bowl. And you mix up some spices and put them in that bowl. Then you have all your ingredients right there ready to drop into whatever you're cooking."

"You mean you actually cook?" he asked, deadpan.

"Of course I cook," she said with tremendous affront, trying to hide her smile. "Do you think the only things I served my daughters while they were growing up were peanut butter and jelly sandwiches?"

"I thought you had a cook and a maid." His expression was just as deadpan as before. She couldn't tell if he actually believed that.

Although Everett had a cook and a maid. But she wouldn't mention that because Everett didn't count. "I cooked and cleaned and earned my own money while I raised my girls."

Although the divorce settlements and insurance payouts had helped.

"Just checking," he said airily, then added, "If you really like them, get them. You need some sort of souvenir."

She had souvenirs. She had all the memories of the delicious things he'd done to her, in the hot tub that first night and the bed last night and everything in between.

But the bowls were nice, and she decided he was right. "Will they fit in the back of the Corvette?"

He stroked his chin, considering them for a moment. "We'll make room for them."

"What kind of souvenir are you getting?"

He grinned and tapped his temple. "All my souvenirs are right up here."

She felt herself blush, full body, realizing he was thinking exactly the same thing she had.

While the saleslady wrapped the bowls, Noreen said,

"Maybe I should get something for the girls. And my sister. And my best friend Tammy."

He looked at her as if he could see right inside her head. "Jewelry. It's smaller. Maybe some turquoise, Santa Fe's signature color."

They meandered through the shops, Cutter pointing out jewelry he liked. The man had exquisite taste.

She found a pretty pair of earrings for Grace, a pin for Valerie who loved to wear scarves, a bracelet for Tammy, and a hand-tooled leather notebook for April.

She stroked the leather. "She'll love this for all her notes."

He smiled. "You've made good choices. Let's dump everything in the car and start touring."

Jamming a hand on her hip, she shot him a mock glare. "That's why you helped me, so I'd get a move on."

He laughed and asked in a deep drawl, "Do I look like I enjoy shopping?"

Yet she got the feeling he'd enjoyed every minute as he'd helped her pick out gifts for her family and her friend.

Just as much as she enjoyed being with him.

Once they'd locked the packages in the trunk, they began their walking tour of Santa Fe. First on the trail was the Saint Francis Cathedral, which reminded Noreen of a Victorian church.

"Is it my imagination, or does it feel like there's something missing?" She tipped her head to take in the site.

Cutter was already reading an interpretive sign outside the church. "That's because it's incomplete. Construction began in 1869, but they ran out of money, and never finished the two towers." He pointed to the bell towers, which should have had spires.

Inside, they stood in sunbeams streaming through the upper windows. Despite never being completed, the church was beautiful. A small adobe chapel on the north side, part of the original church, contained the oldest depiction of the Virgin Mary in the US.

Taking a picture, she attached it in a text thread that included Valerie, the girls, and Tammy. It was ridiculous to send everything separately.

She typed quickly. *Santa Fe. The oldest Virgin Mary in the United States.*

Tammy immediately blasted back. *Are there any virgins left in the United States?*

She laughed, showing it to Cutter. He grabbed her phone, typing his own return. *That is sacrilege.*

It's what she would have typed herself.

They made their way to the Palace of the Governors, a long low adobe building like something out of a movie about the Alamo.

Cutter stopped to read the interpretive sign. The man loved reading signs, go figure. "Did you know that Governor Lew Wallace wrote the classic *Ben-Hur* right here?"

"I thought that was a story out of the Bible."

He rolled his eyes at her. "The movie version with Charlton Heston was the best. He did his own stunts, even driving the chariot. And they filmed that chariot race in one take."

She narrowed her eyes at him. "You're making that up."

"Check it out."

She would check it out, because she'd loved Charlton Heston in *Ben-Hur*. And she loved that the movie was a favorite of Cutter's too.

They wandered through Santa Fe Plaza and into the San Miguel Chapel, which was supposedly the oldest church in the United States, built in 1610. Which meant the Spanish, driven out of Santa Fe by the Pueblo Indians in the Pueblo revolt of 1680, had erected it.

She'd read that fact on an interpretive sign. She could read just as well as Cutter.

The Loretto Chapel was next on Cutter's tour. It was more like the Gothic churches she was used to, with big arches and buttresses and stained glass windows, these imported from France. The miraculous spiral staircase, which seemed to hang in mid-air and had to be at least twenty feet high to reach the choir loft, was roped off from tourists.

"It says here—" Cutter pointed to the sign. "—the builder used wooden pegs instead of nails and that the staircase itself has no visible means of support."

It was truly amazing. She took more pictures and sent those on her text thread, making sure this time not to include Cutter in any of her photos.

"How much farther?" she asked as they walked toward the New Mexico State Capitol.

"The circuit is only about two miles."

"But I'm getting hungry." She rubbed her stomach.

He gaped at her. "You had a huge breakfast at ten o'clock. How can you be hungry?"

"That was hours ago," she pouted. "And we've been walking for miles."

Laughing, he wrapped his arm around her and hauled her in to murmur at her ear. "We'll eat after the capitol. How does that sound?"

She smiled. "That'll make it late enough to be dunch, dinner and lunch."

He laughed at her. "Dunch it is."

Known as the Roundhouse, the New Mexico State Capitol was the country's only round capitol building. Central to the sixty-foot-high rotunda was a turquoise and brass mosaic of the seal of New Mexico, and the ceiling skylight of blue and pale pink cast glorious prisms of color over the travertine marble floor.

A docent approached them, an older woman with permed white hair, to give them a few details. "The skylight represents an Indian basket weave." She pointed up. "And the blue and pink of the stained glass represent the sky and the earth." She spoke in soft, reverent tones, and though the woman must see this spectacle every day, her gaze was one of awe.

"It's beautiful," Noreen agreed.

"We're very proud of the Roundhouse here in Santa Fe." Her smile was as glorious as the sun falling through the skylight. "It's one of the most stunning buildings."

Noreen didn't mention the magnificent Louisiana State Capitol, though the Roundhouse was no less impressive. They were just different and yet both grand.

From the capitol, they made their way to the Santa Fe Railyard with its landmark water tower. It now housed a large art district with galleries, performance spaces, and cinemas, as well as restaurants and antique shops.

They wandered the shops once more, the sidewalks crowded with tourists.

"You didn't buy yourself any jewelry," Cutter said as they looked into the front window of a jewelry store.

She held up her wrist. "I'm not really a jewelry girl except for these." She wore several beaded elastic bracelets she'd purchased online—she and Valerie were addicted to them. She mixed and matched the different color schemes and could wear them with just about anything. And the best was that Everett had scorned them because they were cheap.

Cutter raised a brow. "I thought you were wearing those because you didn't want to get your good stuff stolen on the trip."

She raised an eyebrow. "I get the impression you think I'm some sort of prima donna with a lot of fancy jewelry and a cook and a maid."

He shrugged. "I can't say I really ever thought about it."

Wow. That put her in her place. So he hadn't thought about her in the last forty years. She didn't stalk away, didn't even turn around. She just shut her mouth.

He touched her arm. "I didn't mean it like that."

"Like what?"

"Like I've never even thought about you since you left."

She blushed at his guess. It must have been written all over her face.

"I wasn't thinking that." But she stumbled over the words.

He reeled her in. "I thought about you a lot. I wondered about your life. And I always imagined you in a McMansion with lots of kids and a fluffy designer dog like a poodle or Lhasa Apso, with a cook, a maid, and a gardener, and a driver who chauffeured you around in an expensive Mercedes."

She laughed out loud, but of all the things he'd mentioned, she picked on only one. "A Lhasa Apso?"

He nodded. "Or one of those little teacup poodles you could carry around in a doggie bag."

She laughed out loud. "It's not a doggie bag. It's a doggie carrier. You are so crazy. You never thought any of that."

He smiled. Then his eyes darkened, turning molten, and he lowered his voice. "I can't tell you what I was really thinking, especially not here. There are children close by."

Her skin heated. And she liked the thought that he'd never forgotten her. Just the way she'd never forgotten him.

She had no idea what else Cutter might have said because her stomach growled, loudly enough that he put his hand on her belly as if an alien might suddenly burst out.

Laughing, she said, "It's almost happy hour. I can't help it if I'm suddenly starving."

They found a rooftop cantina that overlooked the town and all the tourists on its streets, and ordered mezcal margaritas, supposedly a specialty of the Southwest. The drink had a sweet, smoky flavor, different from a regular margarita.

"Tequila is made only from blue agave and then steamed," their waiter told them, his hair a buzz cut and his nose pierced. "Whereas mezcal can be produced from any type of agave and is grilled or roasted, giving it that smoky flavor you taste."

"Thank you for the explanation," Noreen said, adding after the man left, "I'll have to try this at home. It's good."

They people-watched before ordering dinner, the sweet and smoky margarita putting a stop to the rumbles in her stomach. Cutter leaned back in his seat. "Have you thought any more about selling me the XB-70 and coming out to visit her when you like?"

Why did it shock her every time he asked about the Corvette? She knew how he felt about the car. She even knew he wouldn't stop asking. It was just... well... It was the sex.

She couldn't resist asking, "Is that why you're having sex with me? So I'll sell you the car and come out quarterly to get serviced?" She spoke with a smile, as if it was a joke, and yet there was the sting of tension inside her. It couldn't be all about the car. Could it?

Cutter laughed. "Exactly. I'm attempting to make myself totally irresistible so you'll sell me the XB-70 just in order to have my body several times a year."

He *was* joking, and she played along despite the pressure in her chest. "Actually, you're the one who finds my body totally irresistible and you won't be able to stop yourself from flying out to California every quarter to get your fill of both of us."

He smiled, leaned forward on the table, his eyes a glittering blue blaze. "I guess we'll just have to see who can hold out the longest."

It was a challenge, but a challenge for what? To see who could make the sex the best it could be? He'd already done that. She was hooked.

But was he hooked?

She broke the game they were playing by picking up a menu. "What are you going to order?"

"I'm having the Cedar Plank Salmon."

"But we had salmon last night."

"Salmon can be good two nights in a row," he told her loftily. "And salmon slow-cooked on a cedar plank is what you would call to die for."

So she ordered the same.

"You are so right," she said as she savored the juicy, flaky salmon. The fish lay on a bed of wild rice, accompanied by maple-roasted Brussels sprouts. "I'm not normally a Brussels sprouts woman, but these are out of this world."

And while they enjoyed the salmon and Brussels sprouts, there was time to continue bickering about the car and who should own it and who would fly out to which coast for the sex she had a feeling they both craved. But she wasn't about to cave in.

She was tipsy on the way back to the shipping containers, but she still knew they'd taken a wrong turn. "Where are you going?"

Cutter just smiled. He was such a sneaky man. She imagined he'd try to seduce her in some sexy, out-of-the-way spot, another gambit to get her to hand over the car.

After the turn, he wended his way through scrubby desert, the road curving through a small housing development, and finally...

"Is that a university?" She couldn't make out the identity of the buildings, but maybe that was her fuzzy brain.

"It's the community college."

Instead of driving into it, he went around it, pulling up near a great blue thing outlined against the desert.

Noreen climbed out of the car. "What is it?"

Cutter snorted a laugh. "It's a blue whale, can't you tell?"

Of course it was. A great whale in the middle of the desert, shimmering blue in the fading light.

"She's made entirely of recycled plastic," he told her. "They call her Ethyl, after the polyethylene trash she's made from."

The more Noreen studied the life-size, eighty-two-foot-long blue whale, the more the details came out, the sculpted mouth, the lines down her long throat, even her eyes, which were colorful strips of plastic shaped around soulful black orbs. It was Ethyl's eyes that grabbed Noreen, almost as if the whale were real.

"This is so cool. How did you even know about it?"

He shrugged, giving her a lopsided grin. "Just surfing on weird stuff around Santa Fe. I'm surprised you haven't heard of her. She was crafted out near you, at the Monterey Bay Aquarium. And she was on display for months in San Francisco's Presidio."

"I totally missed it."

"It was a project to raise awareness about our excessive plastic trash and what it's doing to the oceans."

"She's beautiful." She touched Cutter's arm. "Thank you for bringing me to see her."

He laughed. "So does she make you want to stop buying plastic water bottles?"

She put her hands on her hips. "I'll have you know I have a reusable water bottle at home. I should have brought it with me."

"Your conservation habits deserve a bonus." He grabbed her then, kissed her, his taste sweet, his body hard.

And that night, they both tried to outdo each other to prove the point. As she fell into an exhausted sleep, she was sure they were both winners.

The question was whether she could live without this.

Because the things Cutter Sorensen made her feel were addictive.

WAS SHE WEAKENING?

Cutter pondered the question as they headed to Sedona the following day. He had a suspicion *he* was the one weakening. He smiled at her constantly, even now in the car with the wind blowing through their hair. The phantom of her sweet taste lingered on his lips. Coffee didn't get rid of it. The sickeningly sweet pastry he'd forced himself to eat this morning hadn't done it, nor had the ketchup-and-relish hot dog he'd stuffed down when they stopped for lunch.

And still he tasted her.

She was in his head now, in his blood. And when she was gone, he was pretty damn sure he'd never get her out of his head again. Just like it had taken years to stop pining for her the last time.

They arrived in Sedona in the early afternoon. He'd gotten her out of bed early for the drive. Getting a move on was the only way he could stop himself from keeping her in that bed all day.

She'd grumbled prettily, half asleep for at least another half hour. And that allowed him to do the driving.

If he was going to lose the XB-70, he wanted to get in as much driving time as he could. And that left her time to scour her phone for a place to stay.

She booked a resort in a vortex.

"What the hell is a vortex?" he said in a harsh whisper as the clerk finished checking them in.

"It's a mystical spot where you can feel the convergence of all the energies. They're all over Sedona. People come here just to feel a vortex."

He laughed, and she clamped a hand over his mouth. "People believe in this stuff," she hissed.

He steeled his expression, but couldn't help licking her palm or the shit-eating grin when she squeaked.

After they'd settled in, when he thought it might be the perfect time to show her exactly what he could do for her—

and what she'd be missing when the trip was over—she said, "We have hike out to the vortex. Just to see if we can feel anything." She smiled as she spoke, hopefully proving she didn't actually believe this crap.

"Don't you want to get in the hot tub?" He pointed to the tub out on their private patio.

"Afterward." The word sounded like a promise.

And he smiled right back, thinking about the fun they could get up to in a vortex.

They headed out, Noreen wearing hiking shorts with numerous pockets to hold her phone, tissues, and small snack packages. A wide-brimmed hat covered her face and neck, and she'd rubbed sunblock over her arms and legs. A baseball cap sufficed for him.

She was a damn good hiker, he'd give her that. She marched like a drill sergeant. It didn't matter whether they went up or down, she maintained the same speed.

They climbed switchbacks along rocky ledges, leaving the canyon far below.

"I'm not feeling any mystical energy," he called out.

And she threw over her shoulder, "We're not there yet."

The best thing about the hike was the view as he walked behind her. The woman had a gorgeous ass that fit perfectly in his hands. They'd reached the ridge when the sky began darkening, a rolling smatter of gray clouds at first. But Cutter had heard how fast thunderstorms could hit in the Southwest, and he caught up with her, asking, "How much farther?"

"I don't really know." She pulled out the map the reception clerk had given her. "Here it shows up as a loop, and we'll go back down the other side," she said, pointing to the opposite wall of the canyon. "We've got to be almost halfway."

He pointed a finger toward the darkening sky. "I'm not sure we'll make it."

"Oh." Then she smiled. "It's still gathering. We'll get back before it lets loose," said by she of the ever-present optimism.

Turning back now wouldn't help; they were too close to the midpoint. The only thing to do was soldier on.

Then they stepped out of scrub and onto a magnificent plateau made up of the famous red rocks of Sedona.

The view down the canyon was stunning. He lived on the Florida Keys, with spectacular views and sunsets every day, but this stole his breath. With a sightline straight back down along the canyon, it then opened onto a vista of gleaming red rock buttes. Even he took out his phone for a picture.

Noreen held her arms out to shoulder height. "Do you feel it?" she said almost reverently, her voice soft as the hairs on her arms rose.

Then he felt it too, a zing across his skin, a hum through his body, and when he looked down, the hairs on his arms had risen.

"It's the vortex." She turned in a circle. "Close your eyes." She stood with her head back, her arms out. "It's amazing."

He wouldn't say amazing, just weird. And he had a feeling it was all about the storm gathering overhead, the electricity in the air, the clouds darker now.

"I don't know why no one else is here," she murmured, eyes still closed, face up to the heavens. "I mean, it's a vortex, for God's sake. There should be a bunch of people up here meditating."

He touched her arm, and when she looked at him, he pointed to the dark sky. "That's why no one's here. Everyone else looked at the weather report." Then he added, "We don't want to be up here if lightning strikes."

He grabbed her hand, pulling her to the path on the other side. It didn't matter which trail they chose; it was equidistant either way. When the rain began, it didn't start with a drizzle but came down in a deluge.

Noreen shrieked and ran, but she didn't go far, turning back to him. "I don't think we can outrun this."

"We can't."

A tremendous clap of thunder boomed in the distance, and he prayed the lightning was a long way off. The only thing he was grateful for was the temperature of the rain. If it had been colder, they'd be frozen by the time they made it out of the canyon.

But after a while, even that didn't matter. They were completely soaked, and a chill burrowed deep into his bones. Once they were down in the canyon, the trees overhead at least lessened the rain's pummel, and for now, the lightning was far in the distance.

Noreen was a trooper. She didn't complain, even as the rain fell down her back in rivulets, soaking her clothing and dripping from the bottoms of her shorts. She marched on without a moan or a whine.

If she could do it, he certainly wasn't about to be outdone.

22

The deeper they fell down into the canyon, the colder the rain became, sluicing down the trail like a river.

Cutter wanted to run to catch up with Noreen, having let her get too far ahead while he watched every step. But now he was afraid he'd lose his footing. Besides, if lightning hit, it was better they were far apart. Still, he matched her stride as they hiked along the canyon's bottom, inches from the small stream that had become a torrent.

He still couldn't believe how fast the storm had come on. When they'd started out, there hadn't been a cloud in the sky.

Finally, he made out the adobe structures of the resort climbing up the walls of the canyon. And the rain abruptly stopped. Like a tap turning off, it was just gone, leaving behind humid air that made his wet clothes steam.

But the water still rushed down the canyon stream, and his shoes sloshed on the muddy trail. Noreen trudged ahead, though he rapidly gained on her. They'd almost reached the resort gate and the tarmac beyond when the sun broke through, its brightness on the concrete almost blinding.

Catching up with Noreen, he grabbed her arm. "Are you okay?"

She turned to him, her face pale, her lips a sickening shade of blue. "I'm fine," she tried to say, her words slurred, her mouth almost immobile.

He reeled her in, cupped her face. "You're frozen."

She touched his cheek. "So are you." A lopsided smile creased her face. "We need the hot tub."

Grabbing his hand, they ran, their shoes squishing on the concrete.

They toed off their muddy footwear on the doorstep, and Noreen glanced around. The entry alcove was visible only from the road, and when she saw no one out there, she keyed in the door code, threw her sodden hat on the flagstone, slipped out of her soaked shorts, and pulled her see-through T-shirt over her head.

"Last one in's a rotten egg."

It took him only a second to shed his clothing, leaving it with hers on the doorstep. He kicked the door closed behind him, following her wet footprints to the open patio door.

She was already in the tub, the bubbles frothing, her panties and bra on the marble tile. With high walls on either side blocking the view from other patios, he stripped out of his briefs. Then he sank down into the water.

It was splendidly hot, his body so cold that his skin tingled with the heat.

Noreen grinned at him, her lips still slightly blue and her skin pallid. "Isn't it the most amazing feeling getting in a hot tub when you're so cold? It's like those little fish you see in pedicure salons where they eat all the dead skin off your feet."

He grimaced. "Please don't tell me that. It's grotesque. Especially when I'm sitting in water." But it felt like tiny fish nibbling on him.

Her smile lit up her face. "I've done this before. The cold

plunge and then into hot water. It's amazing, and it's supposed to be really healthy for you. The Swedes do it all the time." She cocked her head. "Although I don't know if you're supposed to get in hot water right after the cold plunge. Maybe you're supposed to do the cold, then get out and dry off."

He didn't care. "This is freaking amazing. And I don't need to get cold again."

Then he reached out with one long arm and reeled her in. "You're amazing. And that hike was amazing."

In the circle of his arms, she said, her tone awed, "It was the vortex. It gave me all the energy I needed to get back down."

"I'm pretty sure that was the storm and the electricity in the lightning that we felt."

She shook her head, her hair a mass of tangles she hadn't bothered to fix. As if she knew that no matter how she looked, even with mascara smudges under her eyes, she was gorgeous to him.

"All right," he agreed. "It was incredible that we got all the way down without a single mishap." He dipped his hands in the hot water, raking them over his face. Then he cupped her cheeks, running his thumbs under her eyes, wiping away the makeup. She was beautiful no matter what makeup she wore, no matter whether her hair was blow-dried or wind-blown or mashed down by her hat.

"Your lips are blue. We need to warm them up."

And he kissed her, long and sweet, her taste delicious, like berries, her lips freakishly cold against his, the feel of her mouth under his miraculous.

He kissed her until his skin heated and the imaginary fish stopped nibbling and her lips warmed. Then he drew her up and over him, pulling her in to straddle him on the bench, her breasts bobbing on the water.

Instead of taking her right then, even as his little head screamed for it, he whispered, "What do you want for dinner?"

"You want to know that now?" she asked, astounded, as if *her* little head was clamoring too. "I don't know. What do you want?"

"Chile rellenos," he blurted. "How hot do you like them?"

"Very, very hot."

"Me too." He pushed himself against her, holding her down, letting her ride the hard ridge of him for just a second. "Do you like it with meat?"

She shifted on him, her smile hot and naughty. "A lot of hard meat. That's exactly how I like it."

She made him laugh. In all his dreams of her over the years, he couldn't have imagined how much better it would be with her now than it had been that summer.

"And I like mine really wet."

She made a face. "Chile rellenos should not be wet," she said dryly. Then she giggled. "But everything else should be. Like a mezcal margarita. Do you think they make them here?"

"If they don't, I can make them as wet as you want."

She was silent for a long moment, as if he'd stolen her breath with their mutually sexy thoughts.

Then, her hands on his face, everything about her warm now, her cheeks, her red lips, her thighs and everything in between, she whispered, "I think we should order dinner *after* we have the appetizer."

Noreen had thought it would take hours to warm up after that rain hike. The only way her blood hadn't frozen was by putting one foot in front of the other. If she'd stopped, she'd have frozen like a block of ice. Okay, that was an exaggeration. The weather had been warmish, but the relentlessness rain seeping into her bones eventually chilled her.

But Cutter knew exactly how to warm her up. And now, in their resort robes, they were snug as bugs in a rug, as her mother always said. Though the saying never actually made sense to Noreen.

"I suppose we should've gone out to dinner somewhere in Sedona," she said mildly. But she couldn't move a muscle. Not after the hike in the rain, followed by glorious, bone-melting sex in the hot tub. Besides, the resort made delicious mezcal margaritas and chile rellenos.

"Neither of us was in any shape to drive." Cutter picked up his margarita. "And after these, we most certainly wouldn't have been in any shape to get back to the resort."

"True." The resort was way out of town along a winding road, portions of it only one way. "Besides, after experiencing a vortex like that, we really shouldn't be driving or hanging out around other people." She waved her hands across her body. "We should be absorbing the energy."

He laughed. "So you really believe it was the vortex and not an electrical storm."

Actually, it was the fabulous sex, but she said, "The lightning was miles away."

He nodded, turning serious. "We were damn lucky it was so far off. If it was closer, one of those lightning strikes might have hit us."

When they'd run pell-mell along the resort tarmac, she'd noted that the gate to the pool and outdoor hot tub was locked. It could have been very dangerous. But she wouldn't think about that. They were safe now.

"You're such a funny man. Do not bring down my mood with danger that never happened. They call that catastrophizing."

"I'm not catastrophizing." He drained his first mezcal margarita. "But it scared me." He was so serious, his blue eyes turned to indigo. "That's why I let you get so far ahead of me. Just in case there was a lightning strike, it wouldn't get us both."

"You were hoping it got you first?"

"It would be better if it was me."

She couldn't bear to imagine it. She leaned close, kissed his mezcal smoky mouth. "But it didn't happen." She sat back, forcing a smile to her lips. "And these chile rellenos need finishing."

They dove in with renewed gusto.

Yet the look in his eyes made her heart beat faster and brought tingles to her skin that had nothing to do with sex. The effect was purely emotional. That's what had been in his eyes and his voice. Emotion.

They weren't supposed to feel emotion about each other. This was just friends with benefits, right?

And yet, it felt more like a courtship.

BY THE TIME LAS VEGAS APPEARED ON THE HORIZON THE next day, Noreen had decided she was sick of driving. Her back ached, her butt was sore from sitting so long, and the roar of the Corvette's engine rumbled through her ears long after she climbed out of the car. The trip, with its long hours of driving, was wearing on her. The Sedona to Las Vegas leg was only four and a half hours, but the Austin to Santa Fe run, even with the day off, had done her in. And the drive tomorrow was another long one.

From Vegas, they had a straight shot home. Then it was the end of the line.

And the end of her sojourn with Cutter.

She was jittery and on edge, her nerves fractured. It was all the time on the road, unpacking and packing, it was finally getting to her. After eight days, or was it nine, it could even be…

Raising her hands to count on her fingers, she stopped. Did it matter how many days? She'd even lost track of what day of the week it was.

She lost count of how many times she'd made love with Cutter. Even if it wasn't making *love*. They were sex buddies. She couldn't let it be anything else. Her track record with men was abysmal, and she couldn't bear adding Cutter to her list of failures.

"Are we there yet, Dad?" she called out over the rush of the wind.

"You asked me that five minutes ago."

"Yeah, and I forgot what you said."

The question was moot. She could read the road signs. She just wanted him to feel her pain.

"We'll get there when we get there."

She shouldn't have had that third mezcal margarita last night. That was most likely the source of her problems.

They were close now, already on the outskirts of Las Vegas, and she just wanted to get out of the car to stretch her legs. She could feel the relief flooding her limbs when Cutter exited the freeway.

"Where are we going? This isn't it." The skyscraper hotels of the Las Vegas Strip were still far in the distance.

"It's a surprise."

She groaned. "I really don't want a surprise right now."

"You'll love this one."

"I'm going to hate it, whatever it is."

He looked at her, grinning like the Mad Hatter. Or maybe that was the Cheshire Cat. "You sound like a bratty teenager."

"I know." She pasted a smile over her grimace.

They pulled into the parking lot of the most amazing... "What the heck is this place?"

Cutter finished the thought for her. "It's the Neon Museum."

"You're joking." But she relished the opportunity to get out of the car, easing the aches in her legs and giving her ears a rest from the constant rumble of the engine.

Her legs felt wobbly as she stepped out, and she leaned against the car a moment. Yeah, three mezcal cocktails, never again. But it didn't stop her from running her gaze over the sight before her.

Not so much a museum, more a junkyard of old neon signs.

With only two other cars in the lot, a weathered woman, who could have been anywhere from forty to eighty, greeted them in an effusive, gravelly voice. Her skin leathery from the relentless Nevada sun and her eyes a permanent squint, she spread her arms wide to showcase the lot behind her. And her smile beamed like the sunshine she lived in every day.

"Welcome, welcome! Let me tell you all about the place. We've collected signs from all over, but most of them are Vegas. We can't let these iconic beauties go to the dump, right?"

Cutter handed over the entrance fee posted on a sign nearby.

"Thank you, thank you," she said just as effusively. "Some of our signs are in working order and still light up, just like they once emblazoned the Las Vegas skyline. Some, however, need a little more work, and we do our own refurbishing. Hopefully, one day, we'll have them all lit up for everyone to see." She waved an arm expansively. "If you feel like taking one of these beauties home, they're for sale." Then she flourished toward the yard. "Have fun. Look at them all."

"They're all amazing," Noreen said and actually meant it as they stood before a massive guitar from Hard Rock Cafe.

They wandered rows of old signs from Sahara, Stardust, Caesars, Golden Nugget, a huge genie's lamp—wasn't there a casino called the Aladdin?—Marilyn Monroe, and even Porky Pig, though Noreen decided not to ask where that one came from. There were signs from places she'd never heard of, motels, restaurants, wedding chapels. The sight would have been spectacular at night with the working ones lit up. They strolled just the way the lady had told them to, chuckling at a neon cactus, a clock with a woman swinging on the pendulum, a Liberace sign for the famous pianist.

Then she gasped. "Oh my God, I remember that place. La Rancho."

Cutter stopped beside her, hands on his hips.

"My sister and I made a trip out here after graduation."

"High school?"

She shook her head. "College. Valerie was older and had already graduated, but we came out here to celebrate, and we stayed at La Rancho. It was a fleabag. In fact, we called it La Roacha, the roach motel. But neither of us had the money for something really nice." She wanted to tell him her parents hadn't funded them after leaving college. They were on their own. But she kept that to herself. "I never actually saw a roach, but I wore my slippers because the carpet crunched when I walked on it." She laughed at the memories. "We had the absolute best time. I was about to get married, and this was the last road trip. The freedom trip."

"Sounds like a lot of fun," he said drily.

She was so excited that she ignored the odd look he gave her. "Back then, there were still cabaret shows, and all you had to do was buy a drink to see them. The all-you-can-eat buffets were cheap and if you gambled, even playing the slots, they brought you free drinks. So we found penny slots side-by-side and got all our drinks for free." She pulled out her phone. "I have to take a picture for Valerie. She'll be astounded."

Cutter held out his hand. "Give me your phone. I'll take a picture with you in it."

She couldn't say why the sign made her so happy, except that it had been such a fun trip. Life and failed marriages hadn't gotten their grip on her yet.

"We were just fun-loving sisters out having a great time," she told him, smiling for the camera.

Seeing the sign and remembering that trip erased her grumpy mood over the last couple of hours. She looped her arm through Cutter's and pulled him along, seeking other fabulous finds. But nothing touched her like the La Rancho sign.

Still, it was fun, and as they left, she told the woman, "Thank you so much. I found the sign for a motel my sister and I stayed at. It brought back wonderful memories."

The woman's smile crinkled her eyes to tiny slits. "That's what we're all about here, saving memories."

It was midafternoon, with bio breaks and stopping at the Neon Museum, but after looking at the map on her phone, Noreen said, "There's a really cool building nearby. Can we drive by it before we go down to the Strip?"

He shrugged and grinned. "Whatever you want."

"It's pretty close to the Costco, and we can fill up with gas there."

"Sounds good."

They stopped at the gas station, then she directed him down a wide boulevard and had him park across the street.

"That is the strangest building I've ever seen," Cutter said, gazing across the road as cars flew by them.

"It's the Lou Ruvo Center for Brain Health, an Alzheimer's research facility." It looked like misshapen blocks that were melting down, curving, almost giving the sense of undulating. "The structure is supposed to represent the building blocks of a person's mind, or at least of their brain cells."

"Looking at it makes me feel like I'm on a roller coaster."

"My friend Tammy, her mom had Alzheimer's. There was a lot of information on the website for this place. Her mom was having visions problems, seeing double, and we took her to the optometrist for a pair of reading glasses even though she actually had pretty good eyesight. Of course, the glasses didn't work, and she just kept closing one eye all the time. Tammy found a podcast through their website that talked about how the brain stops being able to process images in the same way. It's like monovision. So she was closing her eyes to stop seeing double."

As he gazed at the incredible building, Cutter said, "Getting old sucks."

She groaned. "It totally sucks."

Then he shrugged. "But we're not there yet."

"Right." She laughed. "Sixty is the new forty."

"Yeah. And that means we shouldn't squander the rest of what we have."

She looked at him. "What you want to do with the rest of your years?"

After a deep, thoughtful breath, he mused, "I'd like to find a Corvette of my own and drive her to Baja. And over the great Canadian Highway. And since we just drove the southern route across the country, I'd like to go north, see some of the National parks, Mount Rushmore in South Dakota, The Devil's Tower in Wyoming, and Jellystone too." She laughed at the reference to the old Yogi Bear cartoons of their youth. "Maybe make it all the way to Crater Lake."

"That sounds marvelous. Crater Lake is breathtaking. I

took the girls there. It might be lonely by yourself." She felt nostalgic for this trip, especially now it was almost over.

He looked at her then, something strange in his eye. "Oh, I wouldn't go on my own."

Who would go with him? A girlfriend? Zeke? She was afraid to ask. She didn't want to think of him taking a road trip with another woman. No, he wouldn't want to drive with a woman again. He'd pick a guy friend.

After a semitruck passed, vibrating in her chest, he asked, "What do you want to do with the rest of your time?"

She didn't have an answer. People would say travel or spend more time with the grandkids or work in the garden, grow fruit trees or prize roses. But Noreen honestly couldn't say. She didn't want to give up her career until full retirement age, but since she didn't have a significant other, she'd given little thought beyond that.

And finally she admitted, "I really don't know." Which sounded pathetic. Just because she was alone didn't mean she couldn't have dreams.

But she actually loved Cutter's dream, driving across the country, visiting beautiful parks, hiking, relaxing. Loving.

23

"**E**ven if sixty is the new forty," Cutter repeated Noreen's words, "You still need to get a move on and figure it out." Then he started the engine. "Come on, let's go see the Strip."

She wasn't a teenager who needed to decide what she wanted to do with her life. Yet maybe the decision was even more dire because time was dwindling. She was already two-thirds of the way through her life. If she was lucky and lived into her nineties. It was a fact she didn't want to ponder because right now, the option for the rest of her life was to go it alone. The thought was kind of scary. What if her girls decided never to have children? Even worse, what if they had children and their lives were so busy they barely had time for her?

She couldn't think about it anymore. So she slipped on her sunglasses and waved her hand in the air. "The Strip, let's walk the whole thing."

There was actually an old strip and a new strip. The old strip was the Vegas you saw in black-and-white movies. The new strip was Caesars, Bellagio, Mirage, all the way along to Mandalay Bay.

Noreen had chosen the Bellagio to stay at, getting a good deal because it was midweek and she was booking at the last minute. The hotel obviously wanted to fill up their rooms even at a cut rate. After parking in the underground garage, they checked in, though their room wasn't ready yet. The concierge stowed their bags so they didn't have to schlep them back to the car.

Then they set out on their walk of the Las Vegas Strip and hit the pavement just as the Bellagio's water show was beginning, the fountains dancing and swirling and shooting high to the thrum of the music. Crowds crushed against the railings to watch.

"Spectacular, don't you think?" she shouted into his ear.

Cutter nodded. "It's actually pretty cool."

While she was all enthusiastic words and gestures, he was low-key.

After the show ended, they headed past the Forum Shops at Caesars and the replica of the Colosseum. It was hot, and the throng along the sidewalks was thick. If it was like this midweek and not as crowded, she'd hate to see it at the height of the season on a weekend. At the next corner, a small troupe of dancers put on an amazing show, hand-walking, somersaults, flips, and turns. All to the beat of funky music.

Cutter threw some bills into the big utility bucket the group had set out. "They're really pretty good."

She agreed, but was still surprised he'd contributed.

A man dressed all in gold, his hands, face, and neck painted to match, stood on a plinth as unmoving as a statue. She couldn't even detect his breath. Cabaret dancers in costume took pictures with tourists, ladies with mountains of feathers in skimpy costumes, two wannabe body builders wearing cowboy hats, vests, and chaps barely covering their essentials.

Cutter jutted his chin. "Do you want a couple of pictures with those guys? You could even have them hoist you in the air."

She shuddered. "I'd be afraid they'd drop me."

He winked at her. "Chicken."

The exploding volcano show at the Mirage played only after dark, but all the street entertainment was rollicking fun.

"There used to be a pirate show at Treasure Island, two pirate ships attacking each other. But now it's just a bunch of shops," she said sadly as they passed the hotel.

Crossing the street at the next corner, they strolled back along the other side, stopping at the Venetian for a rather unimpressive gondola ride around the lagoon, and then to Paris to ride the elevator to the top of the Eiffel tower where the view was magnificent. Taking the pedestrian bridge over the road, the facade of New York-New York filled the skyline, and beyond that, the Excalibur, Luxor, and Mandalay Bay.

"My feet ache," she confessed, and Cutter pulled her out to the monorail which went back to New York-New York.

"We absolutely have to do the roller coaster," she said, standing across the street from the big hotel with its replica of the Statue of Liberty. The screams of the riders floated down to them as the roller coaster rolled completely upside down in a loop.

They found that the line wasn't terribly long, and she grabbed Cutter's arm. "If we get the daily pass, we could ride the roller coaster over and over."

Dropping his sunglasses down, Cutter gave her a look over the rims. Then he bought two single tickets. "Once is probably enough." As they climbed on, he said, "You have to hold my hand. I'm scared of roller coasters."

She laughed. "You're such a dork." But she held his hand,

and his touch felt good. She didn't want to analyze just how good he was. Or how she'd feel when he flew back to Key West.

She screamed and shouted and held her hands in the air, taking his with her. And it was exhilarating. "I can't remember the last time I went on a roller coaster," she said as they stepped onto the platform, her legs wobbly.

"What about your girls? Didn't you take them to an amusement park and do all the rides with them?"

She laughed with the memory as they wended their way through the casino and out to the street. "The Santa Cruz Beach Boardwalk in the summers. They had concerts on the beach. We saw The Monkees there." And smiling, she shrugged. "Well, not actually The Monkees. One time it was Davy Jones, and another it was Micky Dolenz. The Board-walk shows movies, too, anything that featured Santa Cruz, like *The Lost Boys* with Kiefer Sutherland and one of the *Dirty Harry* movies, *Sudden Impact*. And we all rode the Giant Dipper, the big wooden roller coaster, as many times as we could."

"You were a good mom."

Everyone liked to think they were a good parent, but she wondered. With her four marriages and all the fighting, had she been as good as she wanted to be? "They're good girls. Really smart, and they've done good things with their lives. So yeah, I hope I was a good mom."

Finally back at the Bellagio, the room was ready. "I'm starving."

After they'd dropped their bags off, he sat next to her on the bed, smiling. "You're always starving." But he grabbed his phone. "I'll find you the best place to eat."

She tapped on her phone. "Not if I find it first."

In the end, he won, locating a Brazilian place at the mall across the street. "Have you ever had Brazilian?"

She shook her head, and he laughed out loud. "Then you are going to love this with your bottomless pit of a stomach."

"I'm not a bottomless pit," she argued, pretending affront.

He pulled her up and reeled her in for a kiss, whispering against her lips, "You've fully demonstrated that your appetites are huge." Reaching down, he squeezed her butt, pulling her tight against him.

"Speaking of appetites," she murmured.

He let her go abruptly, backing up, laughing. "You have to wait to fill *those* appetites."

Suddenly, inexplicably, a pain pierced her deep in her belly.

She was almost home. This trip was almost over. He would be gone soon.

And she would be alone.

But she couldn't let herself think about that now. There was tonight and tomorrow still to enjoy. "Well," she said with a saucy bite in her tone, "If you won't fill *that* appetite, then take me for the Brazilian."

Brazilian turned out to be all-you-can-eat. They chose their salads, their sides, and the potatoes. Then the fun began.

Wait staff roamed the dining room with huge skewers of meat, lamb carved right off the bone, prime rib, filet mignon wrapped in bacon, shrimp, pork tenderloin, chicken drumsticks marinated in teriyaki.

"Oh my God." She groaned. "This is so good."

She ate too much, of course, stopping men with skewers far too often. "My girls would love this."

Cutter got out his phone, typed, scrolled, and finally, he gave her a self-satisfied grin. "I found a Brazilian place that'll be perfect for you. It's in San Jose, somewhere called Santana Row."

She clapped her hands. "That's almost halfway between

Grace and April. I told you April's over in Santa Cruz. Grace can pick me up, and we can meet at Santana Row." She knew the shopping district well and felt jubilant, as if she could give the girls an amazing gift.

She was full, but they got the papaya cream for dessert, fresh papaya with vanilla ice cream, and that was delicious too. Yes, the girls would love Brazilian.

Finally out on the sidewalk, she felt like she was waddling and blew out a deep breath. "Oh, I ate way too much. But it was all so good."

Cutter took her arm. "Let's walk it off."

On the opposite side of the street from New York-New York, they wandered through the MGM Grand and over to the new Tropicana.

Still holding Cutter's arm, Noreen said, "We can't come all the way to Las Vegas and not do a bit of gambling."

Cutter laughed. "You mean a lot of losing."

She shook her head, her ears assaulted by the music and croupiers calling out and the counterfeit chink of slot machines, which were all electronic now.

She leaned in close to say, "Here's my system. I play twenty dollars and when I lose it, I'm done. But if I'm winning, I play only till I double my money. And I always play the penny slots."

"You can't win big on the penny slots," he scoffed.

She widened her eyes and smiled. "You'd be surprised. With the penny machines, you can play all the lines and boost your chances of winning."

He laughed. "Jesus, you're a gambler with a system all worked out."

She smiled. "Only for twenty dollars."

They had quite a search to find it, but finally discovered a small area with a few penny slots, taking two machines right next to each other. And the machine sucked in their money.

"I miss the old days of the one-armed bandits." Cutter sighed.

"Yes, but my arm got tired."

"That means you were winning. Or you'd have stopped playing."

They both followed her strategy, penny slots playing all the lines, and the mechanical sound of coins chunking into their bins filled up the air. Of course, there was no money, just a voucher, but it was still fun to hear the noise when she won.

She was up and she was down, then up again, and finally, Cutter grimaced, "I've only got a dollar left."

"Just play it out," she told him.

She was down to three dollars and the fun would soon be over, but she figured it was her entertainment budget, the shouting when someone won big, the tears when they lost. It was all good fun, almost like going to the movies. She loaded up and pushed the button three more times.

And her machine went absolutely bonkers, bells and whistles and cheers enough to burst her eardrums. And Noreen stared at her winnings, not believing it for a moment.

She grabbed Cutter's arm, pulled him over to see. "Oh my God, I just want a thousand dollars."

Up on her feet without even realizing she'd moved, she jumped around and Cutter hugged her while people crowded close as if being near a winner would rub off.

Having lost his last dollar, Cutter said, "Now you can keep playing for hours."

She shook her head, her body still thrumming, and it wasn't just the thousand-dollar win. It was the way he held her so tightly against his body.

"That's my other rule." She shook her head. "Once I win big, not that I've ever won this big, I cash out."

So that's what they did, printing her voucher and taking it to the cashier.

The moment they vacated the machine, gamblers fought over who would take it over. But after a payout like hers, the slot would probably be a loser for the rest of the night, sucking down all the cash it had just given away.

She got the money in tens and twenties, the cashier looking at her like she was crazy. And maybe she was.

"Better watch out for pickpockets," Cutter said dryly.

"We're going straight back to the room." She tucked the money carefully into her purse and slung it across her body, hugging it tight to her abdomen.

If anyone followed, she didn't see them, and Cutter stayed close, holding her beneath his arm, his eyes sharp.

"It's terrible that we're scared someone's going to rob us."

"I don't know whether it's truly a method, but I've heard that people hang out looking for winners."

They made it back to the Bellagio without being accosted and once in the room, Cutter bolted the door while Noreen took the money out of her bag.

"I've always wanted to do this." Climbing on the bed, she threw the money in the air, laughing as bills rained down on her.

"And I've always wanted to do this." Cutter jumped on the mattress with her, on top of the money, on top of her, and kissed her until she couldn't breathe. Then he stripped off her clothes and made love to her amid all those bills.

And it was glorious.

IT HAD BEEN A PRETTY DAMN AMAZING NIGHT, AND AFTER making love to Noreen on a bed of cash, he'd taken her downstairs for a glass of champagne. She was frugal about the oddest things, and despite her winnings, she didn't buy the best. "I don't want to just throw it all away again."

They went out for a stroll to the Mirage to watch the volcano show, which only played at night. It was thrilling enough, but the Bellagio's water show was actually better, and they went back to watch it once more, different music playing now, making the show altogether different as well.

Finally back upstairs, they'd made love all over again. There was something astounding about rubbing all that money on their bodies, making love in it, falling asleep in it.

In the morning, he laughed when Noreen made sure she found every single bill. And then she left an extremely nice tip for the maid.

Then they were heading home. Her home. They'd arrive before nightfall.

Cutter felt the miles rolling away like a wrenching of his heart.

Leaving Nevada for California, they drove by an abandoned amusement park near the border, its roller coaster idle. And his mood spiraled, as if the dead roller coaster echoed the end of the trip, the end of them.

Farther on, passing a strange art installation in the middle of the desert, brightly colored blocks stacked on top of each other, Noreen cried out. "Go back, go back. We have to stop. We need pictures."

He wondered if she didn't want to go home any more than he did. But no, everything she loved was back in the San Francisco Bay Area. It was where she belonged. Of course she wanted to go home.

Would she ever think about selling him the Corvette?

He thought of ways he could stay in contact. He could fly out to visit the car, make love to her, and one day she wouldn't want him to leave again.

The thought was pathetic. She'd left all those years ago, and he'd been fine. He'd be fine again. Except for the XB-70.

As he watched her dancing like a child around the multi-colored stones—which were probably made of Styrofoam—he wondered just how fine he'd be. He'd gotten used to waking up beside her, gotten used to her kiss, her touch, her taste, her laugh, her arms around him. He'd miss her excitement, her enthusiasm for simple things like colored rocks in a barren desert, neon signs in a boneyard, Batmobiles in a car museum, all-you-can-eat Brazilian steakhouses, the XB-70. And him.

After a late breakfast at a diner in an outlet mall, she shopped but found nothing she wanted. And again, he had to wonder if she was stalling.

But Noreen had only ever wanted a week. Or a summer. She'd sworn off men, at least boyfriends, husbands, and relationships.

He'd gone along with it all, relegated himself to being her friend with benefits and her mechanic. And even if he flew out to the west coast to see her, or invited her back to Key West, he'd still be only a sex buddy to Noreen Kincaid.

It was all he'd ever been to her.

24

The Corvette blew through Barstow, which was about halfway home, when Noreen got the jitters.

It wasn't because she'd had too much to drink last night. She'd downed plenty of water, wanting to make sure she didn't get tipsy.

It was all the miles they'd driven. And the very few they had left.

With each mile the car whirled away from Las Vegas, with each mile they drew closer to San Francisco. And each mile took her farther away from Cutter.

When the trip was over, he'd catch his flight and be gone.

She'd gotten used to having him around. And in her bed. He made her laugh, and God, how he made her scream with pleasure.

How much she'd missed good sex over the years hadn't really hit her until Cutter came back into her life. She'd always remembered how good it had been with him during that Corvette summer. But these last ten days had been amazing, surpassing all her memories, surpassing all her marriages. She honestly didn't know how she was going to live without it.

How she'd live without him.

And she started making plans.

He didn't have to leave right away. They hadn't booked a flight yet. He could stay a few extra days. Yes, that would be wonderful.

Except that he was a working man, and he had to get back or he wouldn't have a job to go back to. Even if he could buy the Corvette, he wasn't made of money, and he couldn't afford to lose that job. Just like he couldn't afford to fly out to see her every three or four months.

But she had the money to do it.

What if he didn't want her to fly out to the Keys? What if he was happy to see the end of their cross-country trek?

God, she'd do anything to make him stay, even if it was just a little while.

They hit traffic in Bakersfield on Highway 99, and then they cut across to Highway 5, stopping to gas up again in Lost Hills.

Cutter asked, "The GPS says we can either continue on Highway 5 and cross at Highway 152, which is faster. Or we can cross over here and get on Highway 101."

"Let's cross here. We can stop at the marker for James Dean. He had his accident on this road." The stop would take time. She'd have a few more minutes to plan.

"Sounds good."

At one time, the highway had been a two-lane road all the way across the valley between 101 and 5, but they'd widened most of it to four lanes, except the central part.

They didn't talk much. She put it down to the wind and the engine. And yet they both seemed mired in their own thoughts. He was probably wondering how fast he could book his flight out.

Coasting down the last big hill, before the James Dean Junction, she imagined the movie star roaring through here in his Porsche Spyder, unaware what awaited him.

Stopping at the memorial just past the junction, Cutter paid homage to another sports car lover.

And they were getting closer, ever closer to home.

Her nerves were actually jangling as the two-lane blacktop split into four lanes again. Paso Robles was only twenty miles. Then it was only three and a half hours to her house.

They would be there before dinnertime.

Of course, he'd spend the night, but...

She couldn't bear for this journey to end.

As they drew into Paso Robles, she said, "Pull over here. I need a Starbucks."

She needed something.

She ordered a mocha, hot, even though it was warm out, and Cutter had a mango dragon fruit. As they sat on the benches outside, she ventured another plan. "I know it's a lot faster to go up 101, but we could cut across to Highway 1 and drive up the coast. That way you'd get to see Cambria and Big Sur and we'll cross the Bixby Bridge. Did you ever see *Play Misty for Me* with Clint Eastwood?"

He nodded. "Yeah, great movie." But a question hung on the end of his words.

"There's a scene where he's driving over the Bixby Bridge in his Jaguar, or whatever kind of car he was driving."

"It's a 1957 Jaguar XK 150 Drophead Coupé."

She laughed. "Of course you'd know that." Then she bit her lip, hoping he'd agree to her idea. "So let's be like Clint Eastwood and drive the Corvette over the Bixby Bridge."

"You're totally on." He held up his palm to high-five her. "I thought about going along the coast anyway."

Thank God. She wanted to punch the air.

They hit Highway 1 just before Cambria and headed

north, passing Hearst Castle. "Do you want to tour Hearst Castle?" she yelled over the wind, pointing to the monument way up on the hill.

He shook his head. "No, just the Bixby Bridge."

They probably couldn't get tickets. The tours sold out weeks in advance.

The highway wound up and down along the cliffs, the ocean blue and bright as they flew by. And all the while, time ticked away. Yes, the coast road would take longer, but she'd still be home tonight.

"I'm starving," she said as they neared Big Sur. "There's a restaurant just up here, Nepenthe, with fabulous burgers and an awe-inspiring view of the ocean. Let's eat."

It was the perfect stopping point. She ordered a BLT while Cutter had a huge burger and they shared fries.

The ocean was incredible, the waves crashing below them. "It's too bad it's not whale season. We might've seen them spouting. They swim right by here."

When they were done, it was time to get back in the car. But she couldn't do it. She just couldn't. She wasn't ready to go home.

She wasn't ready for him to leave.

"I've got a fabulous idea. Let's spend the night in Carmel. It's gorgeous there. We can walk on the beach and eat at Clint Eastwood's restaurant."

"But we just ate," he said, giving her a frown.

"This was a late lunch, so we can do a late dinner. There're some amazing little hotels in Carmel. It's a really cute town. And I'll show you some places they filmed *Play Misty for Me*." She wasn't sure she could remember, but so what, it would be another night. Then maybe another day.

He was looking at her as if he could see right through her, as if he knew she needed one more night with him, especially in a romantic Carmel hotel.

"Yeah. Sure. If that's what you want," he agreed. But she sensed his reluctance in his clipped sentences.

"Do you need to get back right away? I don't want to put your job in jeopardy."

He shook his head. "My job isn't in jeopardy," he said a little too sharply.

And he drove them into Carmel. Passing Point Lobos, she thought about asking him if he wanted to take a walk. The beautiful state park ran along the cliffs with marvelous views of the ocean and Carmel beaches. Or they could walk along the bluffs at the other end, to China Cove, where the water was turquoise and seals cavorted on the sand or slept in the sun.

But there was something about the cast of his face that made her hesitate. Not a scowl, definitely not a glare, just a stoniness that had grown over the miles. If he wanted, they could hike the park in the morning. It was only a couple of hours back home. There'd be time.

She found a lovely hotel that was only a few blocks from the ocean and Carmel Beach. And it had a vacancy.

Spreading her arms wide after they set their bags down in the room, she smiled. Even though he didn't. "This is adorable."

A cozy queen with a thick comforter sat in front of an inviting fireplace. If it got cold when the sun went down, they could light the fire. "And we can take a bath in that delightful clawfoot tub," she added, leaning in the bathroom doorway with both hands on the jamb.

Cutter didn't enthuse the way she did, but he was a guy, and enthusing about a hotel room wasn't in his DNA.

"Would you like to go for a walk on the beach?" she asked, feeling the tension in her voice and hoping he didn't hear it. "We're really lucky with the weather. It's still sunny out, while Carmel is often socked in with fog."

"Okay."

Just that one-word answer. Had she overstepped some invisible boundary by suggesting an extra night? It was just that she wasn't ready to let the trip end. "Is everything all right?"

It was such a typical question. She couldn't remember the number of times she'd asked that in any of her marriages. It was so difficult figuring out what men wanted. Men held everything in while women tried prying it out. It was a dance as old as time.

She just didn't want this dance with Cutter. She'd thought they were different together.

But all he said was, "I'm fine."

So she opted for the walk. Slipping off her sandals when they got to the beach, the sand warmed her soles as she ran down to the water's edge. A wave splashed halfway up her calves, and she squealed at the cold water.

Cutter, still wearing his shoes, bent down to stick his hand in the sea. "Jesus, that's cold."

She laughed. "Of course. It's Monterey Bay. You should try taking a dip in February. Talk about a cold plunge."

The beach was littered with families on blankets, couples strolling at the water's edge, children splashing and shrieking in the waves, dogs chasing frisbees. The sand stretched in a long crescent all the way from Pebble Beach to the Clinton Walker House, designed by Frank Lloyd Wright, on the southern point.

They'd entered in the middle. "Which way do you want to go?"

He pointed south, and they headed that way. He said little. She wouldn't it call grumpy, more thoughtful.

Oh hell, she didn't know what was going through his mind.

Until finally he said, "About the car."

She laughed, not feeling the humor at all. "You're not trying to get me to sell you the car again, are you?"

He looked at her, stone-faced. "Yeah, I am. She ran great on the way here. I can drive her all the way back too."

After everything they'd shared, that he could actually bring up the car now pissed her off. She wasn't even sure why. Maybe because it was the last day and the last night, and the last thing she wanted to talk about was that freaking car.

"I'm hanging onto it," she said stubbornly. "But what about my idea? You can come out here every three or four months, take her for long drives, be my mechanic." She felt her excitement rising. This could work. She could pay his way, pay him to take care of the car. "You can go over all her hoses and her pipes and her pumps every few months and keep her in perfect running order. I'll even fly you out here. And then..." she shrugged, smiled, hoping it was seductive, afraid it wasn't. Maybe it was just silly.

He didn't laugh or even smile. "And then what?"

Okay, so this was embarrassing. But hadn't he enjoyed everything they'd done? Hadn't he said, at least somewhere along the way, how good the sex was? She didn't want to let it go. But now she wasn't sure about him.

She shrugged again and lamely said, "You know." That was all she could get out.

"I can what?" he murmured. "Service you? You'll fly me out here every quarter to service your car and you at the same time?"

They'd talked about this before, even laughed about it. It had been a fun joke. So why was he upset now?

And he added, "You expect me to be your stud?"

She stopped, put her hands on her hips, looked at him instead of the dog rushing by to catch the ball his owner had thrown. "My stud?" Her voice came out harsh, and yes, she was more than pissed now. She was angry.

"Yeah, your stud. Your stallion. Your man toy. Your gigolo."

Her laugh sounded more like a cough. "What is wrong with you?"

"I don't like being nothing more than your piece of meat."

"Well, women have been men's pieces of meat for centuries. Now you know how it feels." She didn't raise her voice, yet people were looking at them. Maybe it was their stance, the anger vibrating in the air around them. "If you don't want to deal, just say so. You were the one who brought up the car."

"I brought it up to make you a decent offer, not an indecent one."

Throwing her hands in the air, she turned back to him, lowering her voice. "An indecent offer? We've been sleeping together for days now." She waited for a couple to pass before she hissed, "Was that indecent?"

"It was sport. But now the trip is over. And you have to decide."

Sport. God, that hurt. "I've decided. I'm not selling the car. I told you that from the beginning." Where the hell was all this coming from? Last night they'd been loving, laughing.

"That's not the decision I'm talking about."

He was angry, just like she was, but there was something else, something deeper she couldn't fathom. "I don't even understand what you're asking."

He looked at her a long moment, his gaze roaming her face, her cheeks, her lips, then finally back up to her eyes. "I'll lay it out for you then. All those years ago, you walked away without a backward glance and never came back."

"But you knew that was my last summer." She shook her head, not getting it at all. "I was going off to college the next year when I graduated high school."

"Right. And I was just a boy toy, your summer fling. And

now it's the same thing all over again. Just your mechanic, your driver, and your friend with benefits."

"I thought you enjoyed everything we did. Back then and now."

She was conscious enough to keep her voice low as two guys passed them, throwing a stick for their dog.

Cutter licked his lips, shut his mouth, opened it again.

"What?" she pressed.

"Let's walk," he said, obviously deciding not to finish the rest, and took off, back the way they'd come.

She scrambled to catch up to him. "You can't just stop right in the middle of an argument."

He didn't even look at her. "Actually, I can. There's nothing left to say."

He walked so fast, she was almost running to keep. "Where are you going?" she called after him when he climbed back up the beach to the parking lot.

"I'm going for a drive," he threw over his shoulder. "You can go to the room."

His voice was so cold, she shivered. "But it's my car."

He stopped then, so fast she bumped into him. "I know it's your car," he said, his tone icy. "But I'm taking it out for a drive anyway."

When they reached the hotel, he drove off without a backward glance.

In her car.

25

Cutter drove down the coast, the wind off the ocean blowing through his hair and hopefully clearing his mind. If that were even possible.

He flew past Point Lobos, Highway 1 clogged with vehicles trying to get into the park, the side of the road packed with parked cars. Cutter didn't stop. He needed speed and a fast car and miles beneath the tires.

Blazing over the Bixby Bridge Noreen loved so much, the ocean beyond was like blue glass, waves rising as they came into shore, the sand dotted with drying kelp.

And still he drove on, something roiling in his gut that only the rolling of the car could appease. The sea here was so different from his beloved Key West and yet it soothed him. And finally he pulled to the side in a turnout with a vista of the ocean. Cutting the engine, he climbed out and clambered up on the rocks overlooking the water, sitting atop the highest with his hands draped over his knees, the fresh sea scent rushing through him.

And now he could think rationally. Why the hell had he gotten so angry?

She was the same person she'd been all those years ago. And maybe that was the problem. He was the same man, finally admitting he had the same dream of old, at least where she was concerned.

He felt her eking out a few extra days, a few more nights. Just like she had when they were young and trying to pack everything into the few days they had left.

He'd never told her what he'd wanted, what he'd hoped, what he'd dreamed. But then she'd never asked. She hadn't wanted to know.

And he was pretty damn sure she didn't want to know now.

He'd never had trouble telling people how things were going to work. He decided to go to university and he'd done it. He'd hated the job he got after graduating and he'd moved on. He'd had affairs with women who wanted completely different things than he did and he walked away. He'd bought his first auto repair, then his second, and he'd never let anyone stop him from turning it into the franchise it was today.

Yet still, he hadn't spelled it out for Noreen. He hadn't said exactly what he needed from her, not then and not now. Maybe that's why he'd gotten so pissed. Not with her, but with himself, for his inability to just freaking say it out loud.

To just tell her he didn't want a couple of weeks every three or four months. He didn't want to just look after her car. He didn't want to be just her stud who serviced her a few times a year.

He wanted it all. The way he had forty years ago.

And had never asked.

THE SCENT OF LAVENDER PERMEATED THE ROOM WHEN HE opened the door. And she was nowhere to be seen.

The sound of gentle splashing drifted from the bathroom. This was bad, really bad. Naked in the tub, she was too hard to resist. If he wasn't careful, he'd slip down into the water with her and forget everything that had to be said.

"You're back." Her face brightened with a smile when he stood in the doorway, as if she'd been afraid he'd drive the car all the way back to Key West.

"I never intended to leave. I just wanted to clear my head."

She blinked, a signal of how badly she wanted to ask. And yet she didn't.

Instead of opening his mouth, he pulled his shirt over his head, let it drop to the tile floor. Her eyes went wide when he shucked his pants, then shoved his briefs down his legs.

The water was gorgeously hot when he climbed in, sliding his legs along hers, and settling opposite her. Bubbles covered her to the neck.

Leaning back, he propped his arms along the sides of the clawfoot. "I want the car."

"I know," she answered just as softly.

"And I want you."

"I want you too," she admitted, and he was damn sure it wasn't the way he meant.

"Not for just a service every few months." An ache squeezed his chest, but he didn't wait for her to deny or qualify. "I let you fly away forty years ago without telling you I needed you to come back."

With a small shake of her head, she whispered, "But we were just friends."

He breathed in deeply. "I was never just your friend. I wanted you that first summer when you were fourteen and I

285

was fifteen. And I wanted you that last summer more than you could possibly know."

"But you argued when I wanted you to teach me how to kiss."

"I argued because I didn't want to be your experiment."

She licked her lips. "I didn't understand."

"Maybe I didn't fully understand until you were gone." He reached out to take her hand in his, lacing their fingers along the tub's rim. "I was too much of a coward to say how I felt. I didn't have the courage to tell you because I was just a grease monkey with nothing to offer you." She opened her mouth, and he couldn't let her deny it; they both knew it was true. "So I worked like hell to get a scholarship and earn my degree."

Something registered on her face, maybe shock. "You didn't have to do that for me."

"Maybe I had to do it for me." In the end, even if he hated the office job, he was glad he'd done it. But he laughed softly. "I had dreams of flying out to San Francisco and showing you my diploma." And the laugh turned into a mocking snort. "But then Mortimer got your wedding invitation."

She didn't say anything. There was nothing to say. But he'd driven back across the Bixby Bridge to say what he should have said forty years ago. Even if the answer was still no.

"I loved you then. And I love you now."

HER PULSE RUSHED THROUGH HER EARS SO FAST SHE COULD barely hear his words, had to read his lips to be sure.

He loved her.

It wasn't possible.

Yet her heart beat harder in her chest, and tears welled in

her eyes. "You don't have to say that just because you want the car."

"I want the damn car only if you come with it."

"But—" She didn't know what else to say.

She wasn't even sure how she felt. She didn't want him to leave, yet she couldn't let him go, with or without the car. But love?

And she said the only thing she knew. "I'm not sure about love. I've made so many mistakes. Hurt so many people. I can't trust myself to know anymore. And I don't want to hurt anyone else, especially not you."

He squeezed her fingers. "You said you have the worst taste in men. But maybe you just gave your trust to men who didn't deserve it." He pulled her in until her legs slid over his hips, and they were seated so closely she could see the silvery flecks in his blue eyes. "But I'm not a wife beater, a cheater, a criminal, or a control freak." He smiled with a hint of sadness. "At least I don't think I'm a control freak."

He kissed her so gently, a tear slid down her cheek.

"All I want is a chance," he whispered. "And you deserve a chance too."

"It's been so good." She only realized she'd said the words aloud when he kissed the corner of her mouth.

"It can be even better."

It could be. But... "I don't understand why you didn't tell me back then."

He closed his eyes, breathed in sharply, shook his head. "Because I was too damn proud. You had everything. You were smart and beautiful and funny and so damn sexy. And I was just a poor local kid with grease under my nails. I didn't want to compete with all your high-brow friends back home."

She snorted a laugh that hurt inside. "I wasn't high-brow."

"You went to a private school."

"Yeah, but that didn't make me better than you." But

hadn't she thought how her parents would kill her if she stayed in Key West with a boy who was a mechanic? Hadn't she judged? Telling herself they were just friends protected her from a decision she could never make.

Then he'd gone out and gotten a college education just to show her he was good enough. And yet he was still a mechanic. Why?

And she was still judging. But if she needed to judge, then she had to admit that he was better than any of the men she'd ever thought she loved.

"It's okay," he said. "We were both who we were. And I don't care. But this time, I'm not letting you go without a fight." He pulled her tight against him, showed her exactly how well he could fight.

"You're a talented cook," she murmured. "And you really know how to treat a girl right, breakfast in bed, appetizers in the bathtub, great choice in music, fabulous choices on places to stay."

"And there's so much more to me you don't even know yet." He smiled wickedly.

"But what Key West versus San Francisco?"

He shrugged. "We could be snowbirds, half time on the west coast, half time on Key West, depending on the weather." He could obviously tell she was weakening.

"But what about your job?"

"I've been thinking that I need a change."

"That easily?"

He nodded. "Yeah, that easily." Then he added. "I've got enough for a good retirement nest egg. I don't have to live off you."

That's what Rodney had said. But Cutter was different. She knew it deep in her soul. In her heart. She'd always known he was good, honorable. That's why she'd trusted him with her body that summer.

And maybe he was right. After him, she'd trusted all the wrong men. "I don't know," she said softly, looking deep inside herself. "I've made so many mistakes for so long." And finally she looked at him. "I've always lived up to everyone else's expectations, my mother's, my family's, even my husbands'."

"Maybe it's time you lived up to your own expectations."

"I'm not sure I even know what they are."

He reached out to run his thumb across her lips. "You know. You just need to give yourself permission."

Could she let herself trust him again?

Was that even the right question?

The real question was whether she could trust *herself*. And whether she wanted to be alone for the rest of her life because she was too frightened to take another chance.

"Do you love me?" he asked so softly it was a caress.

And maybe that was the *only* question that mattered.

"I've thought about you for forty years," she confessed. "And I've always compared the men I was with to you." After a breath, or maybe it was a sigh, she added, "And in the end, none of them lived up to my memories of you."

His eyes seemed to bore right into her. "And that means?"

She cupped his cheeks and met his gaze. "It means that I must have always loved you."

His lips curved in a sweet and naughty smile, he pulled her close as he leaned back, taking her with him until she straddled him. "That's a good enough declaration for me."

And he kissed her the way no man but him ever had.

EPILOGUE

Cutter had been staying with her for five days when Noreen finally decided it was time for a welcome barbecue to introduce him to the important people in her life.

Jitters jumbled Noreen's insides. They'd all love Cutter, of course. He was totally lovable. But she wasn't sure how she'd handle all the questions. She'd told Tammy that he wasn't flying home yet, as well as Valerie, but all she'd said to the girls was that she wanted them to meet Cutter.

And she knew the first thing they'd all hint at was that she might be making another of her infamous mistakes. Her reputation was her downfall.

"I'll make the burgers while you get the salad ready," Cutter said, washing his hands, then slipping one of her frilly aprons over his head and tying it in back. It only worked for her when she wrapped the ties around and make a bow in the front.

She laughed. Then she couldn't stop, tears streaming down her cheeks. Fumbling with her camera phone, she could barely see to take a photo. And suddenly, all the jitters evaporated. "You need to wear that when everyone gets here."

He shrugged, raised his brows. "Of course. I'm cooking the Thousand Island burgers, right?"

That just made her laugh and cry harder. "My girls are going to adore you." She didn't even cross her fingers behind her back.

"Didn't your chef husband wear an apron?" he asked as he dumped spices, bread crumbs, and an egg into the ground beef.

She snorted. "His was a manly barbecue apron when he was at home and one of those double-breasted chef's jackets at the restaurant."

He ran his hand over his chest, impressive even with the frills. "I like pink." Then he plunged his hands into the meat, mixing all the ingredients.

She didn't bother with an apron as she sliced raw veggies for the salad. "So," she said, wanting to sound nonchalant. "What should we tell them about our..." She paused, looking for the right word. "Arrangement?"

In the last five days, they'd discussed their pasts when they'd been apart all those years. They daydreamed about the trips they wanted to take in the Corvette, Canada, Baja, all the national parks in all the states. And they talked about what they each wanted their future to look like. Noreen didn't intend to give up her editing business for a few years, and Cutter seriously considered building another sports car. A Lola T70 replica.

And they would live on two coasts. Together. Maybe they'd drive the XB-70 back and forth. Or maybe they'd leave it on Key West, and Cutter could build his Lola out here. That way he'd have a sports car on either coast.

"You mean like what we're going to say when they ask if

I'll be living off you?" He said it without a hint of sarcasm or derision.

Noreen huffed out a breath. "You're retiring. You have a nest egg. And it's none of their business."

Rolling a clump of ground beef in his hands, he plopped it onto the counter and pounded it flat. "It's not. But they'll ask and you'll be embarrassed."

She popped him gently on the arm. "I will not."

"But I'm not a surgeon or a master chef or a financial wizard or an entrepreneur."

"And you're not a wife beater, a cheater, a criminal, or a control freak either."

He grinned. "You're right. I've decided I'm not a control freak."

"Thank God." She ended with a sigh.

"But there's something I need to tell you." He placed a completed burger on a plate.

And her skin chilled. "What?"

"I told you I got my degree in business but couldn't hack it in an office job and I went back to Key West."

"Yes." Her stomach roiled. And yet this was Cutter. She trusted him.

"And I worked at the same shop for a while." Drawing in a breath, he continued as he rolled another patty. "And then I bought it."

"You mean the same shop where I picked up Uncle Mortimer's Corvette?"

"Yeah."

"Wow. That's great." Then she frowned. "Why didn't you tell me that?"

He slapped the ball of meat down on the counter. "I'm not done yet." She waited until he went on. "After that, I bought some more garages. And I called them Budget Auto Repair."

She let that settle inside her. "You said that chain is all over Florida."

"It is. And then I franchised them." He pounded the ball into a patty. "So they're all under the name, but they're individually owned. Like Zeke's shop."

"Oh." She threw sliced carrots on top of the salad, not knowing exactly what he was attempting to tell her. Or how she felt about it. "So this means... what?"

The patty done, he rolled another ball. "It means that I'm not a mechanic anymore. I'm a businessman, but on my own terms."

"So you didn't have to quit your job?"

"No. I just need to make calls, check my emails, voice-mails." He shrugged once more. "And direct my management team."

"You have a management team?" Wonder laced her voice, and she couldn't define the feeling in her chest, whether it was anger or relief or understanding or joy.

"Yes. Although they mostly direct themselves at this point." He looked at her then, his hands covered in raw ground beef. "So you can see that I meant it when I said I don't need to live off you. And that I can take off when I want, do what I want." He held her gaze. "Live wherever I want."

Her automatic thought was that he'd lied to her like all her husbands. And yet her heart didn't feel the betrayal. It felt... *mystified* was the closest word. "Why didn't you tell me?"

"Why do you think?"

"You were testing me." How did she feel about *that*?

He grimaced, shaking his head. "Not really. But I wanted you to want *me*." He tapped the pink apron right over his heart, leaving behind a blob of ground beef. "I didn't want you to suddenly accept me because you'd decided I'd made a success of myself."

"You mean because you didn't believe I thought being a mechanic was a success."

He smiled sadly. "Yeah. Exactly like that."

For the first time, she truly saw the damage she'd done all those years ago, that she'd made him feel *less than*. It had never been her intention. Yet she'd been just like her mother, who'd always believed Uncle Mortimer was a loser, not that Mom ever used the word. *Black sheep* had been a more palatable term. But Noreen had been afraid to tell her mother she'd fallen for a mechanic, as if a man who worked so well with his hands was worth less.

She stepped up next to him and cupped his cheeks. "I'm so sorry. I was young and foolish. And I'm not one to talk after all the mistakes I've made in my life. You were always the kindest, most considerate man I have ever known." She kissed him softly. "And that's why I love you. Not because you went to university or because you started your own company. I love the man you've always been from the moment I met you."

Holding his hamburgery hands aloft, he wrapped his arms around her. "And I love you for giving me the push to do things with my life. And the will to do it my way."

"Love you," she whispered.

"Love you back." Then he lowered his lips to hers for a long, delicious kiss. "Here's to the next third of our life. Together."

Then her doorbell rang through the house.

HER DAUGHTERS WERE AS BEAUTIFUL AS SHE WAS, THE younger one, April, with olive skin, curly dark hair, and a loving smile, the older, Grace, blond and tall like her mother, and perhaps just a little warier than her sister. But Grace was like her name, gracious and trying to be accepting.

Noreen's sister Valerie could have been a clone except for the extra worry lines on her face and the weariness in her eyes. She had sons who'd chosen not to attend the barbecue, and perhaps the sons were part of the worry and weariness. But her strong handshake and her smile welcomed Cutter.

It was the best friend Tammy who threw her arms around him for a big hug, then a kiss on the cheek that her handsome, beefy husband didn't seem to mind. "I've heard so much about you. It's wonderful to finally meet you." She winked with long lashes and tossed her dark hair back off her shoulders, smiling at him with full, ruby red lips.

And he wondered exactly what Noreen had told the woman.

When she said, "Noreen and I were college roommates, in case she didn't tell you," he had a feeling he knew exactly what Noreen had said. Everything about that Corvette summer.

Then the adoring husband shook his hand. "Frank Barlow. Good to meet ya." And he reclaimed his wife with an arm around her shoulders.

Cutter smiled and said his own greetings, then set about finishing the burgers while everyone helped themselves to drinks as if they were regular guests. Which they were. All of Noreen's loved ones. She was a package deal, and he wanted acceptance, not just for her sake, but for his. Because she loved him. She truly loved him. After all these years and all his dreams, he finally believed it with all his heart.

Mortimer would have been happy.

And while the others had gone outside to set the table, start the barbecue, lay out the arrays of salads each of them had brought, he pulled Noreen close. "I like your family."

She smiled, kissed him. "They like you."

"And I think I know exactly why Mortimer left you the XB-70."

She tipped her head in question.

"Because he wanted this, us, together. A family. If he'd sold me the car, none of this would ever have happened." He was getting sentimental, but it sounded like the truth.

Leaning against him, she put her head on his shoulder. "I think you're right." Then she laughed softly. "Too bad he didn't do it forty years ago."

Cutter shook his head. "I don't think either of us was ready back then. So maybe his timing was exactly right."

She sighed. "And I wouldn't have Grace and April. So yeah, Uncle Mortimer's timing was spot on."

FRANK HELPED CUTTER GRILL THE BURGERS, TALKING sports and cars, wanting to know all about the XB-70.

Noreen eavesdropped shamelessly until Tammy leaned into her and whispered, "Oh my God, he's delish. Don't let him get away again."

"I don't intend to," she said, watching the two men. "They seem to get along."

"Sports and cars." Tammy laughed and shrugged. "What else do you expect?"

April and Grace splashed in the pool even though Noreen hadn't turned on the heater. Even in May, the water could still be a little cool. And Valerie stepped through the French doors onto the deck, her features drawn.

"Everything okay?" Noreen asked.

Her sister smiled brilliantly, though it was obviously painted on like she'd paint on her lipstick. Yet despite her drawn features and the dark circles under her eyes, she said,

"It's great. I just forgot to ask Jake to turn on the alarm if he leaves the house."

At the ripe old age of twenty-nine, Jake, Noreen's younger nephew, had moved back into the house just before Noreen left for Florida. His job hadn't worked out. Jake had a lot of jobs that didn't work out. He was a nice kid, but he seemed to have problems finding satisfaction in his work.

Noreen suddenly had a bright idea. Maybe Cutter could talk to him. He'd hated his first job out of university, couldn't stand working in an office, missed Key West, missed working on cars. And he'd found his place, taking a route that gave him the satisfaction he wanted. He would have brilliant advice for Jake on figuring out what he wanted to do with his life. Uncle Mortimer was a good example too. He'd made a life he loved.

Of course, Valerie would kill her if she told Jake he should live in a shack on the beach and charter fishing boats.

And yet it had worked for Uncle Mortimer.

Later, when she had Valerie alone, she'd mention the idea of getting Cutter and Jake together. Maybe it would ease the fatigue on Valerie's face.

Dinner went well, extremely well. Cutter told funny stories about Key West, and the girls asked all about Uncle Mortimer. Then they wanted details about their trip across the country in the Corvette. And Frank was practically hyperventilating as he begged to help when Cutter mentioned building a sports car from the frame up. Tammy winked at Noreen.

As the sun set, they all donned their swimsuits for a little hot tub time.

God, she was happy. She couldn't remember this kind of bliss since her Corvette summer with Cutter. Why had she never recognized it as love?

But she knew why. She'd built her life around so many

expectations, from her parents, her friends, society, her own. Yet now, she no longer had to live with those expectations. Now she could love on her own terms.

And she loved Cutter with all her heart and soul.

CUTTER SORENSON ROSE OUT OF THE HOT TUB, WATER sluicing down his body. "Cold plunge," he called out, holding his hand down to Noreen.

"You're joking, right?" she scoffed. "I don't get in that pool unless it's at least seventy-eight degrees."

"Come on, Mom. It's not that bad." April waved her hand at Grace. "We went in."

Noreen shuddered dramatically. "The sun was out when you went in."

But Cutter leaned down, grabbed her hand, pulling her out of the hot tub and into his arms. Noreen squealed just as he jumped.

She shrieked the moment they surfaced. And then she laughed, loudly and lovingly, as Cutter swam to the far end of the pool with her still in his arms.

"They're like little kids," April said, a smile on her pretty lips.

"They're like a couple in love," Tammy said, watching the two with stars in her eyes until she turned her gaze to Frank.

"I'm a little worried," Grace said, eyeing the happy couple as they drifted farther out of earshot. "I mean, Mom doesn't have a stellar track record with men."

Observing her sister, a shadow darkening her eyes, Valerie mused, "Actually, she doesn't have a stellar track record with marriage." Then she looked at Grace. "There's a difference."

Grace didn't seem to see that difference. "But he was just

Uncle Mortimer's mechanic. What if he's got dollar signs in his eyes when he looks at her?"

Tammy snorted and looked pointedly at her best friend and Cutter. "Those aren't dollar signs. They're hearts."

Grace pursed her lips before saying, "I just worry that her judgement is impaired because she knew him when she was young. But all he's done with his life is fix cars."

April put her hand on her sister's shoulder. "Your privilege and prejudice are showing," she singsonged, then added, "And look at Uncle Mortimer. Everyone thought he was a loser, but he had a fabulous charter business going."

Grace huffed out a breath. "Right. So that means Cutter Sorenson has followed in his footsteps."

Frank leaned in to kiss his wife's cheek. "Maybe you should just tell them and put them out of their misery."

All eyes were on Tammy. She breathed in, then huffed out a sigh. "All right. I looked him up."

"You think I didn't?" Grace asked.

Tammy shook her head sadly. "I'm sure you did. But I have better resources." After all, she was an executive.

"So?" April urged her on.

Tammy paused as if she were waiting for a drum roll. "It seemed he's an amazing mechanic, and that could be why he owns a very profitable franchise of auto body shops in Florida." Tammy smiled when Grace's mouth fell open, and she dropped the bomb. "His net worth is larger than your mother's."

"You're kidding," Valerie murmured, now openly staring at her sister.

"Did you tell Mom?" April wanted to know.

Tammy shook her head. "There are some things your mother needs to figure out on her own. And the first is not to judge a package by its wrapping." Then she turned to look at her best friend. "And I'm pretty sure she's discovered that gem all on her own." She smiled at them all. "Even if it took forty years."

The *Once Again* series, where love always gets a second chance.

Coming, *Book 9* **Cruising the Danube**: He never thought he'd risk his heart again. Until he saw her and she stole his breath. A sexy mature romance!

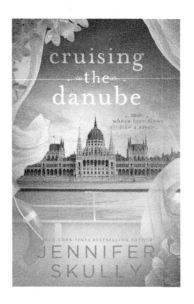

Once Again
Dreaming of Provence | Wishing in Rome

Dancing in Ireland | Under the Northern Lights
Stargazing on the Orient Express
Memories of Santorini | Siesta in Spain
Top Down to California

And coming
Cruising the Danube
Beachcombing in the Bahamas

Get 3 free books just by joining the newsletter for Jennifer and Jasmine! Plus updates on sales and exclusive subscriber contests. Sign up at **http://bit.ly/SkullyNews**

ABOUT THE AUTHOR

NY Times and USA Today bestselling author Jennifer Skully is a lover of contemporary romance, bringing you poignant tales peopled with characters that will make you laugh and make you cry. Look for *The Maverick Billionaires* written with Bella Andre, starting with *Breathless in Love*, along with Jennifer's new later-in-life holiday romance series, *Once Again*, where readers can travel with her to fabulous faraway locales. Up first is a trip to Provence in *Dreaming of Provence*. Writing as Jasmine Haynes, Jennifer authors classy, sensual romance tales about real issues such as growing older, facing divorce, starting over. Her books have passion and heart and humor and happy endings, even if they aren't always traditional. She also writes gritty, paranormal mysteries in the Max Starr series. Having penned stories since the moment she learned to write, Jennifer now lives in the Redwoods of Northern California with her husband and their adorable nuisance of a cat who totally runs the household.

Learn more about Jennifer/Jasmine and join her newsletter for free books, exclusive contests and excerpts, plus updates on sales and new releases at **http://bit.ly/SkullyNews**

Pretty In Pink Slip

Stand-alone

Baby, I'll Find You | Twisted by Love
Be My Other Valentine

Books by Jasmine Haynes

Naughty After Hours

Revenge | Submitting to the Boss
The Boss's Daughter
The Only One for Her | Pleasing Mr. Sutton
Any Way She Wants It
More than a Night
A Very Naughty Christmas
Show Me How to Leave You
Show Me How to Love You
Show Me How to Tempt You

The Max Starr Series

Dead to the Max | Evil to the Max
Desperate to the Max
Power to the Max | Vengeance to the Max

Courtesans Tales

The Girlfriend Experience | Payback | Triple Play
Three's a Crowd | The Stand In | Surrender to Me
The Only Way Out | The Wrong Kind of Man
No Second Chances

The Jackson Brothers

Somebody's Lover | Somebody's Ex

Somebody's Wife

The Jackson Brothers: 3-Book Bundle

Castle Inc

The Fortune Hunter | Show and Tell

Fair Game

Open Invitation

Invitation to Seduction | Invitation to Pleasure

Invitation to Passion

Open Invitation: 3-Book Bundle

Wives & Neighbors

Wives & Neighbors: The Complete Story

Prescott Twins

Double the Pleasure | Skin Deep

Prescott Twins Complete Set

Lessons After Hours

Past Midnight | What Happens After Dark

The Principal's Office | The Naughty Corner

The Lesson Plan

Stand-alone

Take Your Pleasure | Take Your Pick

Take Your Pleasure Take Your Pick Duo

Anthology: Beauty or the Bitch & Free Fall

Printed in Great Britain
by Amazon

18739587R00181